POWER PLAY

An Aviators Hockey Novel

SOPHIA HENRY

Krasivo Creative

TO HENRY
ONE OF THE STRONGEST, MOST WONDERFUL MEN I KNOW

#BeKindLoveHard

CONNECT with Sophia:
SophiaHenry.com

AMAZON // BOOKBUB

#BeKindLoveHard
I stand with Ukraine 🇺🇦

Chapter One

GABY

RULE ONE: THERE'S NO SUCH THING AS LOVE AT FIRST SIGHT.

Lust at first sight, sure, but not love.

Don't get me wrong. I love love.

I love love so much, I've dressed up as Cupid for Halloween. But real love takes time.

Just some unsolicited advice from Gabriella Bertucci, Queen of Having It All Figured Out.

Except my own life, of course.

It's easy to give advice and boast lofty ideals when no one pays attention to you.

"Hey, Gabs!"

I know the voice. Landon Taylor is the only person on God's green earth that calls me "Gabs." But when I look up from the "Lions and Tigers and Red Wings, oh MI" T-shirt I've been folding, I have to do a double take. "You got your haircut."

He runs a hand over his dark blond faux-hawk and grins. "Yeah. It was time to lose the mop top."

"Looks nice." I say, as heat burns my cheeks.

I grab another shirt out of the cardboard box filled with our most recent shipment of T-shirts from Totally Detroit, a local screen printer. If I lift it high and fold it in front of my face, Landon might not notice my annoying habit of hyperventilating whenever I talk to him.

Though he and his family have been clients at my family's stores for years, my palms still break out in a sweat whenever he walks through the door.

"Do you guys have any more of the Tigers Legos?" Landon asks as he digs through a tiny box of toys next to the register. "My brothers are obsessed with them."

"Yeah, I know. Your mom was in here last week and bought us out."

"Damn." His dark blond eyebrows knit in defeat and he turns his attention to a rack of kids' T-shirts.

"You could buy them an actual tiger," I suggest.

"Animal or baseball player?" Landon glances up to shoot me a wink, then resumes pushing hangers aside, obviously not impressed with our selection.

I grab a stuffed tiger with the state of Michigan embroidered in pink across its chest from a nearby table and throw it at Landon.

"RAWWR!"

It bounces off his freshly shorn head and lands on the floor.

"Geez, Gaby! You've gotta tell a guy when you throw a damn tiger at him."

"Now I see why you play hockey." I wiggle my fingers at him before rushing behind the register to help another customer. He can't retaliate while I ring up someone's purchase, but I'll have to remember to take cover after.

The Taylor family has shopped at Eastern Market, Detroit's historic, outdoor public market, religiously every Saturday morning for as long as I can recall. They always buy a bushel of apples from our stand and eat them as they weave through the aisles under the covered sheds. Once they finish browsing, they come back and load their old red wagon with their produce for the week.

That was back when Bertucci Produce was just a small, but thriving, stand in Shed One at the market. Years before Mama and Papa decided they wanted to open 313 Artisans, the small store I currently run, which began as a way to feature local artists as well as Mama's own artistic creations.

That was back when Landon was just a kid strolling through the streets in one of Detroit's oldest communities.

Now, he's Landon Taylor: superstar defenseman for the Detroit Aviators. Detroit's next NHL-bound player.

Rule Two: Real love is between two people. If it's one-sided, it's just infatuation; a crush.

Which is why I can't use the word "love" to describe my feelings for Landon.

Sure, my forehead breaks out in a cold sweat and my heart pumps and thumps like a rock 'n' roll drumbeat every time I see him walk through the door.

But since I don't seem to have the same effect on him, it can't be love.

In defense of my hormonally charged reaction, every time I see him now he looks like a fitness model who just left a photo shoot.

Today, for instance, a blue Under Armor shirt with the Aviators logo skims the curves of his chiseled chest, and black basketball shorts swish against his muscular thighs. I even know he's wearing little white ankle socks inside his gray and blue Brooks running shoes.

Because I'm that ~~obsessed~~ observant.

I doubt Landon notices anything about me, except that I can sling a stuffed tiger with NFL quarterback–like precision. As the only girl in my family, getting overlooked has become as regular as the sun setting in the West.

My brothers will argue that I'm the princess, and I may have been when I was younger, but it's far from the truth anymore. If my dad has his way—and I'm sure he will—my brothers will be the heirs to the Bertucci Produce legacy.

Even though I'm the only one who knows the stores inside and out. Heck, I'm the one who updated—or created—most of our procedures to bring the business into the 21st century. Old-school handshake deals and recording finances on paper don't cut it anymore.

"You guys gonna win the Calder this year?" Papa's voice booms from the other side of the store. Papa's voice always booms, but it's exceptionally loud in a large retail space with one customer.

"Hope so, sir. This city needs a championship right about now," Landon answers.

"You've got a lot of work to do with Varenkov gone." Papa weaves through the narrow space between product displays to stand beside Landon.

Landon sets the stuffed tiger I threw at him on the counter to shake the outstretched hand Papa offers him. "Charlotte drafted Bryan Girard this summer. He's a sick left wing. So, we're hoping he makes up for Varenkov. And Gribov got sent back here."

Papa grumbles, obviously unaware of Pavel Gribov's recent demotion. "When are they calling you up?"

"Charlotte's D is pretty young, but I'm hoping I get my chance soon." Landon moves his hand to the top of his head and rubs it.

"You're a solid, stay-at-home defenseman. Stick to your game and you'll get there." Papa slaps Landon on the back before moving to the other side of the counter. He taps a few keys which generates the buzz of a report printing on receipt paper.

I know exactly what he's printing: the sales report. Daily sales, weekly sales, sales since we opened this store six months ago. He mulls over the numbers in silence. The stress from a stupid piece of paper is going to kill him.

I scan the back wall of the store, contemplating where I can hang the rest of the T-shirts that won't fit on the shelf. We need one of those torso-only mannequins to show off how the T-shirts fit.

Out of the corner of my eye, I see Landon move toward the door and my heart sinks. He has no reason to stay any longer since we don't have the gift he wants, but I want him to linger anyway.

If only I were well versed in small talk like Papa.

What if I picked up the box of T-shirts at my feet and "accidentally" fell? Would big, strong Landon Taylor rush to my rescue?

Better yet: Landon could stay and use his fitness-god good looks and physique to model for our store. Instead of a weird headless, legless mannequin on display we could pop a shirt on Landon and have him walk around. If customers could see his real-life muscles expanding and contracting under the fitted T-shirt, it would cause a "call-911-this-store's-on-fire" sellout of our stock.

Rule Three: If you're infatuated with someone it's super creepy to come up with ways to make him stay longer in your presence.

Super creepy, Gaby.

"See you soon, Joe! Later, Gabs!" Landon calls out, pushing the door open with one arm, while raising the other in a farewell gesture.

Papa lifts his left arm, but instead of returning Landon's wave, he grimaces and clutches his right bicep. His head drops, his chin hits his clavicle, and his shoulders slump over the register.

"Papa?" I ask, unable to conceal the screech in my voice. "Papa?"

My heart stops. Drops. Implodes.

I knock over the display table, tipping a mountain of freshly folded T-shirts onto the floor in my haste. "Papa!"

Papa lifts his head and tries to speak, but no words come out. I can hear the quick, sharp intake of breath from across the room. As I get closer, I notice drops of perspiration beaded across his forehead like raindrops on a windshield. When I reach him, I swing my arm across his shoulders.

"I'm calling nine-one-one, Gaby." Landon appears next to me, cell phone already against his ear. I hadn't even noticed he came back in the store.

"Papa!" I whisper, not by choice. My voice completely left me. Tears roll down my cheeks as I hold my dad. "Maybe I shouldn't touch him. Landon? Landon, what do I do?"

"I don't know. I think he's having a heart attack. I don't know. Um, Eastern Market." Landon keeps his calm as he explains the situation to the operator. "Gaby, what's the address?"

"Twenty-five-oh-eight Russell."

"Twenty-five-oh-eight Russell," Landon repeats. "It's a store in Eastern Market called Three-one-three Artisans. Male, probably fifties, six-foot something. I don't know, he's not overweight or anything."

"The ambulance is on the way, Papa. Stay with me," I whisper to my father.

Papa nods. It's slight, but at least he's responsive.

Landon stays on the line with the 911 operator and I hold on to Papa until the ambulance arrives. The emergency medical technicians charge through the door wheeling an empty stretcher, and other non-essential people follow. It makes me sick to think that people are coming in just to get a glimpse of the "action."

Strong arms pull me away from Papa to allow the EMTs access to him. I collapse against Landon's chest and he wraps me in his arms. He smells like too much cologne and stale beer, which wasn't what I ever expected.

Though staying in Landon's arms is the easy response, I wiggle free of his grasp and spin around, knowing I'd be upset with myself if I didn't watch the two EMTs lift my dad onto the stretcher.

My stomach rolls and I sway forward. Landon grips my arms, holding me firm. "You gotta stay strong, Gabs," he whispers.

I nod and attempt to analyze every action the EMTs performed with a nurse's clinical eye, rather than from a daughter's terrified perspective.

The ridiculous number of situations the medical technicians need to be prepared and properly trained for boggles my mind. They have to know a bit of everything. The difference between life and death depends on each tech knowing exactly what to do for a heart attack, a burn victim, or a gunshot wound. The list is endless, since they could be called to any scene. They save lives every day, yet I bet they don't make one third of what a doctor makes.

"You coming with him?" The shorter, smaller tech nods at Landon.

"I am." I speak up. "No, wait, the store. I—" I survey the store. "I can't leave."

"I'll stay," Landon says.

I whip my head around to look at him. "What?"

"I'll stay. I mean, if that's okay with you. I can hold down the fort until you can get someone here."

Make a decision, Gaby.

I watch the EMTs glide the stretcher through the open door. I have to get going.

"Are you sure?" I ask. Wasted words. Wasted seconds. Time to go.

"Yes." Landon squares his shoulders before taking both of my hands and looking me straight in the eyes. "Gabriella, go with your dad."

"Okay." I slump in his grip, before finding the strength to straighten again. "I'm going to call my Uncle Sal. I hope he can get here soon."

"Just go. Everything will be fine." Landon spins me around and guides me toward the door.

I know Landon can handle the store since I'd be surprised if any browsers come in, let alone customers who'd make him try to figure out the register.

Before following the EMTs to the ambulance, I remember my purse hidden away in the cubby under the register. As I retrieve it, I fumble for words. "Thank you, Landon. I don't even know what to say."

"Go, Gabs. I got you."

I give him a small smile and push through the doors.

Chapter Two

GABY

I stand an inch away from Papa's stretcher, watching as one of the EMTs prepares the back of the ambulance before they lift him into it.

Papa grabs my arm and squeezes. I put my hand over his, patting it softly. "It's okay, Papa. You'll be okay."

My words mimic the silent matins in my head. *He'll be okay. He'll be okay.*

Instead of a nodding, Papa snatches his hand out from under mine and pushes aside the oxygen mask covering his mouth. "Get . . . your . . . ass . . . " Deep ragged breath. Deep ragged breath. Deep ragged breath. "Back . . . in. . . that . . . store."

"Mr. Bertucci, you've gotta keep the mask on, sir," the EMT next to my dad says—Jones, according to his name tag.

"Go, Gabriella," Papa commands.

"But, Papa—" I stammer, wiping at the tears in my eyes. My own father doesn't want me to ride in the ambulance with him. Should I listen? Ignore his pigheaded command?

"Call Mama." Papa pauses to take another deep Darth Vader breath. "Tell her where to meet me."

I turn to Jones and hit him with my best Puss in Boots pleading eyes.

He shrugs, though his expression flashes a bit of sympathy. "We'll take good care of him. Call your mother and tell her he'll be at Receiving."

The second EMT jumps out of the back of the truck, forcing me to take a few unsteady steps away from the stretcher. He and Jones lift Papa into the ambulance.

Jones gives me one last half smile before closing the doors in my face.

With the click of the doors, my entire body shuts down. My brain stops delivering commands. My heartbeat slows. My emotions cease.

Zombie-fied on the streets of Detroit.

An asteroid of dread smashes into my stomach. The ambulance is long out of sight before I can even move.

My phone vibrates in my back pocket, shocking me to life. I glance at the notification.

Social Media Alert: @DetBreakingNews Ambulance called to #EasternMarket business. Follow for details.

Word travels fast in the age of social media. Shaking my head, I swipe the bottom of my screen and press my thumb against the sensor on my phone until it unlocks.

"*Ciao, mio angioletta.*" Mama answers the same way every time I call. It translates to "Hello, my little angel."

The tears roll with my words. "I think Papa had a heart attack. He's in an ambulance. He wouldn't let me go with him. They're taking him to Receiving," I ramble without taking a break.

"What? Gabriella, slow down. What about Papa?" Mama's voice escalates from confused to frantic with each word.

"Papa had a heart attack. The ambulance is taking him to Receiving." I take a deep breath. "You have to meet him there. Right now."

Her car keys jingle as she clamors around in the background. "I'm on my way. Where are you? At Three-One-Three?"

"Yes. He wouldn't let me go with—" A lump sticks in my throat.

"It's okay. Please call your brothers. I'll call you when I find out what's happening." Mama pauses. "I love you, *angioletta*."

After hanging up with Mama, I call my brother Drew first.

"What's up, Duckface?" Drews asks.

Typical big-brother way to answer. I posted a duck face picture on social media once.

Once.

"Papa just went to the hospital. I think it was a heart attack. Mama's on her way there." I pace back and forth in front of the store.

"What?" Drew sounds like he just woke up. "Where is he? *How* is he?"

"I don't know how he is, I mean, he was talking, but I don't know. The ambulance was taking him to Receiving. I'm calling Uncle Sal to see if he can watch the store. I'll be there as soon as I can. I gotta call Joey."

"Do you want me to pick you up?" Drew asks.

"No, Papa's car is out back. I'd rather not leave it here."

"Okay, see you over there."

I hang up with Drew and tap the phone icon next to the number I have stored for Joey, hoping it's really his. As the oldest in our family, you'd think he'd be the most responsible and connected.

Nope.

A few years ago, he packed a few bags—and any familial responsibility—and moved to Colorado to be a ski instructor.

I have no problems with anyone leaving home to make a life for themselves doing what they love. And he probably would've been an awesome instructor, if he'd actually applied at any resorts.

Instead, he's been couch-surfing, smoking pot, and playing video games. At least that's what he's doing according to the one social media account he updates. He never returns calls let us know what he's really up to.

As expected, Joey doesn't answer. An automated voice tells me what number I've reached and instructs me to leave a message at the beep. Why couldn't he have a personal voice mail message so I'm sure know I reached his phone?

"Hey, Joey, it's Gaby. Papa had a heart attack and he's in the hospital. Call me when"—I pause, since I'm not sure if I called the correct number—"or *if,* you get this."

Finally, I call my Uncle Sal to see if he can come down to watch the store. My uncle manages the produce store in Grosse Pointe and says he can't leave, but he promises he'll send Sammy, my cousin.

The bell above the door chimes as I walk back into the store, feeling scared, helpless, and rejected.

Landon looks up from his phone. "Gabs, what are you doing here?"

"My father kicked me out of the ambulance."

"He what?" Landon stuffs his phone into his pocket and crosses the room to meet me.

"He told me to get my ass back in the store and to have my mother meet him at the hospital."

It's only been a few minutes since I spoke with Mama. Though I know she's barely had time to back out of our driveway, let alone reach the hospital, it doesn't stop me from checking my phone, waiting for it to ring or buzz with an update.

"I can't just stand here." I spin around, glancing at every wall of the store. "I can't work. I can't think. What if they can't save him? What if—"

Landon grabs my shoulders as he had earlier, squaring my body to his. "He's gonna be okay." He doesn't blink as he reinforces the mantra that kept me strong until Papa was in the ambulance. "He spoke to you. He was alert. That's a good thing, right?"

The way Landon's eyes hold mine reminds me of when I'd taken figure skating lessons as a kid. My coach taught me spotting; picking a focus point so I wouldn't get dizzy in my spin. Landon's mocha-colored eyes serve as my focus point so I don't get dizzy. For a brief moment, he's my spot—my safety.

"Yeah." I close my eyes and take a deep breath. "Yeah, I'm sure that's good."

He lets me go and digs into his pocket. "I just searched 'heart attack' on my phone and watched this video that says ninety minutes is the key."

"The key?"

I miss the warmth of his hands on my shoulders. I miss the safety I felt standing close to him. I miss the focus point I had staring into his eyes.

"Yeah. If he gets treatment within ninety minutes, he has a better chance of recovery."

I swallow my tears and reach up to rub my neck with both hands, exhaling as I whisper, "You can do this, Gabriella."

"You *can*," Landon confirms. "Now get in your car and go to the hospital. I'll wait here for whoever is coming to take care of the store."

"Papa would kill me if I left right now." I glance at the door, the register, and finally back at Landon.

"You make decisions every day for this store. You've got to trust yourself."

Still, I stall, because I usually have more time to analyze the pros and cons of my decisions and how they impact the store, and, most important, what Papa will think of the choices I've made. To me, going to the hospital is a no-brainer, but Papa made it clear he didn't approve of my leaving the store in Landon's hands.

Who is Landon Taylor, anyway?

A long-time customer, sure. A hockey player. A nice guy, based on the interactions I've had with him. A crush. An infatuation. A friend?

Can I call someone I've made small talk with for years, but didn't really know anything about, a friend? Can I trust our store to a person I barely know?

No. If I left a stranger at our store by himself Papa would have a heart attack.

Or . . . another heart attack?

"I'm going to stay until Sammy gets here," I say, my voice firm.

"Are you sure?"

"I wasn't thinking clearly, Landon. It was ridiculous to ask you to take care of the store. You don't know anything about it." I put a hand to my forehead. "And I barely know you."

Landon's slight wince catches me by surprise. But he recovers quickly, catching my eyes and holding them, as if searching for a fissure to pounce on.

He won't find any cracks in my shell though. The hurt expression that crossed his face when I refused his help is minuscule compared to Papa's wrath if I leave our store in the hands of a customer.

"Please, Gabs, let me help."

"I appreciate your offer. I *really* do. But leaving the store in the hands of a stranger wouldn't be a smart decision."

"'Stranger?'" Landon's voice squeaks with genuine surprise. "We've known each other our whole lives. My parents wheeled me to the Bertucci Produce stand in a stroller before you were even born."

"Where did I go to school?" I ask, thinking by stumping him I'll prove my point.

"St. Paul's. Then that all-girls high school. I forget the name."

How the hell does he know that? The only reason I know where Landon had gone to school was because I'd practically memorized every word written about him in local newspaper features.

It might sound lame, but I liked the thought of knowing a professional hockey player before he was famous. Maybe I'll be interviewed if he ever makes it into the Hockey Hall of Fame.

"When's my birthday?"

He'll never know that.

"July thirteenth."

Damn.

"Favorite hobby?"

"Reading."

Easy guess.

"Favorite band."

"Drowned World."

Aha!

"They aren't my favorite." I gloat in his defeat.

"But you like them. You're going to their concert in a few weeks."

WTF?

"How did you know that?" I glance past him as a slight movement outside the door catches my eye, but no one walks in.

"Told you we weren't strangers."

"You're creeping me out. Seriously." I thought I held the championship belt for scary stalker, but I have a reason. He's Landon Taylor, my vote for sexiest man alive and hottest hockey player in the AHL.

But there's no reason for him remember random facts about me. "I'm not—anything."

"Or maybe you're everything."

"What?"

My brain doesn't have the capacity to wrap itself around everything going on right now.

My dad had a heart attack. The man I fantasize about alludes to me being everything—whatever that means.

Can't think.

Storage limit maxed out.

"I pay attention when it comes to you, Gabs." Landon slides his phone into his pocket and moves toward the door.

"But why?" *Surreal* doesn't even begin to describe this moment.

"You were my first kiss."

After sprinkling that confusing seed in my head, Landon spins around and walks out. Through the front window, I watch him thread his fingers together behind his head, then raise them toward the clouds in a stretch as he disappears from my line of sight.

So calm. So self-assured. He probably drops bombs on unsuspecting fan-girls all the time.

Meanwhile, I scour my brain for the memory of kissing Landon. It never happened. I definitely would've remembered a kiss.

I never would've washed my lips.

A dust bunny rolls past me, a reminder I haven't swept today, or yesterday for that matter. I retrieve the broom from the closet in the back office.

As I sweep, I recall my life in kisses. There have been only a few and they were all with the same person, Jude, a guy I met while playing soccer with Drew and his friends at Kerby Park.

Jude could have been my first boyfriend, until Papa made a horrifying comment about how we Italians knew the best places to hide bodies, especially in Detroit, where no one really cares or questions.

Mafia jokes have never been Papa's style. Must have been something about his little girl going out with a boy instead of a group of girlfriends that brought on the dash of dark humor. He's usually full of life. Full of love. Full of making decisions for the good of his family.

And all of that comes with stress. The kind of stress that causes a heart attack.

I stop sweeping the stupid floor and rest my forehead on the tip of the broom handle.

He'll be fine.

He'll be fine.

He'll be yelling at me again soon.

I straighten and resume my manic cleaning. Every time I sweep the stiff bristles across the painted concrete floors, the dust bunnies bounce and flurry to areas just out of my reach.

Out of my control.

Reports. The idea comes to me so suddenly, the broom slips out of my hands, making a loud *thunk* when it hits the ground.

I'll take over the reports so Papa will never have to worry about them again. I'll figure out what we need to do to make 313 Artisans profitable and able to stand on its own. If I can take the stress of this place away, Papa can focus on Bertucci Produce again and everything will be fine.

I stoop down and pick up the broom, running through problem-solving scenarios while I sweep.

How do I make this place profitable?

Get customers in the door. How?

Advertising. Marketing. Word of mouth. Spokespeople?

Too busy brainstorming ideas and sweeping like a maniac, I don't even hear the chime to alert me that someone entered the store.

When there's a tap on my shoulder, I spin around, raising the broom in self-defense. We haven't had any problems here, but it's still Detroit and I have to be vigilant. On a normal day I'd never be working alone.

My family rarely lets me be alone anymore.

"It's just me, Gaby." My cousin Sammy lifts his hands in front of his face, shielding himself from being knocked upside the head with a broomstick. "Sorry about Uncle Joe."

I let out a breath and lower the broom, relieved I'd almost assaulted my cousin instead of a customer.

Sammy surveys the store like a policeman scanning a scene he's been called to. "Were you here alone?"

"Yeah. Just for a few minutes though," I add quickly. "It was just Papa and I here today. There was one customer in the store when Papa went down. He's actually the one who called nine-one-one. Then he stayed until right before you arrived."

"Good. That was the right thing to do." Sammy nods.

Seems silly to defend my being alone in the store. Though we try to have two people working most shifts, there are times when one person manages the store on their own.

It's never me, though.

"Thanks for getting here so fast," I continue, leaning the broom against the wall. "I'm so sorry to take you away from the main store."

"Don't even waste your words. We're family, Gaby. Family." Sammy pounds his chest over his heart with a fist. The Italian horn charm dangling from the thick gold rope chain around his substantial neck bounces with the vibration.

Sammy exemplifies one of the many reasons I love my family. Always there. No questions. No hesitation.

Well, except Joey, my estranged older brother.

Chapter Three

GABY

"Joey's flying home. He'll be here tomorrow." Mama never looks up from scrolling through her texts, as if she doesn't want us to see the red-rimmed eyes we know she's hiding.

It feels as if she needs permission to show emotion and I want to give it to her. She doesn't have to "be strong" for us. We'll get through it together, as a family, like we always do.

Drew lowers the waiting-room copy of *Sports Illustrated* he's been reading. "Who paid for that?"

I pinch his bicep. Sure, I wondered the same thing, but I'd never say it out loud. It's not the time to complain about our slacker older brother. At least he's coming home. I don't think anyone expected him to drop his life in Colorado to come back.

"If you can't be civil, why don't you go sit in your car, Andrew?" Mama snaps.

Drew raises the magazine again, hiding his scowl.

"Gaby, Papa will be counting on you to help Joey while he's out."

"What's he going to be doing?"

"He'll be taking over for dad."

"At the shed or at one of the stores?" I ask.

Over one hundred years ago, my great-grandfather, Salvador Bertucci, partnered with his best friend, Ben Mitchell (who started his life as Blaise Mangiaracina, but changed his name at Ellis Island because he didn't think he'd be able to get work with such an Italian name) to set up a produce stand in Shed Once at Eastern Market.

It was a perfect arrangement. Sal ran the stand, while Ben supplied the product from the farm his family started when they first arrived. That little produce stand quickly became one of the busiest ones in the market, and continues to be today, thanks to loyal, long-term customers.

The success of the stand allowed my *Nonno* (grandfather) Sal to expand Bertucci Produce into two free-standing grocery stores, which are currently run by Uncle Sal and Papa. It also allowed Mitchell Family Farms to relocate to Monroe, Michigan, and operate into one of the largest farms in the state. The Bertucci and Mitchell clans have been like one family for years.

Until three years ago, when one of the Mitchell boys I considered family raped me at a college party.

"He'll be at Three-one-three."

"Wait. What?" The horror in my voice slips out. I'd just warned Drew to shut up and I can't rein it in myself.

Mama lifts her eyes to me. "He'll be at the new store."

Papa chose Joey to take over for him at 313 Artisans? *Joey?* The new store opened only six months ago. Joey has never set foot in it. Why would my parents think letting him run it would be a good idea? Drew had a better chance at running it than Joey.

"I'm the one who's started the store with Papa. I know every inch of that store."

Mama toys with the string of colorful, chunky beads at her neck. "He'll figure it out. I'm sure it's what your father wants."

"Figure it out? We don't—"

Drew stands up and kicks my leg. Hard. I double over and grab my shin, rubbing the bone as if that will ease the pain. "Let's go get some drinks. Mama, you need a water?"

"Grab me a coffee, please."

Drew nods. When I rise from my chair and take a step, my kicked-leg buckles under me. Drew throws his arm out and catches me, propping me up until I can walk on my own.

"Jerk," I mumble, but I don't refuse his assistance, leaning on his shoulder for the next few steps until the pain subsides.

"You deserved it. You were about to start a huge fight with Mama and get her more upset than she already is. Plus, you know there's no way in hell Papa's gonna let Joey run the new store. Just let it all play out."

Drew has a good point.

Mama and Papa would never trust the store to Joey. Firstborn son or not, Papa would never put our family's brand-new, faltering business in the hands of an irresponsible, pot-smoking wannabe ski instructor.

WHEN OUR OLDEST brother saunters into Papa's room just after noon the next day, Drew and I are both surprised.

Joey, being Joey, hadn't answered any of the texts Drew or I sent. He didn't tell either of us when his flight was getting in. Nor did he tell either of us if he needed a ride from the airport to the hospital.

"Joey!" Mama cries. She throws her arms around him as if he's Mighty Mouse—here to save the day.

"Hey, Mama." Joey returns her hug. He gives me a slight nod over her shoulder.

I would've nodded back, but my brain is murky from the contact high I received when he walked in the door. I swear I can see a cloud around him, like Pig-Pen from *Peanuts,* except he emits a haze of smoke rather than dust. The stench is so powerful, he must've just smoked a bowl behind one of the massive bushes near the entrance to the hospital or something.

Couldn't Mama smell it? It overtook her signature Chanel No 5 scent. Marijuana might make people happy and mellow, but the pungent odor makes me want to vomit.

Don't get me wrong, I'm not anti-weed. Do what you want.

I'm fed up with my older brother and his inability to grasp the reality of adulthood. I'm nineteen and I have a full-time job. I can afford to buy the pot I smoke.

If I smoked it.

"Hey, man," Joey says to Drew.

Drew reaches an arm out, offering Joey his knuckles. Joey knocks his fist against it.

Our family shatters any birth-order stereotypes people may think of. As the oldest, Joey should be the reliable and structured one on the path to the NHL, and Drew should be the screwed-up middle child acting out for attention by smoking pot and moving to Colorado to be a ski instructor.

But Joey had always been a calm kid, into reading and hanging out alone. My parents started Drew, their high-energy middle son, in a hockey program at an early age and he loved it. He's been focused on the game ever since.

I don't even think he drinks. Well, he doesn't drink around us. Not even the ever-present glasses of wine everyone in the Bertucci family sips with every dinner.

Joey, on the other hand, had always been more of a gamer—something that irked Papa to no end. Papa didn't want us kids to sit around the house with eyes glued to the TV all day. He wanted to lock us outside from sun up until sundown.

Joey didn't like playing hockey, or rather, he didn't like the ice-skating part of it. Mama loves to tell the story of his first—and last—skating lesson, where, five minutes into class, he told my Mama that the ice was "too slippery" and stomped off. He tried a few other sports, but never found one he enjoyed enough to stick with long term.

Maybe he was jealous because Papa was ecstatic at Drew's sincere interest and obvious talent. Maybe he just wanted someone to notice his talents lay in areas other than sports.

Like the guitar and the piano and, well, video games. They were the only things that kept his attention.

Mama and Papa pushed him to go to college. They were hell bent on him being the first Bertucci to graduate from university. After one semester, he dropped out, packed up his things, and moved to Colorado. He's only been home twice in five years.

And now he's back.

In Papa's hospital room.

Joey inches toward Papa's bedside, taking baby steps as if he's afraid our father will reach out and grab him zombie-style.

"Come on over, Son, I'm not going to break," Papa's low voice fills the awkward silence since Joey's arrival.

"How're you feeling?" Joey asks. He's finally taken a full step toward the bed and stands close enough for our dad to take his hand. A very un-Papa-like thing to do.

"Save me, Joey. They're treating me like I'm an invalid."

"You had a heart attack, Pop."

"A mild heart attack. Very mild," Papa snaps, shooting an annoyed glance Mama's way.

"Point your dirty looks somewhere else, Giuseppe Bertucci. A heart attack is a heart attack."

Papa rolls his eyes. "I'm fine. Doctor said I'm going home today. I'll be back at work next week."

"Like hell you will," Mama mutters.

"We're going to take care of everything while you're resting, Papa," I tell him. "You won't even have to think about work."

"I can do a lot from the computer at home."

"Drew moved the computer out yesterday. Absolutely no work for you, until after your checkup with the cardiologist next week."

Mama is a brave lady for dropping the no-computer bomb on him. I expected her to stay mum until he got home. But if he's going to wig out, better to do it at the hospital while under a physician's direct care.

"Why would you do that, Celeste?"

"You know why. You can't jump straight back into a stressful situation. You're lucky I'm not sending you to the Caribbean to relax for a few weeks." Mama takes a spot next to Joey.

"Yeah. Because *that* would suck," Drew deadpans. A chorus of chuckles slice through the awkward tension in the room.

"You haven't enjoyed a vacation in fifteen years." Mama slides her hand against Papa's forehead. So tender even when they're at each other's throats.

I want a relationship like that.

"Well, if the boss lady says I'm out of commission, we'd better figure out a plan."

"I've already got all the shifts covered at Three-one-three," I tell Papa, happy to be able to bring some stability to the work front. "I'll be opening and closing every day. I'll manage the orders and schedule the cash pickups. And Sammy and I will coordinate with the Mitchells for the stand's produce shipments."

"Whoa, whoa, back up a minute, Gaby." Papa stops me. "Those are the things that I do."

"Yeah, I know, Papa, but you won't be at work, so I'll take over the stuff you would normally do and delegate—"

"Gaby. Stop," Papa commands.

I cock my head in confusion. Despite Mama's warning yesterday, I went rogue and figured out what needed to be covered, managed, and handled at the new store. Other than Papa, I'm the only person who knows 313 Artisans from storage closet to front register. And since he can't work for at least three weeks, maybe longer depending on the limitations his doctor set for him, I've taken the reins to make sure everything is in order.

"Joey's going to take over at Three-one-three for me while I'm out."

The blaze of startled confusion in Joey's eyes is as intense as the angry confusion in my own.

"But Pop, I—I—" Joey stammers.

"Joey will take care of my role, and you, Gaby, will resume your current role and manage the schedule. I don't want to hear another word. It's final."

Arguing with Papa about it makes no sense. Arguing with him never makes any sense, but especially not today when he's laid up in a hospital bed, anxious to be released. It would be my luck that a stupid squabble would make him relapse.

It's almost as if Papa planned the whole thing. I can almost picture him sitting in the tiny office at the back of the store, elbows on the desk, tapping his fingertips together.

How do I get Gaby not to freak out about telling her I'm handing the store over to Joey? Oh, I'll tell her while I'm in the hospital after I've had a heart attack. She couldn't possibly argue or get upset with me in my fragile state. And my diabolical plan to keep Bertucci stores run only by male members of our family continues on. Moohoohahahaha . . .

Okay, I know it's my insecurity talking rather than how my father really thinks. And I shouldn't be so selfish, especially now. We should focus on working together until Papa gets back on his feet.

"Sure, Papa. I'll do whatever you need me to do," I tell him. I'm still standing behind everyone, almost in the corner of the room. No reason for me to be up in Papa's grill when his beloved lost sheep is home.

Joey stiffens, the veins in his neck popping out as he turns his head toward me. Between the freaky veins, the sideways glare, and the ramrod straight back, his entire body screams sheer terror.

Judging by the look on his face, there might be rotting, undead corpses behind me about to attack. The reaction must come from my easy agreement to leave a store he's never been to in his completely incapable hands.

"Good." Papa shifts in his bed, as if trying to get comfortable. He takes a deep, staggering breath and lets it out. "Tell me about Denver, Joe."

Yes, Joe, tell us about your important days filled with video games and weed. That's a super exciting story. Let me pull up a chair.

For some reason, a desperate urge to speak with Landon hits me. I'm not even sure where it came from, since we don't have that kind of friendship—despite him knowing a shit-ton about me. It's not like I'm privy to having his phone number or address.

Landon has left a few messages on the store's voice mail asking how Papa was doing, but his number comes up as blocked, so I couldn't call him back.

I've had the same group of friends since elementary school and I tell my best friend, Michelle, everything. But she already went back to Chicago for school. So, why would Landon be the first person I thought of reaching out to?

Maybe it's the immensity of him calling 9-1-1 and saving Papa's life?

Maybe it's because my head is still reeling from my genuine surprise that he seemed to know as many random facts about me that I know about him? Maybe it's the weight of him telling me I'd been his first kiss?

Whatever the reason, I want to talk to him now.

But I don't even know when I'll see him again.

Chapter Four

LANDON

It's not like my defense partner, Steve Fabian, to miss practice. But he wasn't in the locker room this morning and he's definitely not on the ice right now.

I skate to the bench, where our captain stands, pulling tape off the knob of this stick.

"Where's Fabian?" I ask him, grabbing a bottle and squirting water into my mouth.

"He got called up."

I turn my head and spit the water out before I choke from surprise. "He what?"

"Don't worry, man. You'll get your chance." He pats my shoulder and knocks his helmet against mine. "Keep working."

Keep working.

Work is all I've done since the very first time I laced up hockey skates. I've spent my entire life working on my skills, endurance, agility. Recently, I added watching videos of games and studying coaching strategies to get better at anticipating plays before they happen.

Why Fabian? Why not me?

I have the best fucking plus minus in the league. Fabian doesn't even come close. The only stat he's beating me in is penalty minutes.

I slam the water bottle against the boards, which grabs the attention of Rick Vincent, our coach.

Fuck.

I'm about to skate back to the next drill, when he calls out. "Get over here, Taylor."

I put my head down, concealing my eye roll as I push off and glide a few inches toward him.

"I don't know what the hell has been going through your head recently, but you need to fucking tone it down."

"Excuse me, sir?" I ask, unsure what I did to piss him off.

He taps his temple. "You're in here too much. And it's fucking with your game. What happened?"

"I don't know, Coach," I say, but I do know.

Ever since I watched Joe Bertucci have a heart attack, my head has been in a weird place.

The dude spent his entire life at his stores. I can barely remember a time he wasn't there when I came in. He's fairly young, and always seemed to be in pretty good health, but had a heart attack out of nowhere. Now, I can't claim to know how he ate or if there were any hereditary family conditions, but still.

It made me realize how precious every minute is.

When I told my dad—who happens to be Joe's cardiologist—he said Joe needed a better work-life balance. Then he gave me an extra-long glare.

"I know everyone yaps that working hard is what it takes to get to the next level, but that's not the only thing. You already work hard. You've gotta work smarter. Get your head out of your ass and get back to the basics—stand up defense. That's what made the Monarchs draft you."

I nod, checked out as I skate to the blue line in front of our goalie, Tyler Campbell, AKA: Soups, to get back into the drill.

Work smarter, not harder. Work-life balance. Watching life pass me because I'm focused only on hockey rather than enjoying the moment.

I sense a pattern.

And then there's Gaby Bertucci—the girl of my dreams—Joe's only daughter.

Watching Gaby, who's always been the epitome of calm and collected, break down when Joe collapsed was like having someone twist a dagger in my heart. Though, I've adored her from afar ever since we were kids, and we've had countless conversations over the years—I've never seen her vulnerable side. And that moment was probably the most vulnerable you can ever see someone.

Ever since then, the way I feel about her started to change—not the attraction. Nope. That's alive and well judging by the way my dick swells and my pulse pounds when I'm around her.

All the reasons I've never taken the chance at asking her out started to dissolve.

Gaby is so down-to-earth and approachable, the moment I started caring about girls, I was hooked.

Once I got to know her, I wanted to know more. Once I heard her laugh, it was my mission to make her laugh again.

And when she looks at me with those big brown eyes and my gaze drops to her deep, pink lips—I can't think of anything but all the ways I want to make her scream.

I'd been so focused on my career that I didn't want to get involved with someone who makes me feel that way by just being in her presence. Hooking up with a girl is much different—and Gaby is not a hookup. If I ever had the chance to feel her lips on mine, I doubt I could walk away.

Which is why I never pursued her.

My entire life is about getting called up to play in the NHL—for the Monarchs in Charlotte, North Carolina. Which means, I'd have to move and she wouldn't be able to go with me. With her responsibilities at her family's multiple stores, she's tied to Detroit.

But now I'm being reminded to create a work-life balance by my father and my coach—and all I can think of is how amazing it felt being the person Gaby could count on in her most vulnerable moment.

I saw her terror. I felt her pain. That's when something clicked. I realized I would do anything in my power to help her—to be there for her. I want to be the one she counts on to make her feel better in the most vulnerable situations.

Maybe that's the part of life I've been missing.

And since I'm already fucking up the "work" part of the work-life balance, maybe I need to focus on the "life" part before I fuck that up, too.

Chapter Five

GABY

"JOEY, JUST LISTEN FOR A MINUTE."

I could be screaming "Fire!" and he still wouldn't listen.

"Hit Credit. Swipe card. It's not that hard, Gaby."

An annoyed growl rumbles in my throat. "You have to manually input the amount into this little machine before you swipe or it won't go through." I tap the black box that prints the receipt and has a hand-held keypad attached for customers to approve the transaction and input their PIN number. "It doesn't automatically do it. The machines don't talk.

"Hold on." He pulls his phone out of the back pocket of his dark skinny jeans and taps the screen, answering right in the middle of training. "Yeah, man. Nope. Not busy at all."

"Ugh!" I slap the counter with my hand, no doubt causing more pain to my own palm than giving Joey an accurate portrayal of my frustration with him.

Most employees are fairly easy to train. Granted, most of our employees, with the exception of a few people, are members of the Bertucci family and have been running a register and working at some type of store for most of their lives.

Still, my brother doesn't follow the easy-to-train pattern. I'm sure he could be if he paid any attention to me at all. He must have magical I-know-how-to-work-a-cash-register powers. Or maybe he has a job back in Colorado he hasn't mentioned.

Doubt it.

The door chimes and I watch an incredible being with arms, legs, and a huge bouquet of flowers for a head walk in.

"Gaby?" A long-haired delivery guy peeks out from around the arrangement.

"Yeah, that's me." I meet him halfway into the store and take the flowers. Curiosity burns my hands, but I set them on a display table.

"Sign in the box." He taps the screen before extending the tablet to me. Using my finger, I scribble a few loops and hand it back.

"Thanks," I call after him. He holds up two fingers, giving me the "peace sign" as he pushes through the door.

The scent of the mixed assortment of blooms assaults my senses as I pluck the card out of the bouquet. Though flowers are beautiful to look at, I hate them.

Technically, I hate the smell they produce. I've yet to find a flower whose scent doesn't make me sick to my stomach.

It's not only flowers, but various fragrances as well. Birthdays and holidays are especially difficult because, without fail, someone always gives me body lotions and shower gels as gifts. I always have to pretend to be excited.

I know I sound like a huge, ungrateful jerk. I'm totally thankful for the gifts, just not the scents. The only flavors I can stomach are vanilla and strawberry. Occasionally apple.

Holding my breath, I turn my back to the flowers and read the card.

To the Bertucci Family:
Thinking about you and wishing Joe a speedy recovery.
Please let us know if there's anything we can do while he gets
back on his feet.
All the best,
The Taylor Family

. . .

"WHO ARE THOSE FROM?"

"The Taylors sent them. They hope Papa gets back on his feet quickly." My lips slip into a small smile.

"Old man Taylor should've saved his money and took it off Papa's bill." Joey says. He'd hung up with whoever he'd been speaking with, and now he's either playing a game or killing ants, judging by how vigorously his thumbs slam against the screen.

"What does that mean?"

"Dr. Taylor is Papa's cardiologist."

"Huh. Didn't know that," I say absently.

"The Taylors have been customers since we were kids. How can you not know what Dr. Taylor did?"

"I knew he was a cardiologist. I just didn't know he was *Papa's* cardiologist. We have a lot of regular customers, Joey."

"Yeah, but none that get you all fired up like that Taylor kid. The hockey player."

"Shut up."

"And he doesn't even know that flowers make you sick." Joey chuckles. Despite engaging in conversation with me, he hasn't looked up from his phone once.

"The flowers are for Papa, not me. And he doesn't get me fired up."

I grab the vase and head toward the office in back, then think better of it, because I can't have them in such a small space with no windows. I'll barf.

"Good." Joey finally looks up and meets my eyes. "Hockey players are fucking pricks. They only want one thing."

"The Stanley Cup?" I ask, feigning ignorance, though I know where he's going with his lame overprotective big-brother act.

Ever since I told my parents I was raped, both of my brothers have carried around a burden of guilt. Drew especially, since he was at the same party when it happened. Whether he'd been at the party or not didn't make a difference. I never blamed Drew or thought he could have stopped it.

We all trusted Jared Mitchell.

"He's a hockey player in his twenties. Think about how Drew acts right now."

Despite supposedly having a girlfriend, Drew's love life can be summed up in one hyphenated word: man-whore. Which is a horrible thing to say about my own brother, but it's the truth. He chases after anything with long hair. And I mean that. He once hit on a guy he thought was a girl.

Drew being such a skirt chaser is somewhat surprising, since he's had a female best friend since grade school. I don't remember him ever trying to make a move on her. Not that I know what the hell he's doing. I'm just the little sister who's went to a totally different high school than he did.

Thankfully, Joey takes the make-fun-of-Drew angle, not the remember-when-you-were-raped-by-a-hockey-player angle. Which I appreciate.

"Even if I *did* like him, I know I'd never have a chance, Joey. So, we can end this conversation."

"If I ever see you with any hockey player, I'll shove his hockey stick down his throat until it comes out the other end." Joey's brotherly guilt always comes out verbally in rather aggressive ways.

"That's really graphic. And gross."

"I'm not kidding."

"I don't even know if that could happen physically."

"End of the conversation."

Joey doesn't see it, but I flip him the bird behind the bouquet before I carry it through the office and out the back door. There's a fifty-fifty chance the flowers will be stolen, but I set them outside next to the door anyway and hope for the best. I'll take them home to Mama after work. She'll be excited for a beautiful fresh arrangement for our kitchen table.

Before I go back into the store, I stop to shuffle through some papers on Papa's desk. The stack holds a few invoices that, I assume, still need to be paid because they haven't been stamped. I lower myself into the well-worn, brown leather chair behind Papa's desk. When we opened 313, Papa brought his favorite chair instead of breaking in a new one.

I love being stuck in the dip Papa's backside had made from years of use. The office still smells of his aftershave, a warm and welcome scent, especially after the flower attack. Although, he might need to tone it down on the Old Spice.

I lean down, unlock the bottom drawer of the desk, and remove the oversized binder holding the business checks. As Papa's replacement, Joey should be paying the invoices, but he wouldn't even listen to me explain how to use the register, so how could I expect him to pay the bills?

Another thing Papa didn't think about.

"Gaby!" Joey calls from inside the store.

"Just a sec!"

Without having a chance to write even one check, I toss the binder back inside the drawer and lock it up.

When I return to the front, I see Joey swiping a credit card once, twice, three times in the five seconds it takes me to get to the register. The customer on the other side of the counter watches him with wide, cynical eyes. Probably wondering how many times the transaction will charge his credit card with all of Joey's manic swiping.

"Just back it out if you can't get it," the man says, grabbing his credit card out of Joey's fingers.

"Sorry, sir." Joey looks at me with panic. "I can't get the credit card machine to work."

I move behind the counter and look over his shoulder. "You totaled it out in the register, right?"

"Yes." His voice drips with annoyance.

I let his cross tone fly over my head. I didn't ask the question to be a jerk. The register has to be totaled out to proceed to the next step. I pick up the handheld keypad. "Did you enter the total into this manually?"

"No."

The customer taps his credit card against the counter impatiently. I look up, catching the V slant of his eyebrows and the frown on his lips. "Thank you so much for your patience, sir."

Then I glance at Joey to make sure he watches how I proceed. I enter the total from the screen on the register into the keypad on the credit card machine.

"I'm so sorry, but I'm going to need your card one more time."

"He already swiped it ten times. How many times will my card be charged?"

"I promise you won't be charged for all those swipes, sir. Our registers and credit card machines don't communicate seamlessly. We have to manually enter the amount. The machine will automatically start printing a receipt for you to sign when the card goes through." I hold up the plastic device. "Joey is a new employee. He's still training on the registers."

With a huff, the man hands over his credit card. I swipe it quickly and the tiny box immediately prints the receipt. I tear the paper off after the first pause in printing and set it on the counter in front of the customer, then slide him a pen. "Sign on the line, please."

As the customer signs the slip, I hit another button and a copy of the receipt starts printing. I grab a coupon from a shelf under the register, throw it in the bag with the receipt, and hand it to the man. "Thank you, again, for your patience. I threw in a coupon for five dollars off your next purchase. Please visit us again soon."

"After this?" He huffs again as he grabs his bag and storms toward the exit.

"I *just* explained the credit card machine to you," I say once the man is out of the store.

"It's a lot to remember, Gaby. Give me a break."

"It would be easier for me to give you a break if you'd paid attention to me when I was explaining it to you earlier. I'm going to instill a no-phone-at-work rule."

"Then what would any of us do?"

I flash him a scowl. "That was a customer. Let's hope he does come back after the crappy service."

"Whatever, Gaby. I'm not even supposed to be up here. I'm going back to the office."

"Good. There are some invoices that need to be paid. Do you know how to write a check?"

"Don't be such a bitch."

I shrug, thankful no customers were in the store to witness our petty sibling squabble. Then again, if there were customers in the store, we wouldn't be having a fight in the first place.

Chapter Six

GABY

AFTER TWO WEEKS OF HELL WITH JOEY AS MY BOSS, A ROAD TRIP TO Chicago to visit Michelle and see a concert is a perfect distraction.

I've never worked in an office environment or the corporate world, but I totally understand why people complain about their bosses. Especially employees who complain when they know more than their boss, because their boss is a huge idiot.

My brother is a huge idiot boss.

Joey can rebuild a car engine and change his own oil. He can fix anything that breaks. He even built an addition onto our house. But the kid has no clue how to run a store. Or bring in customers. Or be civil to the few customers who come in to shop.

We all have our strengths.

He's always been a good brother. He never teased me (too much) or stuffed me in a locker in school. Granted, the only school we attended at the same time was elementary, and we didn't have lockers, but I don't think he would've, and it's the thought that counts.

Thankfully, having a best friend who lives in a ridiculously fun city only four hours away, means I always have a place to go to get away from home, at least for the next few years—or longer, if she stays in Chicago after she graduates.

Somedays, I wish I'd chosen the college route, rather than focus on the store.

I took a few online accounting and business classes last year because I thought they'd help me manage the store better. But online classes took more discipline and time on the computer than I wanted to put in. I realized early, I learn better under the traditional method of sitting in a class and being taught by an instructor.

If only there were a Bachelor of Something in Concert Attendance. I'd ace that. I love live music. I can't play an instrument or carry a tune, but I could definitely make a life out of going to concerts. The people, the vibe, even the sweat—because I always sweat. Even with below-zero temperatures outside, I've got sweat rolling down my back, under my tank top.

If I could capture the amazing hum created by the buzz of a room packed with people listening to the geniuses who create the music and lyrics that speak to our souls, I'd suck it up in a syringe and inject it directly into my veins.

I'm pretty sure that's how addicts feel about drugs. Thankfully, I prefer the natural high of guitar strums, drum beats, and a penetrating, mesmerizing voice rather than a chemical high.

Though I'm be happy to see any number of bands, I especially love Drowned World concerts. Tonight, marks my tenth time seeing them, including a show in Detroit a few nights ago.

Each concert is a completely amazing experience in itself. The guys are so interactive and unique. The first time I'd seen them, the leader singer, Austin, gave the audience members plywood boards and then walked into the crowd. He stood on the boards held up by fans and sang an entire song. It's a lot bigger production now, but it's still magical.

Thousands of damp bodies stand crammed shoulder to shoulder in staggered rows facing the stage at the Aragon Ballroom in Chicago. The temperature in the Spanish village–style concert hall skyrockets as people pack in, pushing and elbowing for position, as we anxiously wait for the band to take the stage. Moisture pours down the crevice of my back, a human shot luge for the streaming succession of sweat.

Michelle and I teeter on our toes, bobbing our heads as we're jostled by the hundreds of other dancers on the floor. Someone behind me keeps bumping into my back, which I understand, to an extent. We're all moving, leaning, dancing. But there is such a thing as concert crowd etiquette, no matter how packed the place is, and this person definitely doesn't understand those unwritten rules.

I throw a quick glance over my shoulder to see what I'll be up against if I confront the pusher. Tall blonde girl, tight black dress, stilettos. Instead of making a big deal of the situation, I focus my attention back to the stage. Then I feel her hand use my shoulder as home base to propel herself upward on her toes. I turn slightly, just enough to make her weeble-wobble on her four-inch heels.

"Sorry," she says, rolling her eyes at me.

Call me crazy, but if someone rolls their eyes during an apology, I'm apt to think it's not a very sincere apology.

"No big deal."

No less than two minutes later, she jostles me again. This time she rams me full force into the person next to me, a short guy in a comedy drama mask mask, which would be a scary sight at any other concert, but Drowed World made theatre masks their gimmick, and hundreds of fans wear them during the show.

"I'm so sorry," I tell the guy.

I think he says, "No worries," but the room is buzzing and he has that stupid mask over his face so it could have easily been "F you."

When I turn around to lash out at the pushy girl, it surprises me to see a familiar face partially hidden by a black Detroit Aviators baseball hat weaving his way through the crowd.

"Landon?" I ask when he gets within speaking range. "What are you doing here?"

He smiles but shakes his head and cups one hand around his ear. Then he beckons me closer with the other hand.

I lean into him and yell directly in his ear. "What are you doing here?"

"Seeing a concert."

Suddenly, the entire crowd roars and pushes toward the stage as the lead singer addresses the audience, and the momentum propels me forward. I stretch my arms out to break my fall and end up smooshed against Landon's chest, which may not have been a terrible feeling if it hadn't happened the way it had.

Michelle grabs my arm to steady me, though Landon's hard, lean body has already done the job. I flash her a grateful smile and stand up straight on my own. The girl in the black dress lays in a heap on the floor at my feet, having fallen in the shoving.

Despite my initial annoyance with her, I squat down and help her up before the audience tramples her in the excitement. It doesn't take a mosh pit or a rowdy crowd to get hurt. Hundreds of people jumping up and down to a blood-pumping beat can be just as dangerous.

Once she's steady, she turns around and elbows her way through the crowd to the aisle that the bouncers keep empty so people can walk to the bathrooms.

No thank you. No apology.

"Are you okay?" Landon asks.

"Yeah, I'm fine." I nod in the general direction the girl walked. "She'll probably have some bruises, but I'm good."

"Why don't we do this," Landon says as he maneuvers himself directly behind me. Then he reaches for Michelle's forearm. Startled by the sudden contact from a stranger, she jerks away and studies Landon under furrowed eyebrows. When I gave her two thumbs up, she relaxes and allows Landon to guide her into the space next to me.

"Do you know him?" she asks, giving Landon a cautious side-eye.

Legitimate question. Friends look out for each other.

I nod. "It's Landon."

"Who?"

"Landon." He answers before I have a chance to say it again.

Michelle's lips rise slightly a telltale sign she realizes it's Landon *Taylor*, my ultimate mega-crush.

Landon's reorganization of bodies means that Michelle and I are now one row closer to the stage, so close we can almost touch the lead singer. *Almost.* Not that I would've—unless he held out a hand.

Another bonus of having Landon behind me is the arm-box he's formed around me when there's a push from the audience. Every time the crowd moves, Landon puts his arms up, caging me in and preventing me from getting pushed around. It's so sweet I want the place to get rowdy so he'll have a reason to put his arms around me.

"I have a confession," Landon says in my ear during a break between songs.

I lean back into his chest, taking comfort in the hard planes holding my weight easily. It takes every ounce of self-control not to sigh and close my eyes. I could get used to Landon's warm, stable body cradling and protecting me.

And then I come back to reality. Dreams like that have no place in real life.

"I've never heard of this band before. They're really good."

I stare, mesmerized as the singer walks to the middle of the stage carrying a ukulele. They're about to play "Open Your Heart," one of my favorite songs.

"Excuse me?" I obviously hadn't heard Landon correctly. Because it sounded like he said he'd never heard of this band, yet he's standing behind me at their concert—in Chicago.

"Well, I mean, I'd never heard of them until I overheard you talk about them at the store." Landon circles his arms around me, holding me against his chest, though there's no crowd surge to make his embrace necessary.

"Why would you drive four hours to see a band you'd never heard of?" I ask, twisting in his arms to study his face.

"Because you're here."

"And?"

"I want you to notice me, Gaby. The way I've noticed you my whole life."

Can someone please tell my legs that buckling is not an option? The girl in the black dress already hit the floor. It's been done.

"Notice you? I've noticed everything about you since the minute I realized all boys weren't like my brothers—horrible devils born into the world to torment girls."

Landon grins, seemingly surprised by my admission. "You barely pay any attention to me when I come into the store. You treat me like every other customer."

"Treat you like every other customer? Landon, I schedule my shifts around the days and times you're most likely to walk in. I keep my hair down and wear perfume those days."

"I just thought you always looked like that."

"Like what?"

"Gorgeous. You should be the model in a Bertucci Produce catalog."

I burst out laughing, thankful that "Open Your Heart" drowns it out. "Produce catalog?"

"Is that not a thing? Okay, ads in the Sunday paper then."

"Can we talk about this after the concert?"

"Oh, yeah, sorry." Landon shakes his head and lifts his eyes to the singer.

"I'm not mad, I swear." I spin around in his arms and, though we're nose to nose, I keep rambling, "It's just loud and I don't have any clue what's going on. I can't form thoughts, let alone sentences right now."

Landon laughs, his entire body shaking me. Then he dips his head and brushes his lips across mine. I can't stop myself from swaying when my knees give out for a split second. He grabs my arms and holds me upright so my head tilts toward his and our lips stay locked.

When he pulls away, he licks his lips and smiles. I can't take my eyes off him, until he grabs my shoulders and physically turns my body toward the stage. I try to twist back around but he holds me firm, before sliding his hands down to my waist.

"Just enjoy the moment," he whispers.

Oh, I'm enjoying the moment. The man I've had a crush on since I was eleven years old just kissed me at one of my favorite bands' concert.

A veteran Hollywood screenwriter couldn't have scripted a better first kiss than that.

First kiss with Landon, I mean. Or second kiss? He still hasn't explained the whole kiss thing, and I haven't had a chance to ask him about it.

As if the buzz of the concert isn't enough to have my insides flipping pancakes, the kiss and his large, strong hands, which switched seamlessly from roaming up and down my sides to circling around my stomach, just threw some bacon into the pan.

Normally, I'm as comfortable at a concert as I am curled up on the couch in my parents' living room reading a book—which is my other happy place.

But Landon's presence has me conscious of everything going on around me. I've never attended a concert with a guy, let alone had a guy behind me, his hands on my hips, swaying and jumping with me to the beat. Millions of thoughts rush through my head, all of which lead to a nervousness sizzle in my stomach that makes me want to throw up.

I want to grab Michelle's forearm and jump up and down, but I can't because Landon is behind me and I have to play it cool.

Although, after all these years, he has to know there isn't a cool bone in my body—and yet, he still kissed me.

And what am I supposed to say to the comment about Landon needing me to notice him?

How could he not have realized I notice every move he makes when he comes to our stores? I know every hockey team he's ever played on, and always have some random statistic or comment ready to spout in case I see him the day after a game.

When the keyboard plays the opening notes of "Guardian," Landon's hands slip down to my hips and he squeezes. "I love this song."

"I thought you'd never heard of them."

"I hadn't. But I've had their albums on repeat since I found out you liked them."

I pinch his bicep.

He releases my hip and shakes his arm out. "Ow! What the hell, Gabs?"

"Just checking."

What kind of sci-fi, alternate-universe portal did I drive through on the way to Chicago?

As if he read my mind, Landon pushes the damp hair off my neck and leans into me. "It's not hard to believe. You're amazing."

And with that I give up. Give up the questions. Give up the disbelief over how I could be in this situation.

Time to live in the moment. And at this moment, all my dreams have come true.

Well, my Landon Taylor dreams.

I lean back and allow my body to sway with Landon's as we watch the band perform "Screen."

I've almost gotten used to being in Landon's arms, watching a concert as if we've done this a hundred times before. Until two guys yelling "Taylor!" body check their way through the crowd and pop our magic bubble.

"Taylor!" the taller guy wearing a black Aviators hat identical to Landon's yells again. "You're gonna get us into so much fucking trouble, dude. We gotta go."

He grabs Landon's arm and tugs him toward the door.

"This is the last song," Landon lies, twisting out of the hold. He leans in and places a kiss on the side of my neck. I can't even smile with the two hulking guys trying to pull Landon away. Judging by the Aviators gear, I assume the guys are his teammates. They don't look like they've been out for a night on the town either.

"It took us an hour to find you, motherfucker! We're all gonna get benched tomorrow," the shorter guy says.

"Don't make me carry your ass out of here," his hat-wearing friend warns.

"I will," says the little guy, lifting Landon off his feet and carrying him toward the door, tottering like a penguin lifting a log in a toughman competition.

Landon twists around. "Guess I gotta go, Gabs. Kiss you later!"

Michelle turns to look at me with wide, questioning eyes and I shrug. Then we watch the guy set Landon on the ground, keeping a hand on his back as he pushes him toward the door.

I spin back toward the stage, relieved it wasn't as big of an incident as it felt like. In fact, no one seems concerned a guy was just carried out by two big dudes.

Chicago and Detroit seem similar in that way. No one blinks an eye. The show goes on with the song, "Car Radio," as the soundtrack to the craziness.

"I'm so glad you came to visit," Michelle tells me as we hurry through the turbulent Chicago winds toward the semi-shelter of the covered station at the Lawrence L stop.

I love Chicago's transit system. Every time I visit, I return to Detroit wishing we had a system where I didn't need a car to get around.

"Me, too. I had to get out of town."

"You better not have been running from that hockey-playing hottie."

"Run from him? I've wanted him to notice me for years. Why would I run from him?" I blow warm air against my frigid fingers. "How much longer?"

"It's just up here." She lifts her arm, but I can't follow her direction. Whenever I look up, the wind slaps me in the face and my eyes start to water. We increase our pace, racing for warmth.

At the station, we stand close, bobbing on our toes while we wait for the train.

"Holy shit! How do you live here?" I joke, as the train pulls in. Quickly, we slip through the doors and settle into seats.

"It's just as cold in Michigan." She rubs her gloved hands together. "Okay. We can talk now. Spill."

"Where do I start?"

"Why the hell is Joey at Three-One-Three?"

"Of course, start with the bad news." I glance at an ad for car insurance on the wall across from us. "Maybe I want to talk about Landon."

"Oh, we'll get to him, believe me. But I get the feeling you need to talk about family first."

Michelle knows almost everything about me. And she has an uncanny way of knowing exactly when I need to vent without me saying a word.

"It sucks. I'm trying to get him up to speed and he doesn't listen to a word I say. He's on this ego trip about how he doesn't need to know the register because he's in charge."

"Yeah, because your dad doesn't know how to use the register." She rolls her eyes.

"I know, right? He's being a total jerk."

"Is that a surprise?"

"Yes and no. I mean, I thought he would be more open to learning everything. He wants the authority but not the responsibility that goes with it."

"Again, I ask, is that a surprise?" Michelle laughs.

"Yeah, as soon as I said it, I realized how dumb I sounded." I look out the window, watching Chicago pass in a blur. "I think he's lost right now. I'm trying to help him, but I don't know what else to do."

"You can't fix everyone, Gaby. Joey's still searching, but he'll figure it out. How's Papa Joe?"

"He's doing great. Still at home resting, but he's recovering well. He's on a new diet and he's ramping up his exercise routine."

"Have I subjected you to enough small talk?"

"Small talk with you is heavy talk."

"That's what best friends are for."

Before she asks, I rush right into talking about the elephant in the room. "I have no clue what's going on with Landon. He was at the store when Papa had his heart attack. He called nine-one-one because I totally freaked out and froze. I haven't seen or heard from him since."

"That's normal though, right? He doesn't come into Three-One-Three that often."

"Usually every other Saturday. Though, I know he still meets his parents at the stand in the market every single Saturday." I glance at her. "When he's in town, because road trips, ya know?"

"You're kinda creepy."

"It's not creepy. It's years of observing their routine."

"That's creepy."

"Not helping."

"Sorry." She shakes her head as if getting rid of the thought. "So, he just showed up here tonight?"

"Yes. Out of the blue. And he said he didn't even know this band."

Michelle reaches into her coat pocket and pulls out her cell phone.

She tugs one glove off with her teeth and taps her finger across the screen.

"What are you doing?"

She holds her phone up to my face. "Aviators play the Wolves tomorrow night."

"Oh."

The Wolves are Chicago's AHL team. Which explains why Landon is in town and how his teammates were the ones who dragged him out.

How completely nonsensical and narcissistic to think he'd driven hours to be at the same concert as me.

"I bet they have a curfew or something. His teammates sounded pretty pissed."

I nod.

"Don't look all dejected, Gaby." Michelle bumps my shoulder with hers. "He broke curfew to see a band he never heard of because you were here."

"Let's play the game where we make up backstories for people." I change the subject, rubbing my gloved hands together as I scan the train. "See the guy over there in the blue puffy coat? He started out at the bar with his friends but then they went to a strip club and he didn't want to go—"

"Because his sister works there and he didn't want to be there to see his buddies ogle her," Michelle finish.

We burst out laughing. Trains and airports are the best places to people watch and make up fictional stories about them.

"I wasn't making up the Landon story and you know it."

My lips quirk into a smile, which I try to suppress but can't. "You think?"

"He didn't just happen to be there. He went on purpose, looking for you. He kissed you!"

My heart flutters as I recall the feel of his arms around me and his lips on mine. "What do I do now?"

"Call him?"

"I don't have his number."

She shrugs. "Ask for it next time he comes in the store."

"I can't."

"He kissed you. I think you can ask for his phone number."

"True." I nod to the guy we created a story around. "You should get blue puffy coat's number?"

"And have to face his sister at work tomorrow night? No way."

"Bahahahahaha."

Best friends rock.

Chapter Seven

GABY

"I'M LEAVING EARLY TODAY, IS THAT COOL?

I'm not asking permission, simply making sure Joey realizes it. He finally figured out the register and most of the ins and outs, and there isn't a soul in the store, so I'm sure it'll be okay to slip out early.

"See you tomorrow, Gaby." Joey doesn't even look up. He's on his phone. Again.

Way to run the store, bro. He's been on his phone more than he's been in the office managing the overhead.

Instead of going home, I want to walk around. The 313 Artisans storefront sits on Russell Street, in the heart of Eastern Market, a block away from the Bertucci Produce stand that started it all.

I love Saturdays at the Market. The vibe of hundreds of people strolling through the sheds send a buzz through me. I never get tired of seeing Detroit alive and humming. Even if it's just for a day; or a few days, since Sundays pack people in as well.

I consider myself lucky.

Have the Bertucci's seen our share of tragedy as one of the families who stayed in the city and tried to pump life and energy into it even if it was in our own small way? Yep.

Show me a person who hasn't been affected in some way by the years of city mismanagement and the downtrodden economy, and I'll show you a liar.

Whether it was violence or arson or loss of work or a family member's loss of work; if you stayed in this city to work or to live, you've been affected. We've all had to dry our tears, square our shoulders, rebuild our homes, and bar our windows—but not our hearts.

Because once we become desensitized to what's going on around us, we might as well move to the suburbs and pretend it doesn't affect us.

A black T-shirt with Detroit street names and landmarks screen-printed in white script across it from every angle catches my eye.

People have asked us why. Why do we stay? Why not move our business and our family outside of the city? And Papa responds the same way every time.

How can we?

Detroit is our city. It's the town, created by the car-manufacturing boom, that gave my great-grandfather the opportunity to work his ass off, and save enough money to start his own produce stand at Eastern Market over one hundred years ago. It's the city that allowed the Bertucci family to open two more grocery stores, one within the city limits, the other less than a mile outside of it.

Sure, Detroit is the city where arsonists burned down our house nine years ago. It's the city where someone shot and killed Papa's best friend while he helped him unload a produce truck early one Saturday morning seven years ago.

It's the city that keeps knocking us—and countless others—down, but also allows us to pick up and come back stronger than ever.

As I rub the soft material of the T-shirt between my fingers, a horn beeps from directly behind me. Startled by the sound, I twist toward the road and watch a sleek, silver car veer to the curb. Seeing Landon's big, brown eyes sends a silent, comforting message through me.

Safety. Warmth.

"Want to go for a ride?" he calls from the driver's side.

Without a second thought, I let go of the shirt, rush to the car, and open the door.

"How's your dad?" he asks.

"He's doing really well. It was a mild heart attack." I reach for the seat belt, slide it over my shoulder, and click it into place. "He's home now, so that's good."

"That's awesome, Gabs. I'm glad he's okay." Landon checks the traffic in his mirrors and pulls back into the street.

"Thanks." I relax in the seat next to Landon. Though still slightly surreal, being with him feels natural. I want to ask him about the concert, but it can wait. "Where are we going?"

"I'm taking you to the place my parents met."

My shoulders tense up, and the end of my sloppy ponytail hits my chin when I glance down at my outfit—ratty jeans and a 313 Artisans T-shirt. "I'm not really dressed for, um, anywhere but work."

"You look great. Don't worry." Landon winks at me. Then he turns onto the service drive and floors it while I take in an eyeful of some of the most unsightly views of Detroit as he merges onto I-94.

My intrigue grows when he exits at Gratiot Avenue. (Which is pronounced Gra-shit for anyone who lives outside of the Metro Detroit area and doesn't know.) Though, it gets better the farther north you drive, this particular part of Gratiot has a dangerous reputation.

Where the heck had his parents met?

"Here we are." Landon announces. My head swivels left and right looking for a landmark or restaurant.

"Where?"

"Right here." Landon nods out the window at a telephone pole in the middle of an overgrown island.

"I'm totally confused."

"My parents met cruising Gratiot."

I burst out laughing. "They what?"

"Crazy, right?" Landon asks, glancing out his window.

"How does that even happen?"

Meeting at the Woodward Dream Cruise, a parade where almost a million spectators watch thousands of people propel their classic muscle cars and hot rods along Woodward Avenue, I can see. But I can't imagine meeting my future spouse while cruising Gratiot Avenue.

It's as if our parents grew up in a foreign galaxy.

"I guess it was cool to drive up and down Gratiot and check out people in other cars and be like 'Hey, girl' to the person in the car next to you. And if the other person was interested, you stopped somewhere to talk and exchange numbers."

"Why would they do that? It sounds so dangerous." An involuntary shiver ripples through my body. "Who knows what kind of nut jobs are out there waiting to jump someone or rape someone."

Landon eyes meet mine and he laughs. "I think they thought meeting people in person was better than the alternative—meeting people online."

"Meeting people online isn't bad," I say. "You just have to be careful. Like with anything."

"Well, the Internet was brand-new back then. Still scary and unknown territory." He pauses. "Are you an online dater, Gabs?" His voice has a teasing lilt, but I know he wants the answer.

"No. I'm not. I'm part of an online book club and—" I stop. I have no shame about my book club or my online book club friends, but I realize how lame I must sound to someone like Landon. "How do you meet people?"

He shrugs. "Usually people want to meet me. I just hang out with the guys and go with the flow."

"Of course." My head drops. Of course, people want to meet him. It will only get worse—or better?—when he makes it to the NHL.

"Tell me about your book club."

No turning back now since I'm the one who brought it up.

"I read this book I really loved and realized there was a social media fan group around it. So, I started talking with some people and realized we enjoyed a lot of the same books. They asked if I wanted to be part of their book club." I love talking about my book club, but it seems juvenile to gush over something that probably sounds so dorky to Landon. "We, um, create a calendar of what we'll be reading and post our reactions and thoughts on an online forum as we read. It's a private forum."

"So I can't see it?"

Silence fills the air as I contemplate out how to answer. The forum morphed from a book club into a place for friends to talk about everything and anything.

Yesterday I posted about "my crush." One of those really long posts where my friends and I analyze every single word Landon has said to me from the day of Papa's heart attack to the unexpected concert kiss.

Landon notices my lengthy pause. "What?"

"Nothing."

"Why so secretive? Do you guys read a ton of sex books or something?"

"Oh my gosh! No. It's mostly YA books."

"Suuure, Gabs." He squeezes my knee. "I don't know what 'YA' means, by the way."

The sudden squeeze makes me jump, but when he keeps his hand on my leg, I can't take my eyes off it. Thankfully, keeping my eye on his hand gives me a focus point so I don't hyperventilate, even though, paradoxically, the hand is the cause of why I'm feeling light-headed.

I gaze out the window, observing each building we pass until it's out of sight. I've been on thousands of car rides, but I've never been so content as being on a drive with Landon.

"Is this okay? I feel bad, like I just dropped in and whisked you away from whatever you had going on today." Landon removes his hand from my leg and places it on the steering wheel. "But now I'm not sure it was the right thing to do."

I miss his hand, like I missed his arms when he released me from the hug after my father's heart attack.

"It was totally the right thing to do," I assure him. "In fact, you don't understand how much I appreciate it. I needed to get out of there. The walls were closing in."

He glances at me. "How so?"

"Papa put my oldest brother in charge of running the store, and he has no clue what he's doing. I'm trying to help him and he brushes everything I say off like I don't know anything. Then blames me when he screws up."

"But your dad knows it's not you, right?"

"Actually, Papa blames me because he doesn't think I should let

Joey screw up. He thinks I should go behind him and fix everything before it becomes an error." I sigh.

"What sense does that make?" Landon asks. "Seems extremely inefficient."

"Exactly!" I exclaim, excited he understands the logic. "Joey should be asking me for help if he doesn't know how to do something. Or I should be doing it myself. It's about efficiency."

"Have you told your dad?"

I give Landon a full-on glare, rather than a sidelong glance. "And upset Papa while he's supposed to be relaxing?"

"Sounds like he's already getting upset."

"He wouldn't listen to me anyway."

"Well, that's a completely different issue." Landon stops at a red light and shifts his body toward me. "Why wouldn't he listen to you?"

"Because I'm a woman."

Landon bursts out laughing.

But I don't.

"Sounds archaic."

"Have you met the Bertuccis? I'm surprised I'm allowed to work at the stores at all. I should be learning to cook and scrubbing laundry on a washboard. You know, the things women are supposed to do."

Landon laughs again, a quick bark as he studies me. When he realizes I'm still not smiling, he continues, "You're kidding, right? Your family can't be that old school about gender roles."

"Then why is my brother, who has never worked at any of our stores, running the newest one?"

"Sounds like we both need a drink," he says as he twists the steering wheel and pulls into the parking lot of a decrepit building I don't want to be stopped next to on the road, let alone walk into. He turns off the engine and jumps out.

As he approaches the passenger side, Landon must feel my tension at the situation. Either that, or he notices the flesh across my knuckles turn a ghostly shade as I grip the door handle with all my might.

"I wouldn't take you somewhere unsafe, Gabs!" Landon yells through the glass. He tries to open the passenger door for me but can't, since I'm not letting go.

When it comes down to it, accepting a ride with Landon wasn't much better than accepting a ride with a random guy I met on the Internet. I know him, but I don't *really* know him.

Aren't there hundreds of television shows depicting super scary situations like this?

Chapter Eight

LANDON

....

ONE OF THE THINGS I LOVE ABOUT THE FLYING BEAVER IS HOW comfortable it makes me feel—which probably sounds like a ridiculous way to describe a bar, but it's been my second home for as long as I can remember. I grew up sitting at the end of the bar doing homework until Mom picked me up for hockey practice.

But now that I'm looking at it from Gaby's perspective, I realize I may have freaked her out by taking her to a deteriorating building in a rough part of the city.

"Gabs, my uncle owns this bar. It's completely safe," I try to reassure her through the window.

Finally, she releases her grip, wiggling her fingers as if helping bring the blood flow back to them after her death grip.

When I open the door, she tucks a loose chunk of hair behind her ear and whispers, "Sorry. I haven't been to many bars."

"I know it looks a little sketchy," I say, grabbing her hand and helping her out onto the broken, cracked sidewalk. "My uncle says it's part of the appeal."

With my fingers laced through hers, I lead Gaby through the door and down a few steps. The warm, dark wood paneling immediately envelopes us as if we've walked into a family member's basement. At least, that's how it feels to me.

"It's a total dive, but it's cool," I tell her as I weave her through the small tables scattered around the room and past the huge pool table. I've seen a shitload of people take a cue stick to the back of the head—or to their face, depending on which seat they'd taken.

"It's got character," she says, eyeing the Golden Tee golf video game looming in the back corner next to a vintage Pac-Man table.

When we saddle up to the bar, I pat an empty seat on the end for Gaby and grab the one next to one of the three other patrons. I'd rather she not be assaulted by regular who's already three sheets to the wind.

Neon beer signs with logos representing every Detroit sports team, as well as a few Michigan college teams, illuminate the bar area.

"Jesus, Landon, it's not even five o'clock," my uncle growls, tromping toward us while wiping his hands on a dingy bar towel. His his more-salt-than-pepper ponytail swings back and forth.

"Yeah, Brian. I know."

"Think your gonna make it to the NHL with this kind of schedule? Don't you have practice today?" He grabs a tall beer glass, sets it under the tap, and tips the PBR handle down.

"Had it his morning."

He complains, and yet—he's pouring my beer already.

"Oh, good. Does this fall under your clean eating routine?"

"It falls under my Steve-Fabian-got-called-up-and-I-didn't routine," I say sarcastically as he slides the beer in front of me.

Instead of comment, or apologize, he glances at Gaby. His demeanor immediately flicks from gruff irritation to warm and welcoming with a simple blink.

"What can I get you?"

"Um, a Sprite?" she stammers. "Please."

"I'm not gonna bite ya, sweetheart." He winks as he pulls a glass from under the bar. After a scoop of ice, he fills it with the soda gun.

"You been running?" Brian asks, setting Gaby's pop in front of her.

He asks the same questions every time I come in. Instead of

answer, I use my manners. "This is my uncle, Brian Taylor. Brian, this is Gaby Bertucci."

"What's the last name again?" He lifts an eyebrow as he fishes a straw out of the pocket in his apron and tosses it onto the bar.

Someone could write a book about my uncle's eyebrows. They have a personality all their own. Full and bushy with gray and white wiry hairs sticking out in every direction. Which totally fits him, because he's not an eyebrow-grooming kind of guy.

"Bertucci." Her voice catches on the word. "Gaby Bertucci."

Brian snatches a credit card receipt off the bar and tucks a pen behind his ear. "I knew I recognized the name. How's your dad doing?"

She removes the straw from its wrapper and pops it in her glass. "He's doing better. Thank you."

After an uneasy start, Gaby seems to have relaxed a bit.

It probably makes her feel better knowing Brian knows her dad. Detroit is a big city, but local, multi-generational business owners are a tight network. It's like a small town where everyone knows everyone.

The Bertucci family are big investors in the city. No matter what the economic climate, they've stayed true through thick and thin. Joe's heart attack probably spread quickly through the community grapevine.

"Glad to hear. Joe's too young for that shit."

She nods.

"Fucking Fabian," I whisper into my glass before lifting it to my lips and taking a sip. Or rather, a chug. I finish half of my beer in one tilt.

Suddenly, Gaby's rubbing my back and saying, "You'll get there. I know you will."

I turn to face her slowly because I don't want to spook her. I can't even imagine how pathetic my dumb-ass looks to her.

Not called up—*again*.

Whining to my uncle and drowning my sorrows with alcohol.

Nothing about this situation screams mentally-strong professional athlete.

When our eyes meet, she must think her touch is inappropriate, because she snatches her arm away as if my back is on fire.

I can't let her think I didn't approve, when, in reality, her reassuring touch is exactly what I need. "Thank you, Gaby. Sometimes I need that."

"Need what?" she asks.

"A pat on the back. A confident word about how I'll get my chance. It's hard to have people riding me all the frickin' time." My eyes flick to my uncle before my gaze drops back to my glass.

"Everyone needs encouragement." She places her hand on my shoulder. "Especially during the hard times."

I lift my beer, draining it in one gulp, before turning the attention away from me. "How about you, Gabs? Do you ever need encouragement?"

"All the time." She removes her hand again. "Right now."

"Why now?"

She pauses, maybe contemplating if she's going to deflect the question or not.

"It's completely surreal to be sitting in a bar with you acting like old buddies when we've never talked about anything but fruit, veggies, or Legos." The words gush out like a busted faucet—fast and without filter.

"It is, isn't it?" I laugh, thankful Gaby lets out her feelings. Too many people I know avoid hard conversations and confrontation, keeping everything in until they explode.

But not Gaby. I can practically see the gears tuning in her head, moving faster than her mouth—which is pretty damn fast.

"Why did you kiss me at the concert? How do you know so much about me? What brought on all this random attention?" She peppers me with questions.

"Whoa! Whoa!" I hold up both hands, hoping to slow her down and give me a chance to explain.

She laughs, then bows her head and tucks a lock of hair behind her ear. "Sorry. That was a bit much."

"When I left the store after your dad's heart attack, you looked absolutely lost. I didn't want to leave, but you insisted. I didn't know what to do. I tried to check in without being too nosy."

"I appreciated your messages and the flowers. They were gorgeous. I wanted to thank you, but you never left your number."

"Yeah." I laugh. "That was a fail on my part. I didn't know my number comes up blocked. Most people I call have me programmed in their phone. Didn't even think about it." I rake my fingers through my hair.

"When I was in the store last week, I heard you say you were going to the Drowned World concert in Chicago. We had a game there the night after so I bought a ticket and—" I lean back and stretch my arms out. "Jesus, I sound *so* fucking creepy."

Gaby nods. "Well, no one has ever tracked me down before."

"That didn't help." I roll my eyes.

"I didn't think it was creepy. But I *am* confused that you chose a concert in Chicago when you can talk to me any time at the store." She pats my upper thigh and my pulse quickens.

"I'm a massive idiot. Is that what you want me to say?"

"No," she says softly. "I want you to tell me the truth."

"The truth," I say with a chuckle. "The truth is, I've never wanted a girlfriend. I've gone out with girls and—" I bite my lip to stop myself because I don't want Gaby to think I'm some kind of fuckboy. "I'm young and focused on my career and never really had time for anyone."

"Okaaayyy." Gaby tries to look away, but I reach out and touch her cheek, gently turning her face to mine.

"Hear me out," I ask when she lifts her gaze to mine. "I've always liked you, Gabs. You're someone I could see myself hanging out with a lot, which is why I never pursued it. I didn't want to start something and not be able to follow through. Or push you aside for my career."

"Well, as far as I know you're still a hockey player and you can't seem to leave me alone. What changed?" she asks.

"Your father had a heart attack. That changed everything."

I lift my empty glass toward Brian, who shakes his head "no" as he fills a pint for another customer. If he's so annoyed by my drinking, why does he serve me in the first place?

"Oh, because you had to talk me though it and call nine-one-one for me?" She drops her gaze to her hands in her lap, inspecting her cuticles. "I froze like a flippin' idiot."

I hate when she's self-deprecating. I wish she could see herself as I see her—hell, as probably everyone who sets foot in a Bertucci store sees her. A bad-ass woman who can run multiple business like a boss.

"No. When Joe had that heart attack—" I pause and take a deep breath to gather my thoughts before exhaling slowly. "I don't know. It's like something clicked. I thought about how shitty it would be if I never told you how I felt about you."

Gaby touches my wrist. "I didn't realize your feelings for me were that serious."

"They aren't—I mean, they weren't." I roll my head back and lift my eyes to the water-stained ceiling tiles. "Seeing your dad go down and Fabian get called up rocked me. And after getting slammed by my coach and my father, I realized I had to make changes. My dad called it work-life balance."

Coach Vincent called it getting my head out of my ass when he railed me during practice after my defense partner left for Charlotte. I thought putting everything into my career was a strength. But evidently, my lows were too low and it affects my play—and the team.

"Interesting." Gaby's rubs her chin with her thumb and forefinger. "Papa's cardiologist told him the same thing."

I laugh. At least my dad's health advice is consistent.

"I've been focusing on appreciating where I am instead of trying to fast-forward to the future."

"How's that working out for you?" she asks a bit wistfully, as if she thinks she needs to do the same.

"I'm here with you, aren't I?"

"I'm part of your commitment to a balance between work and life?" She brings a hand to her heart. "You flatter me."

When I grab her hand, she gasps and looks at me.

"I want to get to know you better, Gaby."

"Oh, come off it. You don't know me at all," she scoffs.

"I thought I proved I did," I say, squeezing her fingers, hoping it triggers her memory of our exchange at the store. The wealth of random information I've racked up about her over the years simply by making small talk.

"No," she pulls her hand from mine. "You proved you're kind of a stalker." Her lips curve into a smile and she turns back to her drink.

"I'm not a stalker," I defend myself. "I'm a good listener. There's a difference."

"I don't eavesdrop on your conversations. Everything I know about you is public information."

My eyebrow lifts, peaked by excitement. "So, you're saying you've looked me up?"

"Well, yeah, I, I mean—" Her cheeks flush a rosy pink as she stutters. "You're a successful hockey player who's been coming to our stores for years. I like to keep up with your career."

"Have you ever searched for 'Landon Taylor naked?'" I nudge her arm with my elbow.

"Nope. I can't say that I have."

"Let me know if you do. I don't want to have that in my search history and I always wondered what was out there on me."

Her eyes widen and she leans back a bit. "Do you have anything to be worried about?"

"Uh, yeah."

"Oh."

Her defeated tone sounds as if I've pierced a balloon of hope in her heart. I'm trying to joke around with her, but she's on edge, so I rush to explain, "I've always gotta be on alert. I have three brothers with access to my baby bath photos. And I've had hundreds of teammates over the years. Hockey players like to play pranks. Mean-ass pranks."

She laughs, relaxing as amusement sparkles in her eyes. "Yeah. Drew has told me about quite a few of those kinds of pranks."

"The X-rated ones?" I ask, doubting her brother shared those.

"Probably not. But I don't need to know about those. There are some hockey traditions that should be left to the players."

"True." I nod. "Muggles just wouldn't understand."

Her head snaps up. "Did you just use a Harry Potter reference?"

"I know you think I'm a dumb jock, but Landon. Can. Read." I lean back in my chair and cross my arms over my chest. "I bet I could be part of your book club."

My comment makes her choke. She thinks the book club posts are always private, but I've seen public page conversations with—

Fuck! I'm totally a stalker.

"Why don't we start our own book club?" she suggests, lifting her drink to her lips.

"Only if I can name it."

"What would you suggest?"

"The Gabs and Landon Erotic Book Club?"

Her eyes flash wide in horror, then she pushes her glass out of the way, folds her arms on the bar, and buries her head into the hole.

I didn't think the joke would embarrass her so much. There's nothing wrong with the books she reads.

"I keep forgetting I have to be careful with you," I say softly, running my palm over her silky hair.

She turns just enough to catch me with a side glance. "I'm not fragile or naive. I'm just reserved."

I snort. "You haven't shut up this whole time."

Gaby lifts her head and sits up, as if regaining confidence. "*Okay*, I'm reserved around certain people."

"Glad I'm not one of them," I say, then nod my thanks as my uncle sets another beer in front of me.

"When people go through life and death situations together, I think they tend to bond quicker."

"That's true. So, let's bond." Feeling empowered by our conversation and my second round of liquid courage, I hook my toes on the rung at the bottom of her chair and pull her toward me. "You have two brothers. One who plays hockey and one who can't run a store to save his life."

She laughs, wiping the side of her mouth with her thumb. "Yep. That sums it up."

"I know Drew," I continue, mentioning her brother who I played with in Midgets. "I never knew he had an older brother though."

"Joey does his own thing. He barely ever went to any of Drew's games."

"Does his own thing how?"

"Smokes weed, plays video games, moves across the country, and sleeps on his friend's floor so he doesn't have to pay rent." She lifts her gaze quickly as if gauging my reaction for tolerance before quickly adding, "Not that there's anything wrong with that."

I grin, knowingly. "Ah. The slacker. Odd for the first born."

"What about you? Are you a typical middle child? Rebellious. Desperate for attention. Stuck in the middle, overlooked by the success of the oldest and the needs of the youngest."

I drop my gaze, picking at my cuticles as her description of middle-child stereotypes hits—hard. I know she's joking, but I can't find the humor. Not right now, when it feels like I got shafted again.

"When you put it that way, it sounds like I'm an ungrateful jerk."

"I didn't mean that. I was—"

"You're absolutely correct, Gabs," I interrupt her apology. "I *am* an ungrateful jerk. I've been in a funk over the last few days. And it's fucking with my head."

The silence between us sits heavy and thick, like a soggy sleeping bag left outside during a rainstorm. But I know enough about Gaby by now to know she won't let it persist for long.

"Want to talk about it?" she asks. "I may not have any answers, but I've always been a good listener."

"When I heard Fabian got called up to Charlotte, it sent my mind into a weird spiral. And I started getting salty about all sorts of things."

"It's understandable."

"Did you know my parents adopted my older brother, Jason?"

It's a total non-sequitur, but with the way my head is right now, it makes sense to me.

"I didn't know that." She leans back quickly, her chair wobbling with the impact. When she reaches for the bar to stop from falling backwards, I grab her chair to keep her steady. "Thanks," she says with a small, grateful smile.

"After a few years of trying and a few years of testing, they still didn't get pregnant. They couldn't afford in vitro, so they looked into adoption. Mom said she never cared if the kids came out of her body. She just wanted kids." I drop my hand to my leg. "They found Jason through an adoption service. A few years later, Mom got pregnant with me."

"That's awesome." Gaby reaches out to touch the hand resting on my leg. Which sends blood pumping through my veins and to my dick.

"Yeah. My parents were both really excited. Surprised, but happy, ya know?"

She nods.

"For the longest time, *I* was the baby. The miracle child they showered with attention. Now, my parents barely notice me."

"Is that even possible? Doesn't being a Charlotte Monarchs first round draft pick make you the golden child?"

"Yeah right," I scoff. "I have an older brother who leaps tall buildings and saves lives for a living. And two younger brothers who need a ton of attention and affection. I'm lost in the mix."

Gaby's eyes widen slightly, which makes me feel like an asshole.

"Jesus, I sound like a selfish prick." I run both hands through my hair. "I'm the only one who was actually born into my family and I'm complaining about my lot in life."

"You're allowed to have feelings, Landon, no matter how privileged you grew up."

"When they adopted Calvin and Nathan, I was stoked. I'm still stoked. Recently, I started having all these jealous—" I pause to take a sip of my beer and shake my head. "Privileged is a perfect word. I'm a privileged douchebag."

"I mean—" she begins quietly.

"Thanks for not judging, Gabs," I say sarcastically.

At first, she looks surprised, as if she didn't think I'd heard her, but then she shrugs.

"Well, I'm sorry, but you do. You're jealous because your parents, who are practically saints, give more attention to two young kids—whose parents didn't even want them—than they do you, a successful *adult* who's known nothing but love your entire life? Sorry if I don't feel bad for you."

Arrow in the bullseye of my heart.

"I know! I *know* I sound horribly selfish. I don't want to be. It's not who I am—or how I really feel. It's the intrusive thoughts I get when I feel like a complete failure. They corrupt my brain and then I dwell."

I let out an exasperated breath and tilt my head toward the ceiling. "I don't know how to make them go away. Every time someone else gets called up to the NHL, I feel like I'm missing an opportunity to make them proud."

"Have you told them how you feel?" Gaby asks softly.

"Well, if *you* think I'm a complete jackass, I can't even imagine how *they'd* feel about me," I admit, louder than I intended. When Brian lifts his head to observe our conversation from the other end of the bar, I lower my voice.

"I love my brothers. I love every kid that's lived with us through the years. I love that we got to be in their lives even if it was for a short time. I still love helping. I volunteer at an after-school program a friend of mine started. I work with the Aviators PR people to coordinate the team's community service." Ticking off my charitable involvements makes me sounds like an even bigger douche. "If I could just make it to the NHL."

Gaby purses her lips and shrugs, as if my last comment catches her off guard. "And then maybe if you score your first NHL goal. And maybe if you get married and give them grandkids. It's always going to be something, Landon. Maybe you should figure out what you want and what makes you proud of yourself instead of trying to please everyone else."

"You driving?" Brian's voice cuts through the air.

Startled, Gaby drops her gaze to her empty Sprite glass. She's confident and professional at work. She rocks out like no one else is in the room at concerts.

Yet, she's so timid around men.

I know she feels crushed by her patriarchal family, but I feel like there's something else—something she hasn't shared.

"Yeah." I push my glass forward for Brain to take. "Ready, Gabs?"

"Yep." She waves at my uncle. "Thanks so much, Brian. It was nice to meet you."

"You too, Gaby. Give your dad my best."

When she jumps off the bar stool, she rolls her shoulders back, which draws my eyes to her chest.

She's got a great rack.

As Gaby follows me out to the car, I bite my tongue so I don't say anything stupid. Well, anything *else*.

I'm still mentally chastising myself for sounding like such an insufferable prick in the bar. She hasn't said anything, so I'm sure she's uncomfortable and wants me to get her back to the store.

I should apologize. I should tell her I'm not usually like this—that I'm upset I'm going through such a rough time right now. But what does it matter?

Perception is reality.

I need to get my head together if I ever want to have a lasting career in professional hockey.

Or any chance with the girl of my dreams.

Chapter Nine

GABY

I MUST'VE PISSED LANDON OFF.

Our conversation completely stalled after I commented about him being jealous of his brothers.

I should apologize. I should tell him it wasn't my business. I should tell him I had no right to call him jealous.

"I'm sorry, Landon," I say after we've settled into his car.

"You have no reason to apologize. You said exactly what I needed to hear." He sighs before pulling his seatbelt over his chest.

Crap. It's worse than I thought.

"But I didn't have a right to say anything. I barely know you."

He groans. "I hate when you say that."

"What?"

"That you barely know me." He starts the car. "Nineteen years is not barely."

"Okay, fine. We're acquaintances. People who casually talk about produce and Legos." I rub my hands together.

"Hey now! I don't talk about produce and Legos with just anyone," he quips.

"Who would? It's not date conversation, is it?"

I'm no expert in topics people talk about on dates since I've never been on one.

"Is this a date?" He presses a few buttons and cold air blasts through the vents. "Damn. I'm probably not getting a second, am I?"

"Second?" The word almost sticks in my throat. "Are we going to talk about getting to first?"

"I said *a* second, as in a second date. Whoa, Gabs, get your mind out of the gutter. We barely know each other." His shoulders shake in a silent laugh.

Breathe breathe breathe.

"Chill, Gabster. I'm joking with you," he says, patting my knee. "It should warm up in a second."

I blame his touch, rather than the lack of heat, for the shivers shooting up and down my arms.

As he wheels out of the parking lot, he speaks again. "Since I've already bared my disappointing soul to you—"

"You aren't disappointing," I interrupt.

"Let's talk about *your* stereotype. You're the youngest and only girl in an extremely 'traditional'--" He uses air quotes on traditional,' letting me know he thinks it's bullshit "—Italian-American family. Princess. Shopaholic. Daddy's little girl who can do no wrong."

"Ha. Ha. Hahahahahaha." I can't help the madwoman laugh that escapes. Though his stereotype may be spot on for many families, he doesn't understand the Bertucci dynamic at all.

"That's a creepy-ass laugh, girl." Landon glances at me before turning back to the road. "Guess I'm wrong."

"Sorry. My parents probably want your stereotype to be true of me, but it isn't. The princess gene skipped me."

"So what's the truth?"

"Youngest. Only girl. Hates shopping and tiaras. I can do anything the boys can do."

"I see. You're the youngest with middle-child syndrome. No one sees you as you are. Only what they think you should be."

"I can run all of our stores with my eyes closed while on vacation in Fiji. But Joey is there right now, fucking up the register, unable to perform credit card transactions, forgetting to make the bank run to deposit cash."

Landon glances at me with wide eyes. "I didn't think you swore."

I fold my arms over my chest in mock defiance. "I can do anything the men can do."

"Touché." He smiles.

Letting out a sigh, I lean back in my seat. "Except get more people in the door. The men in my family get people in the door."

Landon scoffs. "Bertucci built its brand in a time when there were no huge chain grocery stores. Mom and Pop shops were everything. Owned by community members to serve the community. It grew from word-of-mouth, good products, and great customer service. It didn't grow because the men in your family are marketing gurus."

I tilt my head, contemplating his comment. He's completely right. It's obvious, but not something I thought of before. Papa doesn't understand a thing about marketing a new product. He's running a business that runs itself.

"That's true. I never thought of it that way before. All I see is how successful the stores are and how much Three-One-Three sucks right now. No one comes in."

"Hey!" He brings a hand to his heart dramatically. "I resent that."

"I'm sorry! I'm sorry!" I grab his hand and squeeze it. "I truly appreciate our loyal produce customers who shop at Three-One-Three."

Landon smiles. "That's better. I was about to take my money to a huge corporation that cares more about profits than people."

I scoff. "Please don't do that."

"Why didn't you start by selling art and locally made goods at the market? Seems like that would have been the best way to transition to see if the concept could support a brick and mortar."

I swallow hard. "Completely agree. But neither Papa nor my Uncle Sal would get behind it."

It's true, but it's not the whole truth. After I accused Jared Mitchell of rape, my grandfather wanted me away from the produce side of the business. Even though he doesn't work at the business anymore, he's still the patriarch. What he says goes.

"The produce customers are there for produce. They're not necessarily looking for local art," I say, veering the subject away from the sad reality. "We need a marketing plan. A way to reach out to a new group of clients."

"I agree and disagree," London says, which piques my interest. "How many people shop at the market on a Saturday? On average."

"About forty-five thousand." The number rolls off my tongue immediately, having just read an article about it last week.

"Forty-five thousand people choose to go to Eastern Market to shop. If that many people are committed to buying local—they want to buy a lot of things local." He glances at me. "I do agree that you need a marketing plan. Especially since the store is already up and running."

Forty-five thousand people on a Saturday is a mind-blowing amount. Yet, 313 Artisans barely gets any customers. What's the disconnect?

"Did you go to college?" I ask. It's random, and maybe even a bit rude, but I can't help it.

I know how to think critically. I'm good with numbers. Am I completely screwing myself by not furthering my education?

"I'm almost finished at the University of Illinois online."

"Majoring in—" I lead.

"Business administration."

"I probably need to go back to school. Give it a real go this time."

"You already have what people go to school for. You're a successful business and you have a blank slate with Three-One_three to add to the success. You don't need classes for that."

"Maybe there's a marketing certificate program?" I ask hopefully.

"Gabs," Landon begins. "You have it all. I bet you even have ideas."

"I do. But Papa doesn't think we need marketing. He says the Bertucci name is marketing enough."

"The Bertucci name isn't on that store. There's no way for someone to make the connections that it's the same family."

"Exactly! Now try explaining that to Papa." I snort. "Actually, *can* you explain it to Papa? You're a man. He'll listen to you. I'll go get a mani and pedi while the important gender makes the decisions."

Despite my sarcasm, his gaze darts to the chipped black polish on my fingernails.

"Simmer down, Gabs. I'm on your side. We're talking solutions right now."

"I know. I know." I take a deep breath and let it out slowly. "Okay. But my advertising plan is top-secret right now, so if you could keep it on the down low, that'd be awesome."

Landon nods and salutes me.

Discussing my grassroots marketing plan for the store with someone gives me an odd, queasy feeling. A mix of excitement and trepidation, as if I'm doing something wrong. It's been a crazy pipe dream since before we even opened.

I knew we'd need some kind of marketing to bring customers in, but Papa didn't agree with me. He said the reputation of Bertucci Produce speaks for itself. Our loyal customers would come and they'd tell their friends.

The only problem with his line of thinking is that *Nonno* wouldn't let Papa attach the Bertucci name to the store. Very few people, outside of a few regular customers who found the shop through word-of-mouth, would connect 313 Artisans and Bertucci Produce.

313 Artisans isn't a natural offshoot of a produce store—it's a concept that's been Mama's lifelong dream. The store specializes in products created by local artists; everything from paintings and photographs to pottery and T-shirts. Some of our best sellers are iconic photographs of Detroit landmarks past and present, like Tiger Stadium and the Fox Theatre.

It makes the entire extended Bertucci family proud to keep everything in our stores completely local.

Well, everyone except *Nonno*.

"Papa won't drop a dollar for advertising, so I'm investing my own money. I need to create a good quality, effective ad on a budget." I chuckle, unsure if it's even possible. Still, I continue, "My vision is to highlight the city since the store is all local goods, ya know? Maybe take a few pictures of landmarks. I'd love to get a local celebrity endorsement, but I certainly don't have money for that. Don't have money for a photographer either. I've been trying to figure out the fancy camera I got for graduation."

"Can you take classes?"

"I could, but I work weird hours and I can never find a class I can attend consistently."

"I have a friend who's awesome with cameras. I'll ask him if he can give you some pointers."

"Really?"

Landon glances up at me and flashes me a smile. "I want to help any way I can."

The definition of Landon: Eager to help everyone. Community leader. Kindhearted and generous despite his internal psychological struggles.

"Thanks, Landon. I really appreciate that." I continue, "Eventually, I want to run ads in a few local publications. We sell local artwork and gifts, so I thought we could put something in an eclectic newspaper like the *Motor City Nerve*. It would hit a lot of our target market. But I also wanted to try a few other places because we need to market to everyone with Michigan pride, not just artistic types."

"Like hockey fans?" Landon asks.

"Definitely! I'd love to tap into hockey fans."

"I bet I could talk to the PR department for the Aviators. I could get you an ad in our game program pretty cheap. Maybe free."

"You would do that?" Without thinking, I grab his free hand, which has been resting on the gear shift. I let go quickly, chastising myself internally for acting like a silly, giddy girl.

Landon frowns. He reaches for my hand, bringing it toward him and lacing his finger through mine. "Don't let go, Gabs. I like holding your hand. I like getting to know you."

"After all these years," I joke as he rests our joined hands on his thigh. It feels natural.

"And look at us! Talking about more than produce and Legos."

"Oh yeah. Look at us bitching about our perfect lives. Hashtag, first-world problems."

"No shit." Landon squeezes my hand as he chuckles. "Wanna go volunteer at the food bank or something? I need to cleanse myself of my selfishness."

"I need to get home. Serving our community together sounds more like a second date."

"So you're saying there *will* be a second date?"

"If you're asking."

"Actually, I think you asked me." Landon winks. "I like a strong woman who can do anything a man can do."

My heart is humming with happiness when he pulls to the curb in front of 313 Artisans ending a weird, but interesting ride. And we still haven't talked about the kiss. Any of them.

"We've gone this whole time without discussing all the kissing we've supposedly done. How is that?" I ask.

The skin around his eyes crinkles as he smiles. "You never asked."

"I'm asking now."

"I'm gonna get a ticket sitting here." He pulls his phone from his front pocket. "What's your number?" His thumb slides across the screen as I recite the digits. "I'm calling your phone now so you have my info. Call me later."

My heart skips, frolicking in my chest like a prancing unicorn. But I play it cool, responding with a smile and nod.

THE MORE I stare at my phone, the more my nerve to call Landon dwindles. His number taunts me, glowing on the screen since I'd retrieved it from my recent calls list and created him as a contact in my phone.

He told me to call him. So why does pressing the little green SEND icon seem so daunting?

I throw the phone on my bed. Sorting laundry seems like a more constructive use of my time than worrying about calling a guy. I lower myself to my knees and dump my laundry basket.

Flipping two white socks to my left, I start the lights pile. *He has my number.*

Black T-shirt goes into a darks pile on my right. *Maybe he'll call me.*

Khaki pants tossed with socks. *But he told me to call him.*

White underwear with black hearts. Lights? *But what if he's waiting for my call?*

White T-shirt to the lights heap. Now, I can't see the black hearts and I feel better about my decision. *What if he doesn't call me because I never called him?*

A less mundane task might take my mind off the phone call.

Or I could stop being such a coward and call the man.

Pushing aside my nerves, I drop my favorite black tank top onto the darks pile, saving it from becoming a stretched and torn casualty of indecision. Then I grab my phone and press the send button.

"Hey!"

"Hey, Landon. This is Gaby. Um, Gaby Bertucci."

The sharp laughter on Landon's end makes me pull the phone away from my ear for a second. "I know who you are, Gaby."

"Oh, well, um. I'm calling because you mentioned helping me come up with a marketing plan?" I say quickly, twisting a lock of hair around my finger. "Would you, um, do you still want to do that?"

If phone calls are supposed to be easier than face-to-face interactions, why do I sound like a blathering idiot while trying to have a simple conversation?

"I'd love to help you. If you can answer one trivia question."

"Okay."

"How old were you when we first kissed?"

Great, a trick question. He knows I don't remember the supposed kiss. But how could I have forgotten kissing Landon? I still feel the ghost of his lips from the unexpected kiss at the concert.

"Nineteen." It's not the correct answer, but it's the best answer I have since it's the only kiss I remember.

"Wrong."

"Just tell me, Landon. You know I don't remember and you keep dangling it over my head. How old was I?"

"Your kiss turned me into the majestic creature I am today, Gaby. I can't believe you don't remember."

"Well hello, Mr. Modest," I tease.

"One year, my parents dressed me and Jay up for Halloween and paraded us around Eastern Market. I was a frog."

Landon's pause tells me his story should spark some obscure memory of seeing him dressed as a frog. We had to have been kids. When had he been a frog?

"You're killing me, Gaby!"

"I can't help it. I barely remember my own Halloween costumes, how am I supposed to remember a random kid on Halloween at the market?"

"Random kid. Thanks." He chuckles.

"Just tell me."

"Halloween nineteen ninety-nine. You were some kind of Disney princess. I was a frog. Our parents told us that if we kissed, I'd turn into a prince."

His story doesn't ring any bells for me. Back then, I probably thought kissing him would really turn him into a prince, and took one for the team.

"It worked. Just took a few years."

"That is hilarious. *So* freaking hilarious."

"It's more hilarious that you don't remember. I'm offended."

"Well, now that the kiss mystery is solved. Let's plan some marketing." I can't believe Landon remembered kissing me on Halloween when he was seven years old. "Okay, so I thought we could—"

"Damn, Gabs!" Landon hisses. "You are cold as ice."

There's a lump in my throat. "I—what? Why?"

What did I do?

"Straight to business after the frog story."

"What do you want me to say? I don't even remember it."

He laughs. "Talking on the phone is stupid. It would make more sense if you came over to my place. We could put a plan together and make out, maybe create a mock ad."

The phone slips out of my hand, bounces off my shin, and falls onto the floor. *Shit!* I grab it and bring it back to my ear. "Excuse me? What did you say?"

"If you came over we could put a plan together and make up a mock ad. What did you think I said?"

Maybe he hadn't said "make out." Maybe I thought I heard him say "make out."

"I, never mind."

"What did you *hope* you heard me say?" There's a flirty, teasing lilt in his voice.

"Nothing. Stop."

"You're so easy to embarrass."

"I'm not coming over and we will not make out tonight. Can you just help me, please?"

"We're on the fast track, Gaby."

"What does that mean?"

"I like you. Just in case I haven't made that clear yet."

A response catches in my throat. No way Landon Taylor could be that into me. So soon. Or is it soon? Should I be counting the fact that we've known each other our entire lives?

"Your silence makes me wonder if you didn't realize how much," Landon says.

"I'm checking my room for hidden cameras. There may be some kind of reality show filming that I don't know about. *True Tales from the Twilight Zone.*"

The comment makes Landon laugh. I wait until he's regained his composure before speaking again.

"It's kinda weird, right? This sudden interest? I feel like I'm the dog at a dogfight party," I say.

"What in the world is that?"

It would be embarrassing to tell him it's something I'd read about it. Of course, I was because I'm the epitome of a nerdy book girl. He already knows it, I don't have to add fuel to the fire.

"Never mind."

"Fill in the dumb jock."

"You're not dumb. And being a jock, I'm surprised you *don't* know."

"Just tell me."

"It's a party where a guy has to bring the ugliest girl he can find, but he can't tell her. There's a vote and whoever has the ugliest girl wins money or something. It's terrible. It's—"

I should have kept sorting my laundry. Phone calls are not my forte. Opening my mouth in general is not my forte.

"Well, I can't say I don't know guys who would do something like that, because I know a ton of idiots, but I'd be wasting my money if I brought you. You'd be the hottest girl there."

Heat rushes to my cheeks and my heart races.

I've never had issues with how I look. My brown hair doesn't shine like models in shampoo ads, and my eyes are a dull brown, rather than rich and chocolatey, but I'm not bad looking.

I'm cute. Petite. The everyman, er, woman. Whatever.

"If I'm being honest," he continues before I have a chance to respond. "I'd never go to a party like that. Sounds like a major dick-bag thing to participate in."

If I thought his saying I'd be the hottest girl at the party made my knees weak, telling me he'd never be involved in something so offensive has the blood rushing to parts that haven't been excited in years.

"Good answer."

"What would ever make you think that about me?"

"It's not that I thought it was something you'd participate in. The thought crossed my mind because—" I pause, trying to explain my insecurity without saying I'm insecure. "I'm still confused as to why you started talking to me all of a sudden. And not just talking, but the full-court press."

"You act like I'm this celebrity, Gaby." He lets out a deep breath. "I'm just a regular guy. And despite the fantasy you have of me in your head, I'm not great a talking to women. Not until I stood there as your dad had a heart attack. I wanted to be there for you--to show you I cared. It gave me a reason to talk to you. And a reason to stay. A horrible reason. But a reason."

"I don't get it. You're a hockey player. People cheer for you in the stands. They go crazy when your name is announced."

"None of that is real. They cheer for the fictional character they have on a pedestal in their heads. They want the superhero. I'll give them the show while I'm wearing my uniform or at an Aviators event. But off the ice, I'm just Landon. I'm a twenty-one-year-old dude who's spent his whole life around guys. I'm not good at talking to chicks."

His response gives me something to think about.

It's easy to think all hockey players are caught up in the superstar lifestyle. But the everyday Detroiter probably couldn't pick an Aviators player out of a crowd.

"Never really thought of it that way. I guess I've had you on that superhero pedestal since you got drafted into the OHL."

"You've got a pedestal of your own, Gaby. My friends and I have called you the hot Italian princess for years."

Instead of letting his comment sink in, I brush it off with humor because it's pretty funny. "That makes me sound like a spicy sausage."

"Hot Italian sausage." Landon laughs. "Now I'm hungry."

"Oh my gosh, please don't say anything about me and your hot Italian sausage."

"I'm not Italian! How is my sausage Italian?" Landon teases.

"I know. I don't know. I—"

Oh my God! What's my problem? Why can't I shut up?

"You have a dirty mind, Gabriella." He lowers his voice. "I'm gonna have to hack into your e-reader and see what you've got in there."

"I told you I don't read stuff like that."

"Bull."

"Back to the marketing plan," I say. Subject closed.

Thankfully, Landon lets me off the hook, because he wants to talk about marketing for 313 as well. He seems eager to help bring more business to the store, even though it doesn't benefit him at all.

How often does that happen? Someone doing something out of the good of their heart for no compensation?

Landon is a member of the Taylor family, one of the most kind and selfless families I've ever met. I imagine with them it happens a lot.

Chapter Ten

GABY

THE MORE I STARE AT MY PHONE, THE MORE MY NERVE TO CALL Landon dwindles. His number taunts me, glowing on the screen since I'd retrieved it from my recent calls list and created him as a contact in my phone.

He told me to call him. So why does pressing the little green SEND icon seem so daunting?

I throw the phone on my bed. Sorting laundry seems like a more constructive use of my time than worrying about calling a guy. I lower myself to my knees and dump my laundry basket.

Flipping two white socks to my left, I start the lights pile. *He has my number.*

Black T-shirt goes into a darks pile on my right. *Maybe he'll call me.*

Khaki pants tossed with socks. *But he told me to call him.*

White underwear with black hearts. Lights? *But what if he's waiting for my call?*

White T-shirt to the lights heap. Now, I can't see the black hearts and I feel better about my decision. *What if he doesn't call me because I never called him?*

A less-mundane task might take my mind off the phone call.

Or I could stop being such a coward and call the man.

Pushing aside my nerves, I drop my favorite black tank top onto the darks pile, saving it from becoming a stretched and torn casualty of indecision. Then I grab my phone and press the send button.

"Hey!"

"Hey, Landon. This is Gaby. Um, Gaby Bertucci."

The sharp laughter on Landon's end makes me pull the phone away from my ear for a second. "I know who you are, Gaby."

"Oh, well, um. I'm calling because you mentioned helping me come up with a marketing plan?" I say quickly, twisting a lock of hair around my finger. "Would you, um, do you still want to do that?"

If phone calls are supposed to be easier than face-to-face interactions, so why do I sound like a blathering idiot while trying to have a simple conversation?

"I'd love to help you. If you can answer one trivia question."

"Okay."

"How old were you when we first kissed?"

Great, a trick question. He knows I don't remember the supposed kiss. But how could I have forgotten kissing Landon? I still feel the ghost of his lips from the unexpected kiss at the concert.

"Nineteen." It's not the correct answer, but it's the best answer I have since it's the only kiss I remember.

"Wrong."

"Just tell me, Landon. You know I don't remember and you keep dangling it over my head. How old was I?"

"Your kiss turned me into the majestic creature I am today, Gaby. I can't believe you don't remember."

"Well hello, Mr. Modest," I tease.

"There was this one year, my parents dressed up Jay and me for Halloween and paraded us around Eastern Market. I was a frog."

Landon's pause tells me his story should spark some obscure memory of seeing him dressed as a frog. We had to have been kids. When had he been a frog?

"You're killing me, Gaby!"

"I can't help it. I barely remember my own Halloween costumes, how am I supposed to remember a random kid on Halloween at the market?"

"Random kid. Thanks." He chuckles.

"Just tell me."

"Halloween nineteen ninety-nine. You were some kind of Disney princess. I was a frog. Our parents told us that you should kiss me so I'd turn into a prince."

"Oh my gosh." I still have no memory of it. But back then, I probably thought kissing him would really turn him into prince, and took one for the team.

"It worked. Just took a few years."

"That is hilarious. *So* freaking hilarious."

"It's more hilarious that you don't remember. I'm offended, actually."

"Well, now that the kiss mystery is solved. Let's plan some marketing." I can't believe Landon remembered kissing me on Halloween when he was seven years old. "Okay, so I thought we could—"

"Talking on the phone is stupid," he interrupts. "It would make more sense if you just came over to my place. We could put a plan together and make out, maybe create a mock ad."

The phone slips out of my hand, bounces off my shin and falls onto the floor. *Shit!* I grab it and bring it back to my ear. "Excuse me? What did you say?"

"Put a plan together and make up a mock ad. What did you think I said?"

Maybe he hadn't said "make out." Maybe I thought I heard him say "make out."

"I, never mind."

"What did you *hope* you heard me say?" There's a flirty, teasing lilt in his voice.

"Nothing. Stop."

"You're so easy to embarrass."

"I'm not coming over and we will not make out tonight. Can you just help me, please?"

"We're on the fast track, Gaby."

"What does that mean?"

"I really like you. Just in case I didn't make that clear at the concert."

A response catches in my throat. No way Landon Taylor could be that into me. So soon. Or was it soon? Should I be counting the fact that we've known each other our entire lives?

"Your silence makes me wonder if you didn't realize just how much," Landon says.

"I'm checking my room for hidden cameras. There may be some kind of reality show filming that I don't know about. *True Tales from the Twilight Zone*."

That comment makes Landon laugh. I wait until he's regained his composure before speaking again.

"It's kinda weird, right? This sudden interest? I feel like I'm the dog at a dogfight party," I say.

"What the fuck is that?"

It would be absolutely embarrassing to tell him I'd read about it. Of course I had because I'm the epitome of nerdy book girl. He already knows it, I don't have to add fuel to the fire.

"Never mind."

"Fill in the dumb jock."

"You're not dumb. And being a jock, I'm actually surprised you *don't* know."

"Just tell me."

"It's a party where a guy has to bring the ugliest girl he can find, but he can't tell her. There's a vote and whoever has the ugliest girl wins money or something. It's terrible. It's—"

I should have kept sorting my laundry. Phone calls are not my forte. Opening my mouth in general is not my forte.

"Well, I can't say I don't know guys who would do something like that, because I know a ton of idiots, but I'd just be wasting my money if I brought you, because you'd be the hottest girl there."

Heat rushes to my cheeks and my heart races.

I've never had issues with how I look. My brown hair doesn't shine like models in shampoo ads, and my eyes are a dull brown, rather than rich and chocolatey, but I'm not bad looking.

I'm cute. Petite. The everyman, er, woman. Whatever.

"Actually," he continues before I have a chance to respond. "I'd never go to one of those kinds of parties. Sounds like a major dick-bag thing to participate in."

If I thought him saying I'd be the hottest girl at the party made my knees weak, telling me he'd never be involved in something so offensive has the blood rushing to parts that haven't been excited in years.

"Good answer."

"What would ever make you think that about me?"

"It's not that I thought it was something you'd participate in. The thought crossed my mind because—" I pause, trying to explain my insecurity without saying I'm insecure. "I'm still confused as to why you started talking to me all of the sudden. And not just talking, but the full-court press."

"You act like I'm this celebrity, Gaby." He lets out a deep breath. "I'm just a regular guy. And despite the fantasy you have of me in your head, I'm not great a talking to women. Not until I stood there as your dad had a heart attack. And I had to be there for you. I had to show you I cared. It gave me a reason to talk to you. And reason to stay. A really horrible reason. But a reason."

"I don't get it. You're a hockey player. People cheer for you in the stands. They go crazy when your name is announced."

"None of that is real. They cheer for the hockey player—the fictional character they've put on a pedestal in their heads. They want the super-hero. And I'll give them the show while I'm wearing my uniform or at an Aviators event. But off the ice I'm just Landon. And I'm twenty-one. And I've spent my whole life around guys. I'm not good at talking to chicks."

That gives me something to think about. It's easy to think all hockey players are caught up in the superstar lifestyle. But the everyday Detroiter probably couldn't pick an Aviators player out of a crowd.

"Never really thought of it that way. I guess I've had you on that superhero pedestal since you got drafted into the OHL."

"You've got a pedestal of your own, Gaby. My friends and I have called you the hot Italian princess for years."

Instead of letting his comment sink in, I brush it off with humor because it's pretty funny. "That makes me sound like a spicy sausage."

"Hot Italian sausage." Landon laughs. "Now I'm hungry."

"Oh my gosh, please don't make a comment about me and hot Italian sausages."

"You really do have a dirty mind, Gabriella." He lowers his voice. "I'm gonna have to hack into your e-reader and see what you've got in there."

"I told you I don't read stuff like that."

"Bull."

"Back to the marketing plan," I say. Subject closed.

Thankfully, Landon lets me off the hook, because he wants to talk about marketing for 313 as well. He seems really eager to help bring more business to the store, even though it doesn't benefit him at all.

How often does that happen? Someone doing something out of the good of their heart for no compensation?

But Landon grew up in the Taylor family. And since I know their background of kindness, I imagine it probably happens a lot.

Chapter Eleven

GABY

"WERE YOU THE LAST ONE HERE LAST NIGHT, GABRIELLA?" PAPA asks.

"No. Joey locked up. Why?"

Papa shakes his head, dismissing me as he shuffles to the back, still staring at a scrap of printer paper in his hands. The door to the office slams.

"I'm telling Mama!" I yell.

Papa probably can't hear me, but I say it anyway. And I *will* tell Mama. He isn't supposed to be at 313 until Dr, Taylor gives him the all-clear.

How will he recover if he keeps his stress level at a ten?

Pissed and stressed are not the ideal moods for Papa to be in before I present my idea for a marketing campaign. But it's now or never. I don't have a complete advertisement with photos and slogans to show him, but I printed a rough draft of it as well as an outline of the marketing plan Landon and I created together.

We'd fleshed out the details on the phone the previous night. After memorizing the information Landon passed to me from the Aviators sales team, I can recite the statistics about advertising with them like it's the *Our Father*.

For the first time in years, maybe in my entire life, I feel confident. I know my plan. I've prepared for any logical business questions Papa has for me. I'm ready.

I've been bouncing on my toes all morning, waiting to pounce on my father when he emerges from the office. But my confidence declines with each passing minute he doesn't come out.

When Landon walks into the store at lunchtime, it's like the sun burst through a cloud of gloom. His eyes light up and he grins when he sees me. I run around the counter and vault myself into his arms, unable to contain my excitement.

"Hey, Gabriella," he says as he pulls me in for a hug.

"Hey." I squeeze him tight before leaning back and skimming my palms over the sides of his face and hair before cupping the back of his head. The intimacy feels bizarre. But after spending yesterday together and our strategizing phone call, we bonded. It finally feels like we've known each other as long as we have.

Landon kisses my forehead. "You're beautiful."

"You are, too." I wink at him.

"I finally cornered Luke and he said he'd teach you how to use your camera."

"Are you kidding?" I push back. "That's awesome."

"Can you meet him next week?"

"Yes. I can meet whenever he's available. Just let me know so I can change my schedule here if I need to."

London nods. "Did you get in touch with the advertising people?"

"What advertising people?" Papa's voice rumbles behind me. For a large man, he didn't make much noise coming out of the office.

I try to step back, but Landon embraces me once more before he lets go. Though I enjoy it, the hug has contradictory results, giving me a burst of confidence while simultaneously diminishing my professionalism in front of Papa.

"We came up with an awesome advertising idea to talk to you about." I spin out of Landon's arms and move toward my father.

"Advertising for what?"

"For the store."

"What store are you talking about, Gabriella?" The exasperation in his voice tells me he's not interested, or even amused.

"This store."

"We don't need advertising for this store." Papa shakes his head. "I told you that already."

"Papa, we hardly have any business in here. I know you've seen the reports."

"Yes, Gabriella, I have seen the reports. I've been running businesses for over thirty years. We don't need advertising."

Undeterred, I press on. Why not? I've already pissed him off. Might as well state my case.

"You've been running well-known businesses. You never had to advertise. This store is different." I continue talking as I rummage through my purse for the incomplete mock-up ad I created. "No one realizes this store is related to Bertucci Produce, but with this ad—"

"We don't need to advertise. And I don't want to hear another word about it."

"Mr. Bertucci, Gabriella knows this store in and out," Landon interjects. "She knows what it needs to be successful."

"Who are you to talk to me about success?" Papa's eyes narrow on Landon.

I press a hand to his chest. "Landon, it's okay. Please, let me handle this."

"I know you need customers. Look at this place." Landon ignores me, gesturing around the empty store. "And Gab—"

"You should mind your own business, son," my father snaps.

"Papa!"

"Maybe if you spent more time analyzing your hockey skills instead of my store, you might be playing in the NHL right now!" Papa yells at Landon before storming back to the office.

Landon stands completely still, staring at the door as my father slams it.

"Landon, I'm so sorry."

"I'll call you later," he says without looking at me. Then he spins around and walks out.

Papa is overbearing and opinionated and has never been one to keep his overbearing opinions to himself. After nineteen years, I've gotten used to it, but Landon didn't deserve Papa's wrath.

The two most important men in my life are irritated with each other and with me. Though it contradicts everything I just stood up for, I'm glad 313 Artisans has no customers right now.

Because I don't want anyone to see me standing in the middle of the store crying.

Chapter Twelve

GABY

PHOTOGRAPHY HAS ALWAYS BEEN ONE OF MY PASSIONS. EVER SINCE I was a kid, I'd grab my parents' pocket-sized camera or cell phone and snap away. I'm not saying I had talent or understood depth or saturation or anything technical or artistic.

Even now, I just point my smartphone and press the screen to capture an image. If I don't like it, I delete it. If I think it needs enhancements, I send it through one of the numerous photo-editing apps downloaded on my phone. And if I really want to impress myself and others, I'll edit on my laptop using fancy software.

When I received a digital SLR camera, complete with two additional lenses and a beautiful leather case, as my graduation present from my parents, it floored me. I didn't realize that they noticed my passion. I thought they brushed it off as a teenage girl's way of expressing herself in a digital world.

I love the camera. It's my baby. But other than removing the lens cap and pressing the button to take a picture, I have no clue how to work it. I can press the playback button to see the photos I've taken, but I don't know how to analyze them from a photographer's standpoint.

I tried reading the manual and watching online videos, but it all sounded like a foreign language. Aperture Priority. Shutter Priority. F-stop. *WTF?*

"A person who doesn't understand how the aperture works shouldn't even have this kind of camera," Luke Daniels says out loud, as he manhandles my camera. "If you want to point and shoot, use your cell phone."

Okaaaay.

When Landon offered to hook me up with a friend for a few lessons, I didn't realize the friend he had in mind was Luke Daniels, one of his teammates.

Correction: Luke Daniels isn't just a teammate. He's the captain of the Aviators. The face of the team. And rightfully so.

Luke is five foot eleven, and 197 pounds of pure, defined muscle. The thick stubble dusting his cheeks and jaw is the same color as his shoulder-length locks—black coffee with a touch of milk. His voice has a sexy, gruff scratchiness to it as if he swallows knives in a freak show in his spare time.

He barely smiles.

And he's bossy as hell.

This may explain why I've already inched a few feet toward my car when we've only been at it for five minutes. He intimidates the crap out of me.

"Um. Do you hate me?" I ask meekly.

"What?" Luke asks, his voice deep and loud. Though I like it, I keep expecting him to cough and shake the scratch out.

"You're, like, yelling at me, and I don't know why."

I also don't know why I've turned Valley Girl when confronting him. Did throwing in a "like" make me seem more approachable than bitchy?

"I'm not yelling!" he says loudly. Then he catches himself and lowers his voice to an acceptable conversational decibel. "I've been around the lug-heads too much this week. Sorry, Gaby."

"No problem."

Landon told me the team's current four-game losing streak ticked off Rick Vincent, the Aviators coach, so much that he instituted a week of mandatory team events.

Which must've been his way of getting the guys to bond. Lunches, dinners, and movie nights together. Maybe even painting each other's toenails. I don't have any clue how big, bad hockey players bond.

"Okay, so look." Luke points to a tiny wheel with pictures and letters printed on it at the top of my camera. "The camera is built with these presets already. You can use these and your pictures will turn out fine." He turns the dial a few times. "Portrait, night, action."

I nod as he tells me what each icon stands for. I'd read that far in the manual.

"But if you want awesome pictures, you use the manual settings. Photography is the manipulation of light. That's where aperture and f-stop come in. Aperture is the opening in the lens which allows the amount of light to come through. The f-stop is the term used for the different size aperture. There's no specific guide or cheat sheet. I can't tell you to use f/22 for this kind of picture or f/8 for another kind of picture. So many factors go into it. Shutter speed, lens, subject, weather."

Luke stops talking to glance at me. My eyes must have glazed over because he smiles before he continues. "I know it's overwhelming, Gaby, but this is the fun part. This is where you get to experiment."

"What's the difference in the numbers? What do f /22 and f/8 mean?" I ask, eager to learn.

I really want to grasp the concepts. I need to be good at this if I want quality photos for our advertisements without paying out my nose for a professional photographer.

"A smaller aperture will have a larger f-stop number. The opposite is also true, a larger aperture will have a smaller f-stop number."

"Where do I change it if I want to experiment?"

"Right here." Luke flips the camera toward us to show me the lens from the top. "These are the settings. Just turn slowly to get to the next setting."

"Can you demonstrate? I think I'll get it once I start seeing what you're talking about. It's hard for me to grasp the concepts without seeing an example. And I'm not sure how all of this will help me yet."

"Good idea." He jogs backward a few steps and lifts the viewfinder to his eye, putting my face in its sight.

A burning feeling rushes to my cheeks when I hear the *click* of the camera. I lift my hand to cover my nervous smile, but he keeps clicking away.

"I thought you'd be demonstrating on scenery or trees or something."

Luke laughs. "Using a subject is easier for me to explain what I need to. You can flitter off to take pictures of flowers and waterfalls later."

"Waterfalls? In Detroit? Maybe the arc of the water cascading from a firefighters' hose onto a burning building."

"Sadly, that would be an amazing picture."

I nod in agreement. A hollow feeling pinches my stomach from how close to home it hits.

"Remember how I said photography is the manipulation of light?"

No rest for the tortured soul on Luke's watch.

"Yes. And aperture is the opening in the lens that allows the amount of light to come through."

"Right." Luke smiles. "Check this out." He presses a button and an image appears on the playback screen. Then he holds out the camera and shows me the picture.

It's beautiful, even with plain old me as the subject. He'd captured a brightness in my brown eyes and the shy smile partially hidden under the sprawl of my fingers.

A couple is sitting on a park bench behind me, but they aren't in focus, just a blur of peach instead of individual faces. I'm the focus of the picture.

"How did you get that aura-type glow?" I ask, referring to the brightness around me.

"Either you're a saint," Luke teases. "Or I manipulated the light."

That makes me burst out laughing. The camera clicks start again.

"Dude! I'm no saint, and I will make like an angry celebrity and smack that camera out of your hand if you take one more picture of me."

When the camera clicks again, I reach out and rush forward.

Luke shrugs. "It's your camera. I'm betting you won't bust it."

I stomp toward him and snatch the camera out of his hand, turning it on him and snapping a few pictures of my own. Maybe my shots would turn out as magical as his if I didn't touch any of the settings he used.

When I turn on the screen for playback mode, the images are just regular old pictures. No ethereal glow. No sharpness. No bright eyes or bushy tails.

"You're a rookie. Try it again." Luke glances at the sky and moves behind me. "Don't want the sun directly behind me. That'll mess with your light."

I take at least a hundred more shots, listening as Luke directs me where to move the f-stop and how to set the ISO speed. If I'm honest, he's a great teacher. He explains what to do, then stops to show me things to look for in the photo with each change I make to the settings.

Though I began training by taking numerous shots of him, by the end, I've captured strangers, trees, buildings, even the intimidating, oversized tiger statue at one of the entrances to Comerica Park, the field where Detroit's baseball team plays home games.

"Hungry?" Luke asks.

Without waiting for my answer, he starts walking away and slips into a local bar and grill, located at the end of the street where we've been taking photos. I follow him inside.

"Hey, Lukey!" a guy behind the long bar calls out as Luke sits down.

The bartender's weathered face and yellow-white beard make him look years older than he probably is, but the squint of happiness in the lines around his eyes shows his excitement at Luke's presence.

"Hey, Clancy. How's it going? How's Althea?" Luke asks.

Clancy reaches over the bar and shakes Luke's extended hand. "She good. Hasn't been in the hospital recently, so we thanking the good Lord for that."

I slide onto the bar stool next to Luke and set my camera bag on the floor at my feet, hooking the strap around my knee.

"That's good to hear. This is my friend, Gaby. Gaby, this is Clancy, president of my fan club." Luke winks at Clancy as he introduces me.

"Fan club!" Clancy shakes his head as he answers, but his lips hold a huge grin. "Nice to meet you, Gaby. What can I get you?"

"Nice to meet you, too. A water would be great. Thanks."

While Clancy fills a glass, Luke hands me a menu. I look it over while Luke and Clancy continue their conversation.

"How's business been?"

"You know it's crazy for baseball. And football rolls right behind it. Aviators games help out, too."

"Well, with this place down the road from Robinson. It's easy for people to congregate here to talk about how awesome I'm doing."

"You crack me up, Luke. You got yourself a Canadian Eddie Murphy here, Miss," Clancy says, then walks toward the other end of the bar.

His head darts back and forth in search of something. He returns with a bottle of Bloody Mary mix, judging by the thick red-orange liquid dotted with tiny flecks of black pepper and who knows what other spices. Clancy pours vodka and the mix into a pint glass. He finishes it off by dropping in a dill pickle spear and a blue sword toothpick packed with three green olives, then places the drink in front of Luke.

"Thanks, Clancy." Luke gives him a grateful smile before the bartender moves on to serve another customer.

After he takes a sip of his Bloody Mary, he turns to me. "Let's take a look at how you did today."

Suddenly nervous, I reach down and pull the bag into my lap slowly. I remove the camera and hold it out to Luke. When he tries to take it, my grasp tightens.

"Let it go, Elsa."

Startled by his children's movie reference, my grip loosens, and Luke seizes the camera. He zips through my photos, stopping to point out things I should be looking for or how I've improved from frame to frame.

"You're getting it." He nods, pressing the forward button and advancing through the shots.

"Thanks," I say, proud of myself.

Today was a quick lesson. I know I'll have to take thousands more shots to truly understand when I need to use certain settings, but it feels good to have a basic understanding of what I'm doing rather than just pointing, shooting, and hoping it comes out well enough.

"And you can always edit."

"Yeah, I'm good at the editing part. I've been doing that for a long time."

"Do you use software or just phone apps?"

"I use Lightroom."

"That's a good one. Do you have a laptop?" Luke flips the switch to turn my camera off and hands it to me.

"Yep." I place the camera in my bag and zip it up.

"Make sure you bring it to Landon's when you guys work on the ad. I doubt he has that on his computer." Luke continues, "What's up with you and Landon anyway?"

"Nothing. We're friends."

Luke side-eyes me while taking a sip of his drink. "That's not what he says."

"Oh." I lower my eyes to my camera bag as I set it gently on the floor at my feet. Unwilling to let the big, bad Aviators captain see my disappointment.

"Don't get all rejected on me," he warns. "I meant the kid has it bad for you."

"No, he doesn't."

"Do you think I give photography lessons to anyone, Gaby? I'm a busy guy."

I almost laugh, but I realize quickly he's serious about being a busy guy. I mean, I know he's busy and his time is important, but it's still funny when a guy tells someone he's busy. Like he has to drive home his importance.

"Do you drive a Dodge Stratus?"

"What?"

"*Saturday Night Live*?" I ask. "Will Ferrell?"

The empty expression and slight tilt of his head seem to question my sanity, so I give up.

"Nothing." I shake my head, laughing as I think about the old *Saturday Night Live* skit where Will Ferrell tries to make his family realize his importance by yelling, "I drive a Dodge Stratus!"

Instead of explaining, I continue, "Photography is obviously your passion. I just figured you liked to teach people about it."

"Because I seem like the warm, fuzzy teacher type?"

"I honestly didn't think about it, Luke. I didn't realize you were the person Landon was talking about until I met you today. It surprised the heck out of me."

"Well, it's hard to say no when a guy is practically begging at your feet to give lessons to the girl he's had a crush on since childhood."

You'd have thought Clancy accidentally poured straight vodka in my glass, with the way I choke on my water. "What?"

"Oh, Gaby. You're just as naive as he is. I'd say it was cute if we didn't live in a world that barely lets children be naive anymore, let alone adults."

Other than his official title as captain of the Aviators, and his obvious camera knowledge, I don't know anything about Luke. But I'm pretty sure he just confirmed the bomb Landon dropped on me at the concert in Chicago.

"There was no way Landon has had a crush on me since childhood." I dismiss Luke's comments. He's baiting me.

Landon and his family have been customers at our family's stores for as far back as I can remember. If he had any interest in me, it would have manifested years ago, right?

Landon never showed any interest in me until he watched Papa have a heart attack right alongside me.

Any good person would call 911 and stay to see if they could help. His sudden interest could easily be defined as classic White Knight syndrome. I'm not the kind of girl who can keep Landon's attention for long. I'll just enjoy it while I have it.

Luke glances at the doorway. "Speak of the devil," he says, grabbing his Bloody Mary and lifting his eyes to the TV screen above the bar.

I spin around in my seat. Landon stands there, his arm extended, holding the door open for a man walking in behind him. It's probably because Luke's comments are so fresh, but Landon's face seems to light up when our eyes meet. His eyes widen ever so slightly and his lips turn up in a full smile.

"Landon Taylor! What a surprise!" Luke's voice drips with mock surprise. "What are *you* doing here?"

"I was out for a run. Stopped for some water." Landon eases onto the bar stool next to me.

Luke leans over me to sniff Landon. "You smell nice for someone out for a run."

I stifle a laugh. Luke's right. Landon smells like soap and cologne, not sweat. My heart speeds up with the thought that he wanted to see me again.

"I don't have to smell bad."

"Yeah, you do." Luke sips his drink. "You smell bad by nature."

"Fuck off." Landon reaches around me and punches Luke's bicep. The Bloody Mary sloshes around in the glass but doesn't spill.

Landon turns his attention to me. "How did he do?"

"Luke knows his stuff. If I can remember one-third of what he told me, I'll be fine."

"You'll remember, Gaby. And you can always look it up in the manual, now that you know what it all means," Luke assures me.

I nod. I have no clue what it all means; I just hope I remember how to set my camera up as he showed me to get the effects I want because if I try going back to the manual, it would still read like Russian to me.

"I'm surprised you let me help her with her camera since you've been hiding her from us. When are you gonna bring Gaby out?" Luke asks Landon.

"I'm not hiding her. I'm trying to get her to like me before you fuckers scare her off. Or try to steal her."

"Well, you don't have to worry about me, but you know Gribov will be sniffing around like a fucking dog."

"Ugh, why couldn't he have stayed in Charlotte?"

"He needed to get knocked on his ass," Luke says. "Did you see that celly?"

"The one after his first goal?" Landon asks. "Yeah, the fucker needs to act like he's been there before."

"And that's why he got sent back down."

"Such a fucking prick," Landon adds.

Instead of trying to keep up with a conversation that sounds as foreign as my camera manual, I look around the restaurant.

From the outside, it looks like an old-school diner, with its red neon sign above the door and blue horizontal stripes accenting the whitewashed brick. Inside, it has wood finishes and a bar spanning the entire width of the long back wall.

"She's right beside you," Luke says.

My head whips back to the guys.

What did I miss? Something good?

"You've got it bad, man." Luke drains his Bloody Mary and raises his hand to get Clancy's attention.

"I know." Landon places his hand on my upper thigh and I tense at his intimate touch.

Clancy nods and immediately drops what he's doing to make Luke another drink. It seems a bit odd since patrons are elbow to elbow at the bar, occupying almost every seat. Bartenders usually don't stop everything during a rush, not even for their regular customers. I wonder what kind of relationship Luke and Clancy have behind the scenes.

"Looks like you two are official." Luke pushes his empty Bloody Mary glass toward the bartender's side of the bar and lifts his eyes to the T.V. screen again.

Landon ignores him and says, "I thought of an amazing place to do a shoot."

Chapter Thirteen

GABY

TWO WEEKS AFTER HE MENTIONED KNOWING AN AMAZING PLACE TO take photos, Landon and I finally have time to check it out.

"I can't believe I've never been here."

Tourist mode kicks in as I spin in a slow circle, mouth agape at the bleak beauty of the skeleton that was once Michigan Central Station. The train depot stands tall, though it's no longer a bustling hub, but a rundown, graffiti-covered shell of its former glory.

The terminal, with its arches and columns and peaks, is straight out of a Gothic dream. It's such a perfect setting for a ghost story. I can practically see spirits gliding through the hundreds of tiny windows.

"I did a thirty-mile bike ride a few years back. We rode past here. A ton of people stopped to take pictures and check it out." Landon moves closer, now standing under a great arch.

"Can we go in?"

"Can we? Yes." He chuckles. "Are we supposed to? Probably not."

He extends his arm, silently urging me to take his hand. I slide my palm against his and squeeze before following him through the open entryway. A shiver racks my entire body as we walk through. It could be from the touch of Landon's hand or the queasy feeling nailing my stomach as we step inside the dilapidated building. Like we've burst through a mass of ghosts.

I'm glad to be here with him, because never in a million lifetimes would I have crossed that creepy threshold myself.

I've watched too many shows about divers who uncover treasures sunken in the sea. The train station reminds me of the footage of a shipwreck. A manmade marvel now rusted, frayed, forgotten, swallowed whole, and taken back by the land.

When Landon pulls me into the heart of the station, I swallow to keep from crying.

Even with all the building's fractures and flaws, the facade looms, haunting and beautiful, though totally abandoned. The inside is completely wrecked—cracked, broken, splintered, destroyed. The columns are intact but for multicolored words and art spray-painted across them.

Light pours in.

"Wouldn't that be awesome, Gabs?" Landon squeezes my hand. "Gabs?"

I'd been so entrenched in sadness thinking about the once-grandiose building, that I didn't hear Landon. "Sorry. What was that?"

"I was thinking we could take pictures in front of the building. Unless you wanted to take them inside. I don't know if we should highlight how rough it looks in here."

"Yeah, outside would work." I let go of his hand and step toward one of the prominent pillars.

I grab my camera and lift it to my eye, squinting as I snap a picture. I check the image on the screen and shake my head. As I circle the column, I adjust a few settings and take another shot, trying to capture the light just right.

"Much better," I whisper, cracking a slight smile.

I flinch when Landon's stomach presses against my back. "Let's see." He peers over my shoulder trying to catch a glimpse of the tiny playback screen.

I press a few buttons and hold the camera up to him.

"That's sick, Gabs. You're getting really good." In the frigid air of the open station, his breath warms my cheek.

"Yeah, well, Photoshop helps a lot," I say.

"No Photoshop on that one yet."

I can't stop the smile that breaks out across my lips. It seems conceited to say thank you when someone compliments me or my work. I don't take compliments well.

If I'm going to scout photo shoot locations with Landon, I need to rein in my astonishment that he would do this for me and my family.

I circle the room in slow motion. If it's possible to be completely creeped out and in awe at the same time, that's how I feel.

The graffiti scares me a bit. A gang member could walk in, paint cans drawn, at any minute. Then again, I'm pretty sure Mafia guys walk into Bertucci Produce regularly, so I guess danger could be anywhere.

"What are you thinking?" Landon asks. He climbs onto a step at the bottom of one of the columns, wraps one arm around it, and hangs off like someone familiar with stripper poles.

"You don't want to know." I shake my head, laughing at my thoughts.

Landon grabs the column with his extended arm and jumps down. "I do. You're being so quiet. I can't tell if you're freaked out or what?"

"A little freaked out. This place is creepy on the inside. But cool. Creepy cool."

I snap a few more shots of the interior, trying to get the daylight streaming through the windows. I want to capture the haunted feel; a halo, a shadow, something.

"Creepy cool. Haunted. Abandoned. I just described our whole fucking life as Detroiters, eh?" A bitter laugh escapes him.

"I know, right? I don't know one person without a painful story."

"What's yours?"

"Hmm?" I lower the camera.

"What's your story? I see a shy girl from a successful family."

"Success comes with hard work."

"I never said it didn't."

"My story? Arson. Murder. Most recently theft." As I tick off the tragedies my family has gone through, it makes our life sound like a suspense novel. And those were only the ones that affected me directly.

"Holy shit, Gaby."

"I should be in jail, right?" I joke, smiling to lighten the mood. "But this is Detroit."

"Wanna talk about it?"

A beam of sunlight bounces off a piece of broken glass in the debris covering the floor, creating a prism across one of the large columns.

Sunshine and rainbows and murder and arson.

Life. And death.

I kick the pile, sending debris flying, but that piece of glass stays. Stubborn. I bring the camera to my eye and snap a picture of the tiny rainbow against the dirty column covered in graffiti.

"Well, the murder had nothing to do with me. It was Papa's best friend and it took a huge toll on our family. He was shot while helping Papa unload a produce truck one morning. A senseless drive-by. Papa was devastated." I pause. "We were all devastated."

"I'm sorry."

I shrug and continue. "Remember when the night before Halloween was an unofficial holiday to set houses on fire?"

Landon nods. "Devil's Night."

"Yeah, well, evidently no one told the people who burned our house down that it's called Angel's Night now."

"Fuck, Gabs. Recently?"

"Nine years ago. We lost everything. Every earthly possession. Thankfully, we weren't home. A family friend who's a cop called us when he heard our address on the scanner."

"I'm so sorry."

"It's life." I shrug again, dismissing his pity and moving toward the exit of the train station, flipping the off switch on my camera as I walk.

Claustrophobia sets in.

Despite the open air, the hollowed-out station echoes the memory of the hollowed-out shell of our house after the fire.

Too similar. Too eerie. Too close.

"But you didn't leave the city?"

I stop in the doorway, waiting until Landon catches up to me. "Nope. Papa thought about rebuilding, but why build new when we could buy a beautiful old house around the corner?

"We were lucky. We had family to stay with while we house-hunted. We had the means to buy another house. We had the means to buy clothes and toys and . . . *stuff*."

"Doesn't make it any easier. Or justifiable." Landon changes his voice to a low, doltish timber. "These people can afford to rebuild their lives, so let's set their house on fire."

"That's *exactly* how I imagine the arsonist sounding."

Landon laughs. We step outside together. "What do you miss the most?"

"My bedroom." The wonderful memories of my old room fill me with warmth. "Oh, Landon, I barely have words to explain it. Papa built my bed to look like a castle. It took up an entire wall." I spread my arms to demonstrate the enormity of the structure. "There was this wide, short staircase leading to the second bunk. It looked like I was on a balcony when I was on the top bunk. And next to the staircase was a tall, white bookshelf with a pink turret. There was one on the other side by the slide, too."

"The slide?" Landon asks, feeding my excitement.

"Yes. A fat, stubby little slide." I close my eyes and take a deep breath as if the air outside an abandoned train station holds magical molecules that can transport me back to when I was a tiny princess in an enormous castle. "And between the bookshelves, there was a rounded opening, like the entrance to a castle, that led to the lower bunk. I had to sweep aside a sheer, pink drape to get in."

"Sounds amazing."

Landon's voice brings me back to the present and I reluctantly open my eyes.

His eyebrows scrunch together, and a small smile sits on his lips. "I can't see you with a princess room."

"Well, Papa built it for me when I left my crib. I didn't have a choice," I say. "But, heck—who wouldn't want a castle?"

Does a girl ever outgrow a castle? I don't think so. As we age, we want convenience—less pink, more granite.

"What does your room look like now?"

"I miss my Harry Potter books the most, though," I continue without answering his question. "I mean, they were all first editions since Joey got the new book every time one was released. I could easily buy another set at a bookstore, but those were perfectly worn by three sets of grubby Bertucci kids' hands."

Landon slides his hand in mine as we walk to where he's parked. "You miss books the most. Can't say I'm surprised."

The warm feelings from my trip down memory lane melt and disintegrate, just like everything had in the fire. Back to reality.

I squeeze his fingers and whisper, "Don't make fun of me."

"I'm not."

When we stop in front of his car, Landon grabs my hips and lifts me onto the hood. "*You* are the last person I'd ever make fun of, Gabriella Bertucci."

I lean into him, seize each side of his unbuttoned coat, and pull him toward me. I need his air to breathe, after choking on memories of life before the fire.

Landon doesn't disappoint, lowering his head to mine. His lips touch my mouth, but instead of kissing me, he speaks. "You are strong." His hands rove, skim, and squeeze my sides. He dips them under my sweater and his frigid fingers pulse against my warm skin.

I wrap my arms around his neck before he has me sprawled flat against the freezing metal hood.

"You are beautiful." His hands, now warm, slide from my waist up to the wire of my bra, thumbs slipping underneath to caress the soft, sensitive skin.

My feet search for some ledge or opening in the front of the car, but instead, they slip down the sleek, rounded hood.

Damn Landon and his tiny foreign vehicle with no grill for me to rest my feet.

My limbs have a mind of their own, stimulated by each pass of his fingers over tender flesh. Landon must notice my legs bicycling in an attempt to ground myself and takes pity on me. He removes his hands from under my sweater, grabs my legs behind my knees, and wraps them around his hips.

"Perfect." He lowers his head and licks my neck before taking my earlobe in his teeth.

My chest slams against his as I slip my arms around his neck and squeeze his torso with a viselike leg lock.

"Now tell me what your room looks like," he commands, lifting me off the car.

I laugh and kick him in the butt with my heel while tightening my grip on his neck.

Landon meets my eyes before he lowers his lips to my ear and whispers, "I'll find out, Gabriella. Someday I'll see your room."

"I live with my parents."

"They sleep, don't they?"

"Very lightly."

"Not a problem for me, but something tells me you're a screamer."

"Oh my God!" I reel back in embarrassment, releasing my hold on his neck and covering my face with my hands.

With the sudden, unexpected movement, Landon loses his grip. I slip out of his hands and fall backward. My head bumps the bottom of the windshield with a *thud* and I bang my shoulder blades on the hood.

Wincing, I move one hand to rub the back of my head. "Ouch!"

Landon reaches for me and cups his hands under my head, forming a pillow—a bony pillow—but a pillow nonetheless. "Are you okay?" Despite his concern, his shoulders shake with silent laughter.

"Shut up."

"No, seriously, are you okay?" His laugh ceases, but there's a warm smile on his perfectly plump lips.

"Yes."

He leans closer, mouth brushing mine as he whispers, "Never let me go, Gabs."

"Now you tell me," I deadpan.

"I knew you'd be loud. It's always the quiet ones."

"This whole making-me-blush thing is getting old."

"Just let me enjoy it." He pulls back. "Once I officially get my hands on you, you won't be as easy to embarrass."

"You just had your hands on me." Using his coat for stability, I pull myself into a sitting position again.

"Don't make me get dirty, Gabs. You'll just get mad at me for making you blush again." Landon helps me slide off the hood.

"No one talks dirty to me in real life, but I'm a book geek. I've read it all before."

"I thought you didn't read books like that."

"I don't, *usually*, but I *have*." On my way to the passenger side, I inch by Landon, brushing against the front of his jeans.

"Don't do things like that, Gabriella," Landon growls as he closes my door.

Watching him adjust his jeans as he walks around to the driver's side fills me with pride.

Has Landon opened up a comfortable, sexy part of me I never knew I possessed? I mean, I'll never be the sexy librarian who tosses her glasses aside and unleashes her ponytail when it's time to get wild, but it's nice to know there's a sexy side hiding behind my introverted bookish ways.

"Just so you know"—Landon pauses to catch my eyes before he starts the car—"I can be as gentle as you need me to be, but once we get going, you're going to want a mattress, not a car hood, beneath you."

Speechless. Shocked. Scandalized.

And I love it.

Chapter Fourteen

GABY

"MAMA?" I DIP MY HEAD INTO HER BEDROOM. THE OVERHEAD LIGHT is on, and the TV blares, but I don't see her. I tap on the molding as I enter. "Mama?"

"I'm in the closet, Gaby," she calls.

When I reach her, she's standing in the massive built-in closet with various small mountains of clothing surrounding her petite feet.

"What are you doing?"

"Spring cleaning." She snatches a pair of pants from the top shelf.

"It's not spring." I pick up a gorgeous pink cashmere sweater and slide it across my cheek. The smell of Chanel on cashmere describes Mama's elegance in a nutshell.

She smiles and turns to me, holding the pants at my waist as if mentally fitting them on my body. "Well, then it's winter cleaning."

She folds the pants and slings them Frisbee-style onto a stack in the corner of her closet. The piles at her feet are barely a heap. Mama owns more clothes, shoes, and accessories than a small department store.

Trendy, but age-appropriate. Sexy, but classy. Mama rocks every-thing she wears. Never the frumpy car-pool lady who drops her kids off wearing pajamas and a baseball cap. Mama looks fabulous every time she leaves the house.

She can start out in a plain white T-shirt and jeans, slide on a leopard-print belt, wrap her neck in a scarf, pop on some sunglasses, and walk out the door paparazzi-ready. She radiates confidence and beauty.

I hope I'm not making her sound shallow because Mama is anything but shallow. She believes in being ready for whatever life throws at you. The old "wear clean underwear" cliché, but on the outside as well.

"You can have that sweater if you want, Gaby," Mama offers.

I lower the cashmere clutched to my face like a security blanket. "It smells like you."

"After a shower, I hope." Mama winks. Her shoulders drop as she exhales a deep breath. Her eyes scan the closet like a Risk player contemplating which country to attack next.

"Can I ask a favor?"

"Sure, sweets." She reaches for a shoe box. "What'cha need?"

"So, um, I have a date tonight."

"What?" The box slips from Mama's hands and its contents—money in various paper and coin forms—scatter across her feet.

"You have a secret cash stash?" I squeal, tossing the sweater onto Mama and Papa's bed behind me before dropping to my knees to help clean up. "You making a break for it?"

Mama laughs. "Yeah, my collection of two-dollar bills and fifty-cent pieces will almost get me to the border."

I gather the bills and tap them into a neat pile before handing them to her. She gathers handfuls of coins and drops them into the box.

"So, a date, eh?" she asks, trying to sound nonchalant as she replaces the lid on the shoe box and sets it on the highest shelf. "Anyone I know?"

I kick a pair of balled-up socks, sending them into the pile of pants. "Landon Taylor."

"The hockey player?"

I nod.

Mama turns to face me, her eyes squinted in scrutiny. "You have a date with Landon Taylor? Tonight?"

"Geez, Mama, you don't have to sound so surprised. Am I that hideous?" I don't have the confidence she has. I don't have the fashion or makeup skills she has, either.

My glamorous, girly, artsy mother was probably pushed into an early midlife crisis when she realized her only daughter would rather play hockey and work at a produce store than get her nails done and hit the mall.

She reaches out and cups my chin between her thumb and index fingers. "You are gorgeous, Gabriella. Never let me hear you say anything like that again. Got it?"

I nod the best as I can with my face trapped in her grip. She releases her hold and continues, "I didn't realize you two knew each other that well."

"We've been hanging out ever since Papa's heart attack."

"Ahhhh. Tragedy bringing two hearts together."

"Thankfully, it wasn't a tragedy," I remind her.

"True. But still. It's a beautiful way to start out." She clasps her hands across her heart. "You can tell your kids their father saved their grandpa's life."

Mama looks through me, a wistful gleam in her eyes. She's on the verge of going Polonius and I need to put a stop to it. I'm too nervous to listen to a long-winded monologue.

"Come on, Mama! It's a date, not an engagement party. Now can I ask for the favor I need from you?"

"My independent daughter needs a favor from her little old mother? I'm all ears."

"Will you please help me with my hair and makeup?"

Mama draws the back of one hand to her forehead and paws at me with the other, swaying from foot to foot. "I'm gonna faint. Help me, Gaby."

"I don't have time for this. Forget I asked." I spin around with a huff and start back toward my room.

Landon will be here soon to pick me up. I barely have enough time to get ready—even without Mama's antics.

Her musical laugh fills the closet. She grabs my shoulder, spins me around, and pulls me into an embrace.

"I'm so happy you asked me. I'd love to help." She kisses the top of my head and takes my hand. "Come on."

Mama pulls out the chair in the space between the two sinks in the master bathroom and pats the seat. I've watched her apply makeup and style her hair in this chair a hundred times.

I've always loved watching because she makes it seem effortless, but when I try to copy her, it's a disaster. Even countless online step-by-step video tutorials haven't helped my skills. My makeup routine consists of mascara and tinted lip balm. Sometimes I dab on some concealer and powder to mask the occasional zit.

Mama pulls her cosmetics bag from the cabinet underneath the sink and sets it on the counter. She then opens up the top drawer on her side of the vanity and wades through brushes of every shape and size, from flat fans to fluffy and fat.

As she pats my face with a sponge dipped in a silky foundation, regret washes over me.

I set my hand on her wrist. "Not too much. I don't want to look too done up."

"Up." She waves me out of the chair.

When I stand, she turns the chair around so my back faces the mirror. Blind to the products and colors she's laid out, I drop onto the chair, reminding myself that my mother is an artist. There's no reason to question her expertise.

Relaxing against the chair, I present my face as her blank canvas. She works with quick, smooth strokes. The pressure switches from steady and firm while patting my face with the sponge to light and feathery as she dusts a brush across my eyelids.

"You've got a crazy little sparkle in your eye," I say when she stops to dip a brush in something. "You've been waiting for this moment, haven't you?"

"Gaby, I could care less if you wear makeup or not. I don't want to change you. I never have."

"But admit it, Mama, you wish I were interested in all this stuff, right?" I pick up a fan-shaped brush and sweep the tip of my finger across the soft bristles.

"I'm not sure where this is coming from." She leans toward me. "Close your eyes."

I toss the brush onto the counter and obey. "I don't know. Dating Landon makes me feel insecure. About my looks, my job, my hobbies."

"Your job?" Mama quirks one eyebrow." Landon knows our family owns the store you work at."

"I just meant, working at the store instead of going to college."

"Landon didn't go to off college. Did he even graduate high school?"

Looks like I'm not the only Bertucci woman who knows a thing or two about Landon.

The Oshawa Generals of the Ontario Hockey League drafted him when he was seventeen. He played with them for two years before being taken in the second round in the NHL Entry Draft by the Charlotte Monarchs.

"They take school seriously in Juniors, Mama. He's taking online classes, and he's almost finished with his Bachelor's Degree."

"Good for him."

"You should see the girls that chase him. Perfect hair, perfect skin." I pick at the frayed hem of my sweatshirt.

"Stop. You're gorgeous, Gaby."

I open my eyes. "You're my mother. You have to say that. Plus, you're a quintessential hot girl. You'd never have to worry."

"That attitude will make you crazy." Mama pops my nose with a huge fluffy brush, then starts sweeping it over the apples of my cheeks. "He chose you. Just as you are."

"Not too much, Mama."

"Trust me, Gaby."

I wring my fingers. "When can I look?"

"When I'm finished."

"What if I hate it?"

"You won't."

"Do I look like myself or made up?"

"All I'm doing is enhancing what you already have." Mama turns around to grab a black tube from the counter.

After years of watching her, I know lipstick is the final step. My knee shakes up and down in nervous anticipation of the result.

"Stop shaking." Mama conjures her inner hockey player and swings her hip into my knee. She steps back, her eyes narrowing as she scrutinizes her work. Which makes me feel like a painting.

"Okay." She nods with satisfaction. "You can look now."

The words *bad makeup day* don't exist in Mama's vocabulary, so there's no reason for my stomach to pulse with anxiety. I hop off the chair and spin toward the mirror, anxious to see if I'll be joining the circus instead of meeting Landon tonight.

"Holy crap," I whisper to my reflection.

Still me, but enhanced, just as Mama promised.

The eyeliner intensifies my normal black mascara and makes my brown eyes pop. The subtle pink color on my cheeks gives me a soft glow, rather than the round clown circle I expected. My skin tone appears even without looking thick and cakey.

I've always known my mother was a brilliant artist, but she worked a different kind of magic with my simple, subtle transformation.

She brushes behind me to get to the other side of the vanity, which holds Dad's toiletries. "Here." She holds out a small square packet.

As I reach out to accept it, I realize what it is, and promptly drop it as if she's passing me meatloaf straight from the oven and I'm not wearing hot mitts.

No.

No. No. No.

"Grow up, Gaby." Mama bends down and picks up the condom, then thrusts it at me again.

"I don't need it."

"I don't care. It's always good to have one on hand. Just in case."

"It's our first date."

"Not true, Gabriella. You just admitted that you've been hanging out with him. You've had more late nights since your father's heart attack than you've had since you were a newborn. I just didn't know what was keeping you out. Or who."

I wiggle away from her as she tries to tuck the condom into my back pocket. "Mama, stop!"

"Humor me, Gaby. We haven't had *the talk* since you were a freshman in high school. And"—she pauses, a silent homage to the enormous elephant in the room—"at least this way I know you're prepared with the tools to protect yourself."

"Don't worry. I always have mace in my purse." I frown as I pluck the condom out of Mama's fingers and stuff it into my pocket.

"I'm not—" Mama stops and shakes her head. "Landon is—" Another pause. Another shake. Her shoulders drop. "Not all guys are out to hurt you."

"I know, Mama. I know. That's why I like Landon. He's gentle. He's compassionate. He understands."

"Has it already come up?"

Mama begins tossing the makeup back into her cosmetics bag while waiting for my answer. Her seemingly nonchalant question holds the weight of an F-150 hauling cinder blocks.

Rape is never easy to talk about. Not *when* it happens. Not *after* it happens.

Mama won't even say the word. It's always *it*, and I know exactly what *it* means. My family and I will dance around *it* for the rest of our lives. Or at least until *it* is finally a scar instead of a scabbed-over wound.

"No, but we've already had some intense discussions."

Bending down to pick up a silver tube that rolled off the counter, I contemplate how to change the subject in a light, but tactful, way.

"What's wrong?" Mama holds out her hand, and I drop the mascara into it.

"I'm trying to figure out why Dad has a box of condoms in his bottom drawer. Frankly, it's grossing me out."

Mama laughs as she zips the cosmetics bag and sets it back on its shelf under the sink. She has a specific place for everything. "We have two sons and a teenage daughter. We've had a box since Joey turned thirteen."

I pat my back pocket as I walk out of the bathroom. "Not the same box, I hope."

"Smart ass." Mama swats my butt as she follows me out.

As we pass the bed, I grab the pink cashmere sweater I'd tossed onto it earlier. "Can I wear this?"

"Of course." She returns to her closet to finish her winter cleaning.

Before leaving the room, I turn around, run to her, and wrap my arms around her. "Thanks so much, Mama. I love you."

"I love you, too, Gaby. Exactly how you are." She returns the hug with a quick but fierce squeeze.

I haven't taken two steps out of the closet when she calls me back.

"Gaby, wait!" Mama pulls down the shoe box with her secret money stash and retrieves a two-dollar bill. After folding it into quarters, she pulls at the collar of my sweatshirt, reaches in, and shoves the bill into my bra.

"What the hell, Mama?" I bat at her hands, but she's too quick.

"For good luck." She winks and replaces the shoe box.

I have a mother who sends her daughter on a date with a condom and a two-dollar bill for good luck. I don't know if I should feel grateful or horrified.

As I fish the bill out of my bra, she puts her hands on my shoulders, halting my search. "I want you to be safe and in control, Gaby. But I also want you to have the time of your life. You deserve it."

Tears gleam in her eyes, another painful reminder of how stupid and out of control I'd been three years ago. A reminder of her inability to stop—or take away—what happened.

My parents hold so much guilt over the choices my brothers and I make. Whenever something bad happens, they analyze every single aspect of their parenting, from infancy to our teenage years, trying to figure out what they did wrong.

Nothing. My parents didn't make any huge mistakes.

They raised me to make good decisions and be a strong person, even if that strength gets hidden under a shy exterior. But after all the analyzing and questioning of what they did—or didn't do—when it came down to it, I made a bad decision.

Because like many teenagers, I thought I was bulletproof. Until something happened to knock me back to fragile human status.

Like countless figures in literature and history, we all have our tragic flaws. t's the way we handle those flaws that make up our character.

And for the lucky ones, life gives us a second chance.

Chapter Fifteen

GABY

"Kurz Dakota Inn Rathskeller," I read the words painted on the side of the large brick building out loud. "I've never been here."

"Shocker!" Landon jumps out of the car and walks to the passenger side to open my door.

"Thanks," I say. "We eat more than spaghetti and meatballs, ya know."

"Suuure."

"We love The Polish Village and Xochimilco," I throw out the names of my favorite non-Italian restaurants, feeling slightly silly defending my food choices.

As we walk, I pause at a window and run a hand over the pretty, powder-blue shutters. The heart in the middle of each one makes me smile. After rounding the corner of the building, there's a quaint peak, resembling the bell tower of a castle. An old-school neon sign advertising the Dakota Inn and quality beer hangs above the entrance.

I laugh. "Quality beer, eh? Too bad I'm not old enough to drink."

"Shhhh." Landon holds the heavy wooden door open for me. "Let me do the ordering."

"Hey, Mindy!" He places a hand on my back as he greets the hostess. The warmth creates a tingle up my back and down my arms.

"This place is awesome," I say as we pass under an arched doorway. Shelves holding multicolored beer steins, animal heads, and animal portraits litter the walls.

"Right? Didn't know you could visit Germany by way of Detroit, did you?"

I slide onto the chair Landon pulls out for me. "That tower-looking thing outside reminds me of somewhere Rapunzel would be hidden."

He bends over as he pushes my chair in, his lips brushing my ear as he says, "A castle for a princess."

A waitress sets two glasses of water in front of us. I'm enamored by the intricate navy embroidery on her traditional blue German dress.

"I told you before, I'm not a princess," I say after she turns away. "Though, my parents tried to make me into one. Pink and frilly stuff everywhere."

Landon nods to my chest. "Pink."

I glance down as fire creeps into my face. Thank goodness for my olive skin tone. *He's looking at my sweater. Just my sweater.*

"Oh, well, yeah, I like pink. But I didn't want pink *everything.*" I laugh. "I wanted to be like my brothers. Joey fixed cars. So, I made him teach me how to change my oil. Drew played hockey, so I played hockey."

Landon chokes on a sip of water. "You played hockey?"

"Not for long. I'm not a clumsy person or anything, but I never felt comfortable ice skating. Too scared to go too fast. Too scared to try the hockey stop."

"What were you scared of?"

I stare at my water glass to gather my thoughts, then shrug. "Falling. Failing. Not being as good as Drew."

Not being as good as anyone.

Landon gives me a half smile from across the table. "Falling hurts at first. Still does sometimes. Depends on who caused it."

Thankfully, he avoids mentioning the failing part.

I continue, "Plus, Papa told me girls should play individual sports." I change my voice to imitate his gruff baritone, "'There's no money in team sports for women.'"

"Wow, now there's a great message for his daughter," Landon teases.

"I know, right? But I wasn't sporty anyway, so I didn't take much offense. I always loved being at the store. Ever since I was little, I've been at my father's side. I observed, asked questions, and learned every single position."

Landon catches my gaze. "Which is why it sucks even more that your dad doesn't listen to you about the new store. He knows produce, but he has to realize he took over a thriving business. He doesn't know how to market a new concept. I wish he would've let you explain your ideas."

Mini coach lights hang from the ceiling, bathing the room in a warm glow, and illuminating his eyes.

I know some people think there's nothing special about brown eyes —that they're just there. But they've never had the opportunity to stare into Landon Taylor's.

His eyes are electric, but soft. Sharp, but warm. Intense, but kind.

His eyes are a direct reflection of his soul.

"Well, once we get the mock-up completed, he might reconsider. If I plan it out rather than throw it at him on a whim, maybe he'll take me seriously."

"Can't go worse than the first time, right?"

"Well, I realized my mistake that time."

"Having me there?"

I laugh. "No. I'm glad you were there. How he treated you was wrong, but I appreciated you backing me up. Professional and logical is what works with Papa. Come at him with the emotional card and he makes mean, sexist remarks."

Landon cocks his head to the side. "Continue."

"Um, well, when women are emotional my dad makes stupid comments about—" I drop my eyes to my lap, refusing to mention PMS in his presence. "Never mind."

"No worries. I get it." He blushes.

Turns out *awkward* is the perfect word to describe my interactions with guys. Which means Drew was right—and I hate it when he's right.

"Welcome to the Dakota Inn. Can I start you with some drinks?" our waitress asks.

I don't know if she heard the awkwardness and came to save me or not, but I'm grateful for the interruption.

"I think we're ready to order." Landon looks at me for permission and I nod. "We'll have a pitcher of *Hacker-Pschorr*, a combo plate, Kurz stack of *Kartoffelpuffer* with sour cream, and the *Kasespatzle*."

To say everything Landon ordered is completely foreign to me would be a bad joke, but it's the truth. I haven't even had a chance to look at the menu to check out the translations.

"Very good." She grabs our menus from the edge of the table. "Be back in a minute with your beer."

"I was thinking we could do some shots at Robinson Arena," Landon continues normal conversation like I didn't just embarrass myself for eternity before the waitress came over.

"Sure. We can take some there." I press my lips together to keep from frowning.

"What?" Landon asks.

"Nothing." I shake my head, dismissing my thoughts. I let Landon's generosity and enthusiasm guide my reactions. "Taking photos at the Aviators' home arena would be authentic and cool."

"But—" Landon leans toward me, his closeness permitting me to unleash the reason for my silent objection.

"Robinson Arena is nineteen-seventies-era u-g-l-y. I mean, the only way we could make Robinson look good is if you stood naked in front of it holding Bertucci Produce in each hand," I say.

Landon's deep burst of laughter makes people at other tables turn toward us, which says a lot, considering the thunderous noise level in the restaurant. Landon certainly hadn't picked a place known for its quiet, intimate setting.

"Naked? Really?"

"You two are going to overshadow the entertainment." Our waitress places a pitcher of beer in the middle of the table "No underage drinking in here," she says, setting an empty beer stein in front of Landon—and a full glass of milk in front of me.

My stomach drops as I stare at the milk—utterly embarrassed.

"The beer is for me, Aunt Vera," Landon tells the waitress.

Vera folds her arms across her chest. "Well, then you'd better give her your car keys, Landon Charles."

This time I'm the one laughing. The thought of cranking the engine and sailing down I-75 in Landon's sleek, black Audi convertible makes me giddy.

"I tried," Landon apologizes as he pours beer into his glass. He glances the way his aunt had walked. "You can have a sip when she isn't looking."

"It's okay." I hold up a hand. "I don't drink."

Not anymore, almost slips off my tongue, but I'm not ready to lead Landon down the yellow brick road of doom. Yet.

"At all?"

"Does the wine at church count?" I ask.

"No."

Siting up straight, I shake my head. "Then no, I don't drink at all."

"Does it bother you if I do?" Landon raises his full glass.

"Nope," I say honestly, making a motion for him to tip his glass back. Each sip gets me closer to driving his car.

"Your staring is making me paranoid."

"Oh, geez, sorry," I stammer, lifting my glass to my lips, trying to mask my embarrassment at being caught. As soon as I get a whiff of the milk, my stomach rolls. "I was just—it's—you're really cute."

He glances around the room as if looking for spies. Then leans toward me and lowers his voice. "Did you just compliment me?"

"Yeah, why?"

A sexy smirk slides across his luscious lips. "Do you like me, Gabriella?"

"Isn't it obvious?"

Or does he make out on the hood of his car with all his friends?

"No. And it drives me crazy. I can usually tell when a woman is interested in me."

"I like you, Landon. I really, really like you."

"Good."

"I'd like you even more if you got me a Sprite. I hate milk."

Landon slides the glass to the edge of the table. "Sorry about that. Pretty lame thing to do."

I can't even make him feel better and say someone in my family would have brought him a glass of milk if he were underage, too, because Bertucci's are raised with a glass of red wine next to their dinner plates.

"No worries." I shrug. "You can't help what your aunt does. Is it really your aunt? Or, like, a family friend or something?"

"No, she's really my aunt."

"Are you introducing me to your family one person at a time?" I tease, poking his rib.

"You've already met most of my family over the years. Mama thinks you're perfect, by the way. So if you want to marry me, she'd be totally cool with it."

Marriage? Why are both of our mothers using the m-word already?

"Ummm, yeah, how 'bout them Aviators?"

I've never been good at transitioning away from awkward conversations.

Luckily, Landon rolls with it. "Have you been to a game yet this year?"

"No, I'm always working."

"Can you get a night off? I want you to come see me play."

My pulse pumps and a squeal of excitement hangs on the tip of my tongue. I hold it in.

"Yeah. Yes. I can definitely take a night off. I didn't know if I'd come across as too clingy if I came or whatever." I fiddle with my knife and fork, pretending to straighten the already straight silverware.

"Clingy? Gaby, I've dreamed of looking into the section where the wives and girlfriends sit and see you there cheering for me. Maybe whipping your shirt off and waving it around if I score."

Though I'm caught totally off guard by his comment, I can't stop the bark of laughter.

"It was a really good dream." Landon winks. "I love seeing you blush, Gaby. I love being the person who makes the color rush to your cheeks."

"There are a million ways to put color in my cheeks, believe me."

I bury my face in my hands so Landon can't see the new blush attached to my accidental innuendo.

"Check, please." He lifts his arm, pretending to motion for Aunt Vera.

Suddenly, a man clad in a blue and white gingham button-down shirt and suspenders holding up navy blue short pants stands up and raises his beer stein, shouting something in German. The crowd cheers and yells a response.

With the raucous roars, an electric vibe courses through the crowd. The man pushes a large easel to the front of the room. An aging poster board filled with words and pictures rests against it.

Behind him, a man in a camel-colored suit starts playing a tune, and the crowd sings along with gusto as the man in short pants uses a stick to point to the words.

I scan the restaurant, taking in every genuine smile and laugh. Then I turn to Landon who's singing along with everyone else, only he doesn't have to look at the words.

Beer stein in the air, Landon sways from right to left as if we're sitting in a beer hall in Germany. He has a great sing-along voice – which means, he's good at yelling and laughing in German.

Landon catches me looking at him and points toward the board with the words for the sing-along. He's grinning like a little kid who just talked his mother into letting him do something he normally isn't allowed to do.

I turn back toward the front, watching the man leading the crowd with gusto. My heart races and my stomach lurches, slightly uncomfortable in this situation.

My nerves begin to calm when I scan the crowd again. People of all ages, all walks of life, all having a blast singing a silly German song about *"fette sau"* and *"schnickelfritz,"* which, according to the pictures on the poster, means a pig and a kid.

I can't even tell what some of the pictures are supposed to depict. But it's amusing, and obviously meant to be silly entertainment to get the crowd involved, rather than a way to find the next local singing star.

Still, I ease into it slowly, pretending to sing by mouthing the words. It hits me immediately that you can't fake it here. You have to go all out, or not at all.

As everyone around me sings happily, the urge to join pulses through me, almost permitting my mouth to open. When my brain realizes what I almost allowed my voice to do in a roomful of people, I promptly bolt my lips together with an invisible staple gun.

Suddenly, Landon grabs my hand. The strength of one simple squeeze prods me to step out of my comfort zone. It gives me the courage to let go of my embarrassment and sing out loud.

It feels amazing.

Within minutes, my singing rings almost as loud as anyone's in the pub. But not quite everyone, since there are a few with rich, loud voices in the group.

When the song ends, the hall blazes with laughter, smiles, and cheers. I turn back to Landon, who isn't immune to the merriment. He raises his eyebrows, silently asking me if I'm enjoying myself. I can't keep the stupid grin off my face as I nod like a maniac. I have half a mind to grab Landon's beer stein and raise it in the air like the majority of the crowd, but I catch myself.

No underage drinking here.

And no drinking around men for me.

Ever.

When Aunt Vera seats a group of four at the table next to us, Landon scoots his chair closer to me to give them more room.

He leans in, his lips right on my ear. "You okay?"

"Yeah," I say, nodding in case he can't hear me.

He slides his arm across my shoulders and squeezes me. "I'm glad you like it."

Having his arm around me feels natural, like we do it all the time.

"How many times have you done this?" I grab a sesame seed–coated breadstick out of the glass mug in the middle of our table and bite into it.

"Hundreds. I've been coming here since I was a kid. Perks of having an aunt who works here."

"It's so fun."

"Just wait." He pushes his chair away from the table and stands up. "Be right back."

While I wait for Landon to return, I pull my phone out, curious to Google more about the history of the restaurant. Just as I'm about to look it up, I notice a text from Michelle waiting for me. I stop to read and reply quickly.

Michelle: How's it going? Where did he take you?

Me: The Dakota Inn

Michelle: Is that a hotel???

Me: NO! It's a German Beer Hall.

Michelle: Oh. OK. I was about to drive from Chi-town to kick his ass. Is it fun?

Me: Having a blast. Just sang a song in German.

Michelle: Since when do you know German?

Me: They have a poster board with the words. It's a sing-a-long. So fun! We have to come back next time you're in town.

Michelle: Hook me up with one of his hot, hockey-player friends and you have a deal.

Me: :) Gotta go. L is coming back.

Michelle: Be good. :P

Me: Always. <3 Love you.

Michelle: Love you, too.

Quickly, I tuck my phone into my purse as Landon sits down.

There's no need to do an internet search on the history of the bar, since I can ask him. I'm sure he knows the story.

"Here you go." Landon hands me a yellow thing with some red feather-type stuff on top and a red flap hanging down on each side. I turn it over in my hands, inspecting it.

It's a chicken—a chicken hat, to be exact. He sets a white hat with blue feathers and flaps on the table in front of him.

"What is this for?"

"You'll see," Landon says with a silly spark in his eye.

Mystery still hangs in the air when Aunt Vera appears with a tray filled with steaming food. She sets three large plates on our table: one in front of Landon and me and one in the middle, near the mug of breadsticks. I have no clue what any of it is, but it looks and smells so delicious that my stomach roars like the lion on the Kurz Family coat of arms hanging above the bar.

"We can share." Landon points to the plate in front of him first. "This is *kasespatzle*. Noodles with caramelized onions and Swiss cheese over sauerkraut."

He continues, "You've got the potato pancakes in front of you." He uses his fork to point to the plate in the middle. "And that's bratwurst, knackwurst, hot German potato salad, and sauerkraut. It's all amazing. Dig in."

Landon starts with a forkful of the *kasespatzle*. So, I grab a potato pancake and dip it in the little cup of sour cream on the plate next to the three pancakes.

The meal tastes as amazing as it smells and within minutes, I've eaten so much I'm full to bursting. Still, I want ten more potato pancakes.

"How'd I do?" Landon asks.

"I could eat here every day for the rest of my life."

"You could never give up homemade Bolognese." Landon laughs.

"True." My full stomach almost growls again at the thought of Papa's red sauce. "Okay, *six* days a week."

"You may have some German in you."

Not yet, but maybe someday, I think. But instead of verbalizing the sexual thought, I say, "I may be German somewhere down the line. Mama's a mutt. She just goes along with the overbearing Italian that is Papa."

Landon looks up with a smile. "Get ready to put your chicken hat on, Gaby."

I'd almost forgotten about the silly thing I'd banished to the corner of the table when our food arrived.

That's when I hear it: the opening chords of the Chicken Dance.

Patrons wearing crazy chicken hats of all colors jump out of their seats and rush to the front. I have no intention of putting on the hat or getting out of my seat, but Landon has other thoughts, grabbing my hand and tugging on it.

I shake my head. My heart pumps so loud I can hear it, and so fast I think it might escape from my chest. Landon pulls again, persistent in his mission.

How can I tell him that his insistence I do the Chicken Dance makes me want to barf, without offending him or the amazing meal I'd just devoured?

"It's all silly fun, Gabs. No reason to be freaked out." He stops tugging on my arm but keeps my hand in his while he waits, allowing me to make the choice.

Everyone in the bar has a smile, a laugh, and a funky little chicken hat. No one's paying any attention to me.

I slide off my chair, like liquid Gaby. Landon swipes our hats from the table before leading me into the circle of chicken dancers.

He plops the stupid hat on my head, then secures his. I can't even pretend I don't know the Chicken Dance. Everyone knows the Chicken Dance. I haven't done it since I was a kid, but it's not something you forget.

Of all the images I'd conjured of what we'd do if I ever had the opportunity to be on a date with Landon Taylor, cupping my hands to make a bird beak, flapping my arms like wings, and shimmying to the floor had *not* crossed my mind.

Well, not shimmying to the floor in this way.

Damn! The sexual thoughts needed to stop.

Suddenly, some random person hooks my arm with theirs and spins me in a circle before letting go. Then Landon hooks my other arm and spins me the opposite way. Though it caught me by surprise at first, it's fun. I can't help but laugh as I do-si-do with each partner that grabs me.

"You're holding back!" Landon yells across the room, his arm linked with an older lady about a foot and a half shorter than him.

"I'm not!" I laugh as the "round and round" part ends. Landon edges through the crowd of deranged chicken impersonators to stand by me.

"Come on, Gaby. You've gotta really wiggle that ass when you shimmy down."

"A rough, buff hockey player is telling me how to get down? For the Chicken Dance?"

"Or he just wants to see you wiggle your ass." He taps my backside playfully.

When the song ends, Landon snatches the chicken hat from my head. Then he laces his fingers through mine and leads me toward the door, throwing our hats and some cash on our table as we pass. Aunt Vera waves to us as we leave. I wave back and try to yell "thank you" on our way out.

"Well, what did you think?" Landon places his arm over my shoulder.

"Grown adults drinking, eating, laughing, and chicken dancing?" I pause before exclaiming. "It was the best date I never knew I wanted to go on."

"Good." He opens the passenger door for me.

I shake my head. "Nope. Give me the keys."

"Gaby. I'm fine. I promise."

"Landon Charles, don't make me go get Aunt Vera because I don't think that would be a good scene."

Without another word, he hands me the keys and climbs into the passenger side. I close his door and round the car.

"I've never driven a foreign car before," I whisper. Motor City guilt and fear of being struck by karmic lightning keeps me from saying it too loud.

"Not living up to my hometown Golden Boy image, am I?"

"Well, you're certainly not the poster boy for the Big Three." I adjust the seat forward so my foot can reach the pedals.

"Audi. Sounds kind of Italian, right?"

"No. Not even a little bit." I laugh. "We better not take any pictures in your car."

"We can take them in my room. I think my bed is American-made."

The car jerks to a stop, yards short of the stop sign, a flashback of my embarrassing first driving test.

Yes, first.

"Kidding, Gabs." Landon closes his eyes and leans back against the seat as a sly smile creeps across his lips. "Maybe."

"Simmer down now, Taylor."

"I said I was kidding. My bed may not be American made, you'll have to check."

"I can't tell if you're trying to get a rise out of me because you like to see me blush or if you're really joking."

"Both." Landon's eyes flash open, intense under the glow of the street lights. "I want you in my bed tonight, Gaby."

There it is. The request I've been longing to hear from him for as long as I can remember. It's also the request I've been afraid to hear. Because that means it's real.

And before things can go further, I know I have some issues to work out.

But I'm willing to do it for Landon.

"Well then, let's see how fast this puppy can go." While halted at the stop sign, I check for cars, then floor the Audi.

Landon jerks forward, looking at me with wide eyes and arched eyebrows, seemingly startled more by my words than the momentum.

But I wasn't kidding, and I hope he wasn't either.

Because if he's offering, I'm ready.

Chapter Sixteen

GABY

ONCE WE'VE MADE IT INSIDE LANDON'S DOWNTOWN DETROIT condo, he leans in and places a soft kiss on my neck. In one deft tug, he pulls me into his arms and presses his lips on mine.

Firm. Soft. Eager.

I wrap my arms around his neck, hoping his mouth can teleport me to another place. A place where beginning a serious make-out with him doesn't bring on a panic attack. A place where I can trust a man.

If I can trust anyone it's Landon, I remind myself.

Landon *has* never hurt me and *would* never hurt me. He's shown time and time again how much he cares about me and how gentle he can be. I know he won't press me to go further than I want.

The problem is me, not him. I want to take this as far as we possibly can. And the thought scares the shit out of me.

After the rape, I thought I shouldn't want sex. I felt guilty for being aroused. Like pleasure was dirty and wrong.

A part of my brain tricked me into thinking I was some kind of sick whore if I found pleasure after something so violating and violent happened to me.

The rape itself, and how people treated me afterward, made me feel guilt and shame about natural human desires.

Therapy has helped me reframe how I think about sex. Healing will take time.

Every step with Landon is a trigger—but it's also an opportunity to reclaim my body as my own.

When Landon pulls away, his lips glisten with moisture from my mouth. He grabs my hands, holding them behind his back as he drags me forward. Though he's moving slowly, it feels like I have to run to catch up. He doesn't stop at the couch in his living room but keeps walking toward the hallway, where I count three doorways.

Landon passes the first doorway on the left, which is a bathroom, I learn after peeking in as we pass. He lets go of my hands to spin around and face me before grabbing them again. Then he pulls me with him as he walks backward through the only door on the right. Once inside, he presses himself against me and covers my mouth with his. With our lips still locked, he reaches behind me and bats the door closed.

Inside his bedroom, the urgency kicks up a few notches. He guides my arms up, and a flash of pink covers my field of vision as he lifts my sweater over my head and tosses it to the ground. His nimble fingers find the button at my waist and pop it open before I can lower my arms.

I knew the kid was fast on the ice, but his speed and skill in getting me undressed has my head spinning. It barely takes him three seconds to shuck my jeans to my knees and push them down the rest of the way with his foot, without taking his mouth off mine.

The kiss intensifies with each piece of clothing he removes. My clothes lay in a pool at my feet, and Landon hasn't even taken any of his off yet.

Dark gray covers every inch of the walls, and continues over to the ceiling. The subdued color combined with his black headboard, black nightstand, and black and red comforter gives his room a cozy, cave-like ambiance. My olive-toned flesh, covered in the appropriate places by matching black bra and underwear, practically glows.

Before he has a chance to go for the clasps at the back of my bra, I grab his shirt and fumble with the top button. I'm not nearly as fast as he is, probably due to how much my fingers shake with the simple, but sensual, task. I try not to compare speed and focus on the buttons instead. Once I have the first two undone, I lift it over his head, hoping he's not wearing a T-shirt under his button-down.

Score! When I lift the shirt, the only things underneath are his impeccable abs. His jeans hang low on his hips, exposing the indent of his belly button amid his hard, muscular stomach. I throw his shirt in the general area where he'd thrown my sweater.

Instead of reaching directly for his jeans, I stop to press my mouth on his and splay my hands across his chest. There's no chest hair, just toned muscle underneath smooth skin.

I want to touch every inch of him. My hands roam up his chest, over his shoulders, and down his back. Slowly, I trail my fingers from his shoulder blades to the jeans resting on his hips.

Which reminds me . . .

When I pop the button on his jeans, his stomach tightens under my hands. He lifts his mouth from mine to bring his lips to my ear.

"Do it," he pleads in a strained whisper.

The tension in his voice and the contraction of his abs spur me on. My fingers slip inside his jeans and brush the area beneath lightly as I pull down the zipper.

And that's when I find out Landon Taylor went commando for our date.

"You're a little vixen, Gabriella," Landon hisses. Then he grabs my hips and lifts me. I wrap my legs around him as he moves us toward the bed. He holds me with one arm, leans over, and pulls down the comforter before dropping me. "I knew you had it in you. Hiding inside that introverted exterior all these years."

Landon leans over me, then reaches around and unhooks my bra with one hand. He pulls the strap down one arm and then the other, taking his time, holding my gaze as he removes it. Once my bra hits the floor, he pauses to observe me with hot, hungry eyes.

I love how he looks at me—fascinated and exhilarated as he inspects every inch of my bare skin. His hair sticks out in every direction, still disheveled from when I pulled the shirt over his head. He bites his bottom lip as his wide, unashamed gaze moves from one part of my body to the next.

He climbs on the bed, hovering over me without lowering his weight. My electrified squirming beneath him gives him silent permission to continue. He lowers himself onto me, our bodies locking together like Legos. Every unclothed inch of him presses against the most sensitive parts of my body, still covered with a thin layer of fabric.

Landon lifts onto his elbows, his lower half still molded to mine, while his hands weave into my hair. He begins to circle his hips slowly, creating an exquisite friction burning between us. He never removes his gaze from mine, gauging my reactions, and asking wordless permission every step of the way.

That's when panic sets in.

The tenderness in his eyes, the affection in his caress, and the phenomenal feel of his expert movements make no difference.

My racing heart has nothing to do with the excitement of our intense, intimate situation.

Landon tries to lower himself onto me again, but I press my hands against his chest, stopping his descent. While his heart beats furiously against my palms, fear courses through my veins.

Being in Landon's arms doesn't cause trepidation; being in this situation does. But my system can't tell the difference.

Too familiar. Too scary. Too trapped.

I swallow, suppressing the bile rising in my throat.

"I'll go slow, Gabriella. I won't hurt you, okay?" Landon's breath blows fast and hot against my face. When he shifts his hips, I feel how much he wants me. Both exhilaration and alarm pump through my chest.

"I'm not a virgin, Landon," I whisper, lips quivering.

I want to respond to his advance without fear without thinking about the past, but my chest throbs.

"Really?" The tone of Landon's voice lowers a few octaves, husky, animalistic. His fingers slide over the fabric at my hip and around to the front before settling between my legs.

My body freezes when it should be thrusting forward and cheering him across the goal line.

Thankfully, he must sense my hesitation, because he raises his hand and rests it at my hip.

"I was—"

The words stick in my throat. Maybe because deep down I still blame myself for what happened, and being in this situation for the first time since the assault floods my mind with memories of my ignorance.

I'm the one who went to a college party as a sixteen-year-old. I'm the one who drank so much I could barely walk. I'm the one who trusted a long-time family friend who was there. I'm the one who led him on by agreeing to go with him when he said he knew a quiet place I could rest. I'm the one who left the safety of my brother and his friends to follow him to a bedroom.

I swallow hard, knowing I have to say something because I don't want Landon to think this has anything to do with him.

"There was this guy at a party. I was really drunk, so drunk I could barely speak or walk. I said no, but I didn't stop him. *Couldn't* stop him. I—"

"Oh my god, Gaby!" Landon climbs off me and backs away, putting frosty space between us.

I can't handle the space. Space says more than any words can. He's horrified I'm not a sweet virgin, but a naive "slut," as I've been called.

My body breaks out in goosebumps where his warm skin had been. I squeeze my eyes shut when the tears come fast and hard as if I'm standing directly under an angry rain cloud of my creation.

"I'm so sorry. I should have told you before this. I know it was my fault. It's why I don't drink and—I'm sorry, Landon."

"Gabs." He moves closer, pulling me against him and wrapping me in his muscular arms. He kisses the top of my head and smooths my hair, his palm starting at the roots and moving down to where the locks end at the small of my back. "Gabs, you don't have to apologize. That was *not* your fault."

"It was. I shouldn't have gotten so drunk. I shouldn't have followed him." I close my eyes, which sends another rush of tears racing down my cheeks. A mixture of salt and mascara runs into my mouth. "I shouldn't have even been there."

Society dictates suffocating rules for women. We shouldn't dress a certain way. We shouldn't reveal too much skin. We shouldn't walk alone at night—or anytime, really. We shouldn't drink at parties. Hell, we shouldn't even leave the house.

We should know better than to bait the ferocious male animal inside with salacious activities like going about our normal lives.

If we do, any situation we find ourselves in is perceived as our fault.

Landon places his palms on my cheeks and cradles my face. "It was *not* your fault. That prick had no right to take advantage of you. He knew you were drunk. Fuck, he knew you were young!"

If it's possible to exclaim while still whispering, Landon has the ability. I feel the strength in his words. Feel the adrenaline, anger, and tenderness transfer through his thumbs as he rubs at the tears under my eyes.

But I still can't look at him.

"Open your eyes, Gabs," Landon commands.

My lashes flicker, heavy with fresh tears. When I look at him, his face hovers inches above mine. His eyes hold the kindness and comfort I've come to rely on from him.

"I want to be with you, Landon. It's—I haven't been in this situation since then, and I didn't realize my reaction would be so—I don't know." I shake my head unable to find the right words.

Will fear ever allow me to be intimate with anyone? Will I always feel ashamed and angry when lying under a man?

"We're not doing anything until you understand what happened wasn't your fault."

"I'm trying," I whisper.

Three years of trying.

"Do you understand that *he* was wrong, not you? You have a right to be at a party and drink and not be raped, Gaby."

I shake my head, though my face is stuck in the vise grip of his hands.

Landon releases me and sits up. "Every night I have women throwing themselves at me."

I wiggled onto my side and up on my elbow, before pushing myself into a sitting position. When the sheet starts to slip, I snatch it and hold it against my chest. Landon doesn't even register the action.

"Girls wait outside the locker room wearing practically nothing.

They follow us to bars. They sit there and get shit-faced with us, hoping one of the guys will take them home."

It takes every ounce of strength I have to keep a poker face, while he casually discusses situations of his life that create feelings of insecurity and jealousy for me.

Why would he bring this up now? Especially after bearing my soul to him.

"So, if a girl who is plastered goes home with, say Luke, and Luke fucks her while she's passed out, does it make it okay because hooking up was her original intention? I mean, she was there to get with one of us, ya know? Wearing practically no clothes, following large, strong men to bars, getting drunk with them."

The sheet pulls taut as I clench my fists. "No. It is to okay. It doesn't matter if it was her original intention or not. Is that what you guys do?"

Landon tries to put his hand on my shoulder, but I bat it away.

"No. I'm trying to make a point. And I'm doing a shitty job of it." He rubs a hand over his head."I'm trying to say *no*, it's not okay. It's never acceptable to assault a woman. Why would you ever think drinking at a party makes you at fault for what happened?"

"Drinking isn't always involved," I say, unwilling to give up the fight yet.

"I know. There's this stereotype that all men are just sitting around waiting to rape someone. If a woman provokes us, we jump on her. It's not true. Most of us know right from wrong. We know how to treat women. We know that the prick who raped you needs to have his head bashed in and be dumped in jail."

I glance down at the cozy black comforter covering my lower half. Telling him about that horrible night three years ago was a mistake. I wanted to be honest because I didn't want him to think I wasn't attracted to him.

Isn't honesty the key to a lasting relationship?

Honesty. Trust.

A boyfriend with seven-pack abs.

I'm massively attracted to him. But now, he'll be gentle and careful and boring with me. Which makes me sound like I'm looking for something wild, and I'm not.

I want normal. I want to be able to touch him and have him on top of me without feeling dread.

I want an experience with someone I love to help me forget the memory of my horrific "first time."

"I need to hear your internal monologue because my comforter's not interesting enough to stare at it that long," Landon says gently coaxing me from my thoughts.

"He did get his head bashed in," I admit, rolling my eyes and shaking my head. "And it's a ridiculously complicated situation."

"How is it complicated? You tell your parents. They take you to the police and press charges on the motherfucker."

If only life were that easy. I lay back down on the bed next to him. The warmth of his heart radiates from his skin.

"You can trust me, Gaby. Nothing you say to me will leave these walls."

I trust Landon with every fiber of my soul.

But rape is a hard subject to discuss with anyone—at any time. No matter how much you love or trust someone, it's not easy to explain the invisible scarlet letter over my vagina.

"I told my parents. And—" I pause. "Well, let me back up. The guy who did it is a family friend. He's from a family whose farm supplies all the produce for our stores. The Bertuccis and Mitchells have been intertwined for so long the women are like aunts, and the men are like uncles. I thought of him as a cousin, or at the very least, a friend."

Landon reaches over and caresses my face, his soothing touch giving me the strength to continue.

Outside of my immediate family and my doctor, no one knows what happened that night. Not even Michelle. My intuitive best friend sensed something had happened, but she never asked, and I've been too embarrassed to tell her.

Instead of telling anyone else, I locked the experience inside and threw away the key, promising never to get myself in a similar situation again. I haven't touched alcohol since. Or been to any parties. Or been on any dates. I lived my final two years of high school as a spinster.

"I told my parents. And they believed me, but my grandfather told them we had to talk to the Mitchell family before we went to the police. He thought going to the police without giving them a head's up would be bad for business."

"Are you kidding me?" Landon removes his hand from my cheek, but I grab it and put it back. His tender touch gives me the courage and confidence to continue.

"The Mitchells didn't believe me, of course. They asked me why Jared would ever do that when he thought of me as a sister. They called me a liar. A slut. A drunk whore."

My breathing increases repeating the names they've called me as if I were a random person they'd never met instead of the girl they'd known since birth and treated like family.

The vile names are burned in my brain, refusing to let me heal and move on.

"What?"

"They told my grandfather that if I went to the police, they would stop deliveries immediately and sever all ties." I shrug.

"Who gives a shit? Any farm in the state would kill for that contract."

"Yeah, well, it's different when you have great-grandfathers who started a business together and grandfathers who continued that business. It's about loyalty above all else."

"Loyalty to who? You're family." Landon's so fired up his cheeks are pink.

"The Mitchells are family, too." I laugh. There's nothing funny about it. I understand the rules. "My grandfather didn't think the situation warranted dissolving a long-standing relationship."

"Fuck him," Landon exclaims, the vein in his neck pulsing with anger.

"Yeah, that's how I felt. I've barely talked to *Nonno* in three years. Papa barely talks to him, either. But they have to communicate for the business. I doubt *Nonno* even realizes I avoid him."

"I can't believe your family put their business ahead of you."

I look up. "You can't? Haven't I explained the archaic Bertucci ways enough?"

"Yeah, I get the business patriarchy thing. I mean—I don't agree—but I believe what you're telling me is real. I didn't realize ignoring his granddaughter's rape fell under those archaic ways. Your family should treat you better than that."

"Yeah, well, that's life." I swallow hard. "Now I understand why women don't speak up. Even if they do, they may have family who will protect the attacker."

It's a fact I'll never forget because I'm reminded of it every morning when I swallow the antidepressant I might not need to take if my family cared about me more than their business.

I'll never forget it because being betrayed and assaulted by someone you think of as a family member isn't something you forget.

I'll never forget it because the entire situation led me to the night I tried to kill myself.

But I won't tell Landon that part of the story. Telling him I'd been raped had to happen, or our physical relationship could never move forward. But I won't tell him about the antidepressants and suicide attempt. No one else needs to know how weak I am.

"Is that why your parents started Three-One-Three?"

"Hmm?"

"To distance themselves from your grandfather? To have their own business without ties to him?"

"I—" I search for words. "I don't—I never thought of that. I thought it was Papa's way to fulfill Mama's dream of selling her art."

"It sounds like there would be huge repercussions for your dad if he crossed your grandfather. Maybe his solution to keep the peace *and* keep you safe was to branch off?"

Had my parents started 313 Artisans as a way to get away from *Nonno* and the Mitchell family?

No. They'd never pour their life savings into a store with a huge probability of failing in an unpredictable Detroit economy just for me.

Would they?

While I contemplate his question, Landon sweeps my hair back, letting his fingers slide through the locks, tugging gently when they catch a snarl of waves. The light tug jolts me back to the moment, and I lift my eyes tentatively.

"Who kicked the guy's ass?" he asks.

"Drew and a few of his teammates. After the talk with the Mitchells, and *Nonno* deciding his granddaughter wasn't worth severing business ties, Drew took justice upon himself. He and a few of his teammates beat the crap out of him. And guess what happened?"

Landon's head tilts in question, but he stays silent.

"The Mitchells pressed charges against Drew. Only Drew."

"What?" Landon bolts up. "That's fucked up. That's *so* fucking fucked up!"

I nod. "But you know what's *even more* fucked up? The kid graduated later that year and started driving the business delivery truck. And for unexplained reasons, they moved our deliveries from mornings to afternoons, knowing I worked at the store after school. I had to see him every single day. And he just laughed and smiled, like nothing ever happened. He even asked me to prom."

"No."

"Yeah." I shudder at the memory, inching closer to capture Landon's warmth.

"What the fuck, Gabs?" Landon notices my subtle scoot and lowers himself back to the bed. Then he wraps his arms around me and squeezes me against his chest.

I inhale his skin, the mix of cologne and sweat relaxing me into a sense of peace after discussing one of the most horrific parts of my life. But not the most horrific. I don't know if I'll ever admit that to Landon.

"I didn't mean to ruin the moment. I just wanted to be honest with you and it turned into this big huge talk about rape and horrible men and puck bunnies and—I'm *such* a buzzkill."

"You're not a buzzkill," Landon says. "You are strong and amazing and I can't believe all this happened and I never knew."

"How could you have known?"

"I would've noticed a change in your personality. I've been to one of your stores every week for almost my entire life. Except when I was in Oshawa."

Before I answer, Landon puts the pieces together.

"It happened while I was in Oshawa, didn't it?"

Chapter Seventeen

LANDON

WHEN GABY NODS, HER FOREHEAD RUBS AGAINST MY CHEST, creating a friction and warmth I want to feel on lower parts of my body. But I'm too pissed off.

How could I have not been there for her when she needed me most?

"I would've bashed his face in. I'll *still* bash his face in. I can't believe I wasn't around."

"It's not like you would have known even if you had been around. We barely knew each other."

A low growl rattles in the back of my throat, but she places a hand on my chest to calm me.

"I meant that I wouldn't have rung up a purchase by saying, that'll be fifteen dollars and forty-two cents, by the way, did you know I was raped last week?"

I exhale slowly and drop my forehead to hers. We close our eyes and lay for a minute breathing together.

Gaby slips a hand in between our meshed bodies, sliding her fingers over my upper thigh before skimming my cock. My dick jumps, pressing against her stomach.

But I'm not fucking her tonight. We can kiss and hold each other, but I'm not taking it any further, even if she begs. Actually, hearing her beg would be fucking sexy—but I still wouldn't fuck her after what she just shared with me. I grab her hand and pull it back up.

"I'm really into you, Gabs. Deliriously into you. But we aren't having sex tonight. Our first time together will be passionate and memorable, not marred by the thought of what that mother fucker did to you. I swear, I'll put him in the fucking hospital if I ever meet him."

"I'll always be marred by him." Her words come out spiteful and bitter.

"Tonight we sleep. Just sleep." I tighten my embrace, hoping to transfer some peace into her despite my racing heart. "I want to hold you until you forget that asshole."

Though it's easy for me to say, I know it's not easy for her to do. She'll never forget what happened, but I hope she can find safety and comfort in my arms.

I'll never rush her or do anything she doesn't consent to. Not all men take advantage of women. And though I have no doubt she's ready to have sex with me, I understand her hesitation and don't want to rush into it. Especially with something so heavy on her heart.

"I'm sorry I ruined your night."

"Gabriella, this is not about me. It's about us."

When I shimmy farther below the comforter, she follows suit, snuggling into me as if she wants to burrow into my chest. Her head rests on my chest, her hand over my heart.

And I feel completely content. Being with Gaby evokes calm and peacefulness in me I haven't felt since I was a child.

"You're still into me, right?" She asks into my skin. "I didn't ruin your feelings?"

"Totally, completely, *stupidly* into you," I say, brushing my hand up and down her back. It's a soothing, not sexual, caress. Well, it's semi-sexual since we're lying in my bed, with nothing but her silky black undies between us. I'm not going to push her into having sex but fuck if I can stop my mind from fantasizing about her.

Trying to direct my thoughts elsewhere, I kiss her head. She tilts her neck to look at me. When our eyes meet, she returns the same look of electricity and desire burning inside.

"I'm totally into you, too," she whispers.

"If you ask really, really nice. I may be coerced into kissing you." I flash her a mischievous smile.

She lifts onto her elbow, testing my self-restraint with a full view of her chest. "Kiss me."

"Was that nice?" I tease, then blow lightly on her exposed breasts. A shiver ripples up and down the length of her body.

"I think my boobs are pretty nice," she shrugs and glances down at her chest.

My eyes automatically veer to her double D's. "I agree. But when you want something, you should use the word *please* at some point. But if you're going to tease, I can tease, too."

I lean over and lick her left nipple, which makes her laugh.

"What?" I ask, surprised by her reaction.

"That tickles." The bed shakes with another musical giggle.

"Oh?" I grab her waist and flatten her on the bed, then lean down to take her nipple into my mouth. At the flick of my tongue, her torso jolts forward, but I hold her firm. "Ready to be nice?"

"Nope." She shakes her head, defiantly giving me a small smirk.

"Why are you making this hard for me, Gabriella?"

She laughs, confirming that she has the maturity of a thirteen-year-old boy when it comes to her sense of humor.

"Fine! Will you please kiss me?"

"Yes." I whip the comforter off us, sending it to the bottom of the bed. Then I place one leg on either side of her and kneel above her.

Her eyes widen and her cheeks brighten, evidently impressed by the full-frontal. She waits, almost hyperventilating in anticipation of what comes next. She thinks I'll lower my mouth to hers, but that's not where my mind is. Instead, I sit back on my calves and lower my head toward the lips I want to lick—which are nowhere near her mouth.

"Landon?"

"You asked me to kiss you. I decide where."

I lean down and kiss the inside of her left thigh. Then, turn my head and nip the inside of her right with my teeth. And if the kiss and nip aren't enough to make her explode, I blow a steady stream of air between her legs before clamping my mouth directly on top of her underwear and raking my tongue against the silky fabric.

"Landon," she gasps my name as her breathing comes hard and fast.

Something else is about to come hard and fast for her if I keep flicking my tongue and sucking in that spot. The thought of making her orgasm has me throbbing.

I lift my eyes to hers. "Is this okay?"

"It's okay. It's just, um." She pauses as if shy or uncertain about what to say.

"This is a safe space, Gaby. I don't want you to fear communication with me. Every step is up to you."

She nods. "I've never done that. I don't know if I'll like it."

My mouth quirks as I try to stop a knowing smile. "Well, I'd bet my car that you'll like it, but I won't do anything you don't want me to do."

"I—" As she contemplates, she squirms beneath me.

Every movement fills me with excitement, but stopping is always an option. I won't move again until I have her permission to pull her underwear off and taste her again.

"Do you want to try?" I ask.

She lifts her eyes to the ceiling and takes a deep breath. I wait patiently as she wrestles with the demons consuming her thoughts, hoping my patience will help her move past any hurdles she has about being able to move forward and enjoy a healthy, sexual relationship.

When she lowers her head back to me, our gazes lock. I haven't moved one muscle. I'll wait as long as she needs before I proceed.

"Yes," she says through her exhale.

I spring forward to kiss her quickly, then lower my head between her legs.

Chapter Eighteen

GABY

THE LAST FEW MONTHS WITH LANDON HAVE BEEN ABSOLUTELY amazing. He's patient and kind—and has taught me that couples can have an amazing sex life without going all the way. Though, we've gotten pretty close a few times.

Waking up in his bed and watching him dress for practice has become routine. It's a good thing he has a job that takes him out of town, otherwise we'd practically be living together. When he's in Detroit, I barely make it home to my parent's house.

"I got you a press pass for tonight," he says, standing next to the bed, holding a black lanyard with a white plastic rectangle dangling from the end.

"A press pass? What for?" I glance at it, surprised to see my headshot already laminated on the card. Where had he gotten a picture of me?

"I thought it would be good practice for you to take photos at the games. Moving targets. Awesome subjects." He winks.

Bolting to my knees, I wrap my arms around his neck and hug him, hoping that squeezing my chest to his will keep my heart inside.

Getting to photograph the Detroit Aviators in action is a dream come true. Perfect male specimens skating and sweating and spinning and scoring. My own photos. No copyright infringement.

"This is completely amazing. Thank you." I pull away slightly so I can reach up and kiss his lips.

Landon responds immediately, enveloping me in his arms as he parts my lips with his tongue. His persistence makes me wish he didn't have to leave for practice in a few minutes. Then again, it's probably a good thing, since every time we touch I want to take it further.

But Landon insists we take our sexual relationship slow. I understand, truly I do, and I appreciate his concern for my internal issues. It makes me respect him even more.

"You make me wanna climb back into bed, Gabriella."

"Aren't you tired?" I tease, rubbing the back of his head, enjoying the feel of his short hair against my palms.

With that, he crouches down, grabs the back of my thighs, and flips me onto the bed. A giggle escapes as my back hits the mattress. Then he pins me with his body and attacks me with kisses and tickles. I try to escape his dancing fingers by curling into the fetal position, but I can't move with his weight on top of me.

"Lan—" I laugh and gasp for breath. "Stop. Landon."

His fingers ease up on the tickling, but his lips don't stop. Once I catch my breath and breathe evenly again, I slip my hands under his shirt and lightly scratch my nails over his back, something I know he can't resist. His kisses halt abruptly and he inhales deeply, his face still wedged in my neck. His back arches into my fingers like an eager cat, bringing the silly, sexy situation to an end too soon.

Landon presses up on his arms, lingering over me as if in mid-push-up.

Now that I think about it, lying under a sweaty and shirtless Landon while he kisses me every time he comes down from a push-up sounds super sexy.

"Feel free to continue that tonight," he says. Then his feet hit the floor and he stands up quickly.

"Feel free to continue with those kisses tonight, too."

Landon grabs my hand, pulling me off the bed and into his arms.

"You don't have to worry about that, Miss Bertucci." He nips at my earlobe before releasing me. "Stay as long as you want."

"I'll leave with you." I jump off the bed and scoop my backpack from the floor next to his nightstand. "Toothbrush," I say out loud as my brain scans the list of things I need to collect.

Landon holds the door open with his shoulder and twists toward me. "It's totally okay if you leave things here, Gaby."

After spending every possible moment together over the last few months, I don't know why it surprises me when he tells me to leave my things. Probably because I've never had a boyfriend before. I've never stayed over a guy's house or apartment or—in this case—a sky-rise condo overlooking the Detroit River and Canada. I've definitely never left my things at a guy's place before.

My heart flutters and warmth rushes to my cheeks as I gaze at him.

"Every time you look at me with those wide, innocent eyes, I want to corrupt you even more. You're killing me, Gaby."

Landon closes the door behind him, leaving me hyperventilating and ready to throw my wide-eyed innocence out the window.

I press my fingers to my mouth and stifle a giggle, as I fall back onto his bed.

Suddenly, the door bursts open, and Landon runs to me, sweeps me into his arms, and presses his lips to mine. As his fingers weave into my hair, our bodies mold together, bringing a jolt of life to my previously relaxed state.

"Okay. Now you're out of my system. Until tonight." He releases me and spins back around, exiting as quickly as he entered.

Stunned. Flabbergasted. Dumbfounded. I never have the right vocabulary to explain life with Landon Taylor.

WHEN I GET TO WORK, I've barely finished tucking my purse under the counter when Papa stalks over to me.

"You forgot this." He drops a pill into my hand. "You should probably keep some with you if you aren't going to come home."

"Thanks." I close my fist and walk around the counter, grabbing a bottle from the fridge next to the register as I pass.

"I assume you were with a friend again?" Papa asks as he watches me toss the pill into my mouth and chase it with water.

"Yes, Papa. I stayed with a friend. Mama knew."

Mama knows every time I stay at Landon's. I tell her everything.

After the rape, my doctor prescribed an antidepressant. The medicine took away my anxiety, but it also robbed me of any emotions and every ounce of personality. I wanted peace from the flashbacks, not to be a lifeless robot.

Though I assured my parents I'd been taking the pills dutifully, I stopped. If they asked, I'd lie or pop one just for show, then spit it in my hand and throw it away when they turned their backs.

The charade went on for about a week. Then things got bad.

Evidently, you aren't supposed to stop the medicine I'd been prescribed cold turkey. You have to wean off slowly with a doctor's supervision. I never thought about the negative effects it could have on my body. I just wanted to feel again, even if feeling meant shame and pain and rage.

Killing myself had never crossed my mind before I started taking those pills, not even in the days after the rape. But after I stopped the medication, the thought of suicide consumed me.

I'll never know if it was withdrawal or timing—because a week after I stopped taking the pills, I started seeing my rapist almost every single day.

And I don't mean that in a schizophrenic, hallucinatory way.

After he graduated from college, he started working full-time at Mitchell Family Farms as their delivery driver. Deliveries that used to come in the morning started coming in the afternoon during the hours I worked at the store.

That's when the harassment started.

And I say harassment because it *is* harassment when your rapist asks if you want him to take you to your prom.

It *is* harassment when your rapist asks if you have a boyfriend.

It *is* harassment when your rapist asks you how you're doing with a smirk on his face.

The constant interaction, combined with jumping off the medication enhanced my depression. I began to feel like the only way to stop everything—the pain, the shame, the harassment—would be to kill myself.

One day, Mama found me on the bathroom floor with an empty bottle of ibuprofen next to my hand. I don't remember anything except waking up in the hospital. I had to have my stomach pumped, which EMTs did at the scene of the overdose. I also had to have an overnight evaluation in the psych ward.

Because I'd never had any suicidal thoughts before being on the medication, my doctor chalked it up to my stopping the antidepressants without being weaned off properly. Instead of starting me back up on the robot pills, she listened when I told her how they made me feel. She switched my medication which made a world of difference.

Now, my anxiety is minimal and I have a full range of emotions. They aren't as intense as they might be if I weren't on anything, but I'll take that trade-off any day.

Still, ever since my suicide attempt, my parents have kept my seven-day pillbox on the kitchen counter. Now they know every time I take my medicine—and every time I don't.

MY FAMILY HAS HAD season tickets for Detroit Red Wings games since the sixties, back when they played at the Olympia, a historic but long-ago torn-down arena. We've always had great seats, too. At Little Caesars Arena, we sit at center ice in the upper part of the lower bowl. I've never complained in my life.

But the laminated rectangular press pass hanging around my neck spoils me within minutes—no—seconds. Do I care that it's two minor league hockey teams gliding across the ice in front of me?

Nope. Same chill. Same noise. Same excitement.

I stand against the Plexiglas, closer than I've ever been to the action, with my lens in the hole cut out for cameras, shivering happily.

Though I've already decided Landon will be the model in the advertisements I create for 313 Artisans, I don't want a memory card full of one player. Especially since being this close to the action gives me the opportunity to capture so many amazing shots.

No one can blame me for snapping of few of Luke Daniels, as an homage to the accelerated learning program he'd put me through. And out of sheer respect for the team captain, of course.

I take a few quick pictures of Pavel Gribov, the team's star center who started the season in the NHL. He'd been called up to play with the Monarchs last year when one of Charlotte's forwards separated his shoulder.

Up and down. Up and down. The life of a minor-league player.

Well, *some* minor-league players.

Landon has never been called up to Charlotte. It's the elephant in the room. The chip on his shoulder. The issue we never speak about unless he brings it up. Which he hasn't.

A lot of players spend time developing in the AHL before getting the call. Some spend four years. Other guys—some of the stars—never set a skate in an AHL arena, they go right to the big league.

But it's hard to keep perspective when you're player who isn't getting called up. I know the weight on Landon's shoulders. It keeps him awake at night. I know because I sleep next to him and see the glow of his cell phone screen at all hours when I turn over or get up to use the bathroom.

Landon doesn't want me try to console him by spouting empty words about how some players take longer to develop or how there needs to be an opening in the lineup. He wants his chance.

As the game goes on behind the glass, I wonder what Landon has to do to get called up to play for the Monarchs. At plus-35, Landon leads the team in plus/minus. That says a lot for any guy—but especially Landon, a defenseman who plays thirty-five to forty minutes a game, including killing penalties and on the power play.

Power play.

Life could be described as a series of power plays.

Not in the sense of being up a man, but in a business sense. People in power have the opportunity to play around with those underneath them. The Monarchs coach and general manager all have the power to move Landon up. But it hasn't happened yet.

My father has the power to let me run 313, but he won't give me the opportunity.

I lower my camera to protect the lens as one of the Aviators players slams an Iowa Wild player into the boards. The glass shakes as two more players from each team descend, all elbowing and pushing as they vie for the puck stuck between their skates. I can't see it unless I put my head against the glass and look down, and that's not going to happen with four huge bodies banging the boards.

Finally, someone kicks the puck free with his skate blade, sending it toward Detroit's goal. One of the Wild players rears back for a one-timer, but an Aviators player dives, sliding across the ice in front of the shot.

Number 6. Landon Taylor.

No surprise there.

The surprise comes when Landon doesn't get up. He lays on the ice, curled in a fetal position, clutching his face with his gloves. The whistle sounds immediately, as the referee, along with everyone in the arena, notices the puddle of blood forming on the ice under Landon's head.

My stomach lurches as I watch the puddle grow into a pool. The Aviators' trainer shuffles across the ice quickly and drops to his knees in front of Landon, blocking my view. I move along the boards until I run into a row of seats and can't go any farther.

"Can you see what's happening?" I ask the fans in the front row without taking my eyes off the scene on the ice.

"I think he took that shot to the face." One of the guys in a Luke Daniels jersey tells me.

Landon rolls onto his hands and knees, and the trainer applies a towel to his face. The crowd erupts into applause as Landon pushes to his feet, allowing the trainer to assist him as he skates to the bench.

My stomach feels heavy, as if I swallowed my heart. In nineteen years of watching hockey, I've seen hundreds of guys hit by pucks. But when it's the man you love bleeding, you can't stop the feeling of dread that seeps into the pit of your stomach.

Landon doesn't sit down when he arrives at the bench. Instead, he keeps walking straight back toward the dressing room.

It takes every ounce of self-control not to run up the stairs and bang on the locker room door until they let me see Landon. The hockey fan in me knows how dumb that sounds.

He got up. He skated off the ice. He's fine.

The girlfriend in me still has to hold back. Or find something else to think about.

As if answering a silent call, someone knocks on the glass directly in front of me. When I turn, Luke is skating in a circle before he has to line up for a face-off. As he skates past the glass again, he twists his glove, lifting his thumb. Then he catches my eye and nods. Shooting him a smile of relief, I nodded back.

Luke Daniels. The epitome of Captain.

And a pretty damn good guy.

"ARE YOU OKAY?" I rush to Landon when he emerges from the Aviators' locker room. My fingertips hover over the gash across his right eyebrow while my other hand rests on his chest.

"I'm fine. The eye area bleeds a lot more than other areas. Makes it look worse than it is." Landon closes his hand over the one I placed on his chest. Then he leans down to kiss my forehead. "Don't worry. I know a good doctor."

Deep down, I know he's fine because he'd returned to the game just a few minutes after leaving the ice, but I feel better after checking him out myself.

"Your dad's a cardiologist."

"I help him keep his career options open. He's been stitching me up for years."

Instead of laughing, I throw my arms around him and squeeze him hard. Landon responds by returning my hug and kissing the top of my head. Since my face is buried in his dress shirt, he'll have two damp black mascara streaks on his blue button-down when I pull away.

I lift my face off his chest and meet his eyes. "No concussion?"

"Absolutely not." He bends his head and presses his forehead against mine. "Just a cut. I promise."

Landon's arms stay locked around me as I exhale a deep, relieved breath. A concussion could lead to bigger health problems and be career-ending.

He lifts his head to look me in the eye. "Wanna go visit Uncle Brian? I need a beer."

"Me too," I joke.

Landon releases me from his bear hug and grabs my hand, leading me toward the arena's concourse. "We'll take your car. I'll leave mine here since our lot has security. Cool?"

I nod. "Aren't you afraid people will recognize you?"

"I'd be fucking stoked if anyone recognized me. But I'm pretty sure most people have cleared out by now."

"Don't be that guy."

"What guy?"

"You know what guy."

"The Gribov?" Landon asks.

"Exactly."

Gribov has a reputation for being a hotheaded showboat and taking badly timed Unsportsmanlike Conduct penalties.

"Could you ever see me acting like Gribov?"

Could I see Landon squat down to one knee and bring his stick to his eye as if peering through the scope of a rifle to "shoot" at a goalie he'd just scored on?

Could I see Landon running his mouth at the referee until the man in black and white stripes would get so pissed that he'd send him to the penalty box?

"No. But fame changes a person," I say dryly.

Landon doesn't seem like the guy who would do a one-eighty, but you never know.

I remember Gribov making some arrogant remarks to the media after being called to Charlotte last season. He sounded like such an egotistical prick, it made me want to fly down and smack him. Thankfully, he got bucked off his conceited horse when the Monarchs sent him back to Detroit.

Gribov finally met karma. Not that it did any good. He still hasn't stopped yapping.

"Yeah, except the fame didn't change him. That's just how he is," Landon says.

"Fame won't change you. But it will give you a bigger platform. The platform you want to prove yourself to the world."

Landon stops abruptly and my arm practically jerks from its socket. He drops my hand. The skin around his eyes creases in concern. "Is that how you think of me, Gaby? Crybaby attention whore?"

The temperature in the concourse of the arena seems to drop a few degrees and a shiver racks my body.

"No. Not at all. Why would you take that comment as an insult?"

Landon's gaze falls to his feet. "Because you're the only one who knows how selfish I am underneath it all."

"I wouldn't use it against you, Landon. Everyone is selfish. I'm selfish. I'm jealous. It's innate."

Landon still hasn't lifted his head, so I grab his hands.

"Landon, look at me." He doesn't, but I continue anyway. "You are one of the kindest, most selfless people I've ever met. Siblings get jealous of each other. We all want our parents' attention."

"I know. But my situation is different. And it makes me feel like an exceptional dickhead."

"What does it say about me that I want my older brother to hit the road so I can have the family business all to myself?" I release Landon's hands and lift my fists toward the air. "Bertucci Produce shall be mine! All mine!"

He shakes his head, but a laugh escapes his upturned lips, so I've diffused the situation. He laces his fingers through mine as we continue to the arena doors.

"For the record"—I glance at Landon—"I meant the NHL would be a platform to show the world what an amazing player and man you are. I wasn't thinking about your family."

"I know, Gabs." Landon shoots me a half smile as he pushes through the arena doors "I had a rough game and I feel like shit right now. I'm wallowing."

"Let's go cheer you up with a depressant!" I exclaim, bursting out into the cold night.

"If you'd rather skip the bar and let me fuck you on the hood of my car, just let me know. I'm confident all the sex endorphins would cheer me up." Landon grabs my hips as he joins me outside. "And I know how much you like that."

Thankfully, the winter wind whipping against my cheeks masks the color his steamy suggestion put there.

Especially since he's right.

And a tiny part of me wants to take him up on his offer.

Chapter Nineteen

GABY

Shit.

My stomach turns and tightens when Landon raises his arm and waves to a large group of people cramped into a large round booth in the far corner of the bar.

Going for a drink at Brian's bar seemed like a great idea. Until I realized we were meeting a group of Landon's friends there.

I scan the people occupying the booth. Two hot hockey players, two puck bunnies, and a girl who looks more natural than bunny.

Apprehension cements my feet to the floor. Landon steps forward but gets jerked back, like the owner of a stubborn dog refusing to walk on a leash. I keep his hand locked in mine without moving from my place. He whips around, eyes wide with question.

"Sorry." I point down. "I thought I dropped my Chap Stick."

Big fat lie. *Huge* lie.

Please don't take me over there. It's a silent plea, but I hope he notices the apprehension in my posture.

Landon's lips curve into the sweet smile he always has for me. He brings our joined hands to his mouth and kisses the back of mine. Then he pulls me forward again. Though I try my hardest to think of another lame excuse to stall, nothing comes to mind, so I have no choice but to follow.

"Taylor!" one of the guys yells as we approach. He lifts his fist and reaches out.

I recognize his face as one of Landon's teammates, but I don't know his name.

"Hey!" Landon leans over the table and pounds his fist. "Everyone, this is Gaby."

A jumbled chorus of "Hey, Gaby" rings out over the loud music flowing through the stereo system.

Landon places his hand on my back, directing me into the crowded booth beside the dolled-up, bleached blondes. One has less meat on her bones than a discarded turkey leg at the Renaissance Festival, while the other girl's carrot-colored skin seems to glow, even in the dark corner of the bar.

Fake tans aren't difficult to spot on March night in Michigan.

As I slide across the tattered vinyl seat, I give the girls a quick, nervous smile. Landon steals a chair from the next table and posts up next to me. He sets a comforting hand on my knee, but instead of calming my nerves, it makes my stomach twist.

Not the good kind of twisting where his hand on my knee means we'll be making out on the hood of his Audi later. Instead, it's the anxiety-ridden, sweat-producing twist of an introvert being thrown into the lion's den. I hate being the new person in a large group of people who all know one another.

The outsider. The misfit.

Soon, I realize I don't have to worry, because the conversation continues around me like I never sat down. The girl next to me didn't return my smile—just turned her back to me and continued her previous conversation.

"What do you think, Gaby?"

"Excuse me?" I look in the direction from where I heard my name called.

"You knew Tay Tay before his haircut. What do you think of it?" The question came from the guy who'd waved us to the table when we walked in.

Tay Tay?

"I like it," I say, though I barely hear my words. I cough and repeat them, slightly louder than the first time.

"Flow is gone. What she gonna grab when you fuck?" Another guy says in broken English. I can't help but recognize Pavel Gribov after the amount of photos I took of him at the game.

Love him or hate him, I can't deny his talent.

"Dirty." The guy across the table from me shakes his head.

"Don't worry about my sex life, Comrade. I've heard you're in a bit of a slump." Landon raises his beer bottle and taps it down on top of Gribov's bottle. A blast of beer bubbles and gushes out over Gribov's hand like foamy lava.

"Fuck off." Gribov jerks his hand away and shakes the beer off. "You owe me this beer."

"Get a round, Taylor. You're the last one here."

"Be right back," Landon tells me before standing up.

I raise my hand to get his attention. "I can help."

But Gribov pushes back from the table and follows Landon to the bar before I have a chance to slide out of the booth.

As the conversation clicks around me, I only catch a sentence here and a roar of laughter there because the bar is loud. A shiver travels from my shoulders to my fingertips and shoots straight to my toes. Perspiration breaks out on my forehead, drops of distress appearing one by one, but I doubt anyone notices the silent SOS.

Freezing and sweating simultaneously. Telltale signs of a misplaced misfit afraid to jump into a conversation with her peers.

"I'm going to use the restroom," I announce to no one in particular since the only person who cares about my presence is at the bar laughing with his uncle and teammate.

When I finish, Landon and Gribov are still at the bar, waiting on their order. Instead of going back to the table without Landon, I head for the door.

Once outside, I take a deep breath of cold, smoke-filled air, as all the nicotine addicts huddle around the entrance puffing on their cigarettes.

Totally worth it for a minute alone to regroup. Between the crowd and the conversation, the bar seemed claustrophobic.

Out of the corner of my eye, I see the two girls from the booth walking out of the bar. The ones who haven't looked up from their conversation to say a word to me since Landon and I arrived.

"What's up with that girl Landon brought?"

"Maybe he lost a bet?"

"I know, right? She must give good head."

"Why?"

"Why else would he be with her?"

Turns out, the fresh air I craved is rancid and bitchy.

Of course, good head is the only reason Landon would choose to be with someone whose hair hadn't been bleached so much horses would mistake it for hay.

"Do you smoke?" I hear a woman's voice behind me. One of the mean girls.

"No." I shake my head.

"Then what are you doing out here?" she asks in a clipped tone.

"Needed some air." I look down the street, ready to hail a cab—if cabs dared to come near this place.

"So, you and Landon are a thing?" she asks.

"We're friends."

"Friends." She laughs. Her brown eyes search my face before lowering to scan the rest of me. "Landon gets bored easily. You might want to try using a mint or something next time."

The other girl snort-laughs. Super classy. Both of them.

An older man next to me throws his cigarette down as he pulls the door open. The still-smoking butt lands inches from my feet. I step on it, smashing it into the concrete with a few rotations of my foot.

"Excuse me, sir. Can I bum one of those?"

"Anything for you, sugar." He lifts a pack of menthols from his front pocket and shakes the box until one pops up higher than the others. Then he plucks the cancer stick out and hands it to me. I nod my thanks as he disappears inside and I pass the cigarette on to the girl.

She scowls. "I could've gotten one."

"But you didn't. I did." I open the door to go back inside, but a petty internal voice gnaws at me. I can't quite leave the situation alone.

As the only girl in a family with two older brothers, I learned to stand up for myself around mean girls years ago, despite my non-confrontational personality. Drew always had a flock following him after his hockey games making snide comments to me because they thought I was his girlfriend.

I can't let two miserable chicks ruin my night.

Using my foot to hold the door open, I dig in my purse for the tin of mints I carry. "Here." I open the container and toss a handful of mints into the air.

She misses catching any of them, and they bounce across the sidewalk like tiny, rubber raindrops.

"You'll need those before I will." I nod to the mints covering the concrete.

"Whatever, bitch." The girl lurches forward. Instead of rushing inside to hide, I conjure every hockey fight I've ever witnessed and step toward her, ready to pull her shirt over her head, hockey-jersey style.

Evidently, she wasn't expecting me to challenge her advance because she backs away.

I laugh and slide inside. Once safe, I press my back against the door and take a deep breath.

My hands tremble. My heart hammers.

I've never been in a fight in my life. I've never done anything that rude in my life. Worried that one of them might try to get in and ram me in the back, I step away from the door and hurry back to the table.

That's when I realize I've painted myself into an awkward corner for when the girls return to the group.

The repercussions of acting before thinking. This is why I stay home and read books on Friday and Saturday nights.

When I sit down, the only other woman at the table, who was tucked between Gribov and another guy earlier, gets up and slides into the booth next to me.

"I'm Caroline. I'm so glad Landon finally brought you out. We were beginning to think you were an imaginary girlfriend."

"Gaby," I say, though Landon introduced me earlier.

"You are gorgeous. Who does your hair?" Without permission, she touches a lock of waves hanging in front of my shoulder. I jump, surprised at the unexpected contact.

"Um, my aunt?" I don't know why I phrased it as a question.

My aunt has been the only one to touch my hair since I was a little girl. Just a trim. No color, no highlights. Nothing except a hot pink extension every October in memory of *Nonna*, who passed away from breast cancer five years ago.

"I'm so sorry. That was creepy." Caroline releases my hair. "I'm Blake's wife." She points to the guy across the table. Blake Panikos is another one of the Aviators' defensemen.

Caroline leans closer and whispers conspiratorially. "I can see why you're the unicorn that nabbed Landon's heart."

"Excuse me?" I ask, flipping my hair over my shoulder and leaning closer.

"You pulled Landon Taylor. He's impossible." She straightens in her seat and raises her glass to her lips.

"I—" How do I respond to a comment like that? I've never "pulled" anyone in my life.

"How the fuck I get rid of this girl?" Gribov asks so loudly he may as well have been asking everyone in the bar.

"That was subtle," Landon says, tilting his beer back. He glances at me and raises an eyebrow.

I smile and nod. I like that he checks on me, even when we're at the same table. Caroline seems much nicer than the girls smoking outside.

"He's talking about the girl he brought, who brought her friend. The ones who haven't spoken to anyone but the guys and each other," Caroline explains.

"I know the ones. We had a slight altercation outside." I admit.

"Really?" Caroline pats my leg. "Tell. Tell."

I give her a brief rundown of my interaction with the girls. Retelling makes me sound pretty badass, even though I'd been running on anger-induced adrenaline.

Caroline elbows Gribov. "I think Gaby may have solved your problem."

"What did you do?" Landon's tone matches the one Papa uses when he scolds our dog, but the gleam in his eyes shows more amusement.

"I turned their stupid joke on them."

"Oh tell them, Gaby! They'll think it's great," Caroline urges.

"I don't really feel, um—" I stammer, slightly uncomfortable telling a story involving blow jobs in front of four men.

"Can I tell them?" Caroline asks.

"Go ahead." I lower my head and wring my hands in my lap, avoiding eye contact with every man at the table.

"One of them made some dumb-ass comment about how Gaby must give good head if Landon is dating her. Then she said he gets bored easily and she should use a mint if she wants to keep him happy. So, Gaby threw mints at the girl and told her she'd need them before her."

"I threw mints into her cleavage, not, like, *at* her," I correct so it doesn't sound like I pelt people with mints.

"You threw mints into her enhanced breasts?" Caroline asks with a snort. "Oh my god! That's even better!"

Though the music still thrums and bumps in the background, the bar seems to take on a moment of silence. Then all at once, a thunderous roar of laughter erupts from everyone at the table. And because my nerves have calmed a bit, I laugh, too.

Once the laughter dies down, I hear Landon's words loud and clear, "And that's why I love her."

Chapter Twenty

LANDON

MY WORDS SLICE THROUGH THE ROAR OF HYSTERICS AND THERE'S complete silence.

Except choking.

There's a forceful hacking sound coming from Gaby, who's hunched over the table. Caroline pats her back a few times as if she can bang out whatever my girl has lodged in her throat.

But she won't be able to. You can't slap out shock.

I wink at her, but Gaby doesn't wink back. She doesn't smile. Just stares at me with wide eyes and flushed cheeks.

"Another man bite the dust," Gribov breaks the silence.

"*And* Gaby got rid of your skanks." Blake raises his beer.

He taps the neck of his bottle to Blake's. "She is useful."

"Game day tomorrow, boys." I stretch my arms above my head and fake a yawn. "I think I've embarrassed Gaby enough for one night."

"It was nice to meet you guys," she says, sliding out of the booth. When she stands up, I jump to my feet and grab her hand.

"Nice to meet you too, Gaby," Caroline calls. "Get my number from Landon. We can sit together at the games."

"That would be great. Thank you."

"Come on, Gabs." I tug her arm. "I need to get you alone."

As we hurry to the exit, Gribov yells, "Do not rush. She have no mints left!"

I roll my eyes and usher Gaby out the door quickly.

ONCE I'VE UNLOCKED the door to my condo, I pull her inside and yank her into my arms. She snuggles into my chest as if reveling in the warmth.

"How I feel about you is real, Gabs. I've never come close to feeling this way. You are everything I dreamed you'd be." I press my lips to her hair.

She pulls away to look at me. "You dreamed I'd be a boring book nerd?"

"Yeah, right." I call her bluff. "A boring book nerd who rocks out at concerts and throws mints at hoes like it's rice at a wedding."

"'Throws mints at hoes like it's rice at a wedding.' That is the best thing I've ever heard you say."

I burst out laughing. "Better than 'I love you?'"

"I stand corrected," she says, dropping her tone. "It's the *funniest*, not the best."

I rub her side with my fingers as my stomach swirls with desire. "Is it better than, 'let's go to bed?'"

She swings her hips gently. "Now I'm singing The Cure in my head."

"The cure for what?" I ask, puzzled.

"Geez, boy. You need a lesson in music school."

"We can play music school tonight. You be the teacher, I'll be the—"

"Don't say student!" she interrupts. "That is so freaking wrong."

She tries to wiggle out of my arms, but I tighten my grip and lower my head to her ear. I nip her earlobe with my teeth, then whisper, "Principal. I'll be the principal."

"Is this going to turn into Landon and Gaby Act Out Erotica?"

"You remembered our book club," I murmur before trailing kisses down her neck. I lick the skin below her earlobe and draw tiny circles on her neck with my tongue. "Miss Bertucci, I need to speak with you in my office."

"Are we really doing this?"

"It's a pressing matter." I tilt my pelvis into hers, showing her just how pressing a matter it is. My dick swells, ready to burst out of my trousers if I don't get them off soon.

"I have five minutes before my next class," she teases before spinning out of my arms and running toward my room.

"I'll get you a sub!" I call, laughing as I chase her.

Though I can't wait to get my hands on her, I slow it down once we enter my room. I know she's scared and I need to take my time and let her be in control.

I lean against the closed door, sizing her up like she's the opposing team's goalie and I have a clear breakaway, scanning every inch of her from top shelf to five-hole. When I move forward, she squeezes her eyes shut.

I stop my advance, giving her a moment to regain composure. Her head swivels from the bed to the floor to me. Suddenly, she takes two large steps before launching herself into my arms. I catch her easily, anticipating the move before she chose it. She wants to move forward as much as I do.

Our mouths meet. Our tongues tangle. Fast. Feverish. I squeeze her ass as I carry her forward and deposit her onto my bed.

As Gaby tugs the hem of her top up and over her head, I strip off my shirt and shuck my pants to the ground. When I look up, she's fumbling around, trying to roll the waistband of her leggings over her butt.

But I can't wait. I need her right now.

Putting my hands on the bed on each side of her, I lean down and place my lips on her breasts which are spilling out of her bra. Her back arches and she lifts her hips, giving me the ideal opportunity to pull her pants past her thighs and down to her ankles. Once I toss them to the floor, I rise onto my knees and grab her hips.

"I love how your body reacts to my touch, Gabs."

"Me, too," she squeaks through a ragged breath as the pace of her breathing increases.

I press my lips against her skin, using the lace at the top of her bra as a guide as I slowly make my way across her left breast, and down the valley between before moving to the right.

The feel of her soft, supple skin sends blissful ripples of pleasure straight to my cock. My hands remain at her hips, alternating between gripping and relaxing every time my mouth meets her skin. She pants, faster and faster as each teasing touch heightens her anticipation of where I'll place my mouth next.

Her muscles tighten under my grip, but instead of assuming its desire, I know better. This isn't about me. And though I won't move away, I won't move forward until she gives me the go.

Suddenly she exhales and relaxes, then grabs the cups of her bra, tugging them down and fully exposing her breasts. She holds the fabric down and pushes toward my face—giving me approval.

I lower my mouth onto her, rolling my tongue over her nipple, and brushing my thumb over the smooth skin of her stomach like a slow windshield wiper. Though her nipple hardens under my touch—then she tenses again.

I remove my mouth and lift my eyes to hers. "Everything okay?"

"Just thinking too much."

"Don't think, Gabs. Feel." I glide my hand down her hip and across her upper thigh before settling between her legs. When my fingers skim her underwear, she arches against me.

"Feeling yet?" I ask. Leaning on my elbow and pushing her underwear to the side as I slip a finger into her, exploring gently.

"Yes," she gasps when I slide a second finger inside. "Yes."

I pick up the speed, rubbing my thumb over her clit as I hammer my fingers in and out quickly. I must hit the right spot because her hips buck off the mattress. I can't handle it. I need to be inside her—to feel her warmth curl around cock.

She groans loudly when I pull my fingers out, but I need to grab a condom before things really get going. I slide off the bed and run to the bathroom. In less than thirty seconds, I'm kneeling over her again.

Her eyes flash open when I tear the wrapper. Fear swirls under her lashes and I know I have to take it slow and wait for her consent. Not that I wouldn't anyway, but knowing her background, I want to do everything I can to make sure she's comfortable and in control.

I hold the condom out for her. With a quick glance at my cock, which is fully prepared to accept the sheath, she grabs the disc. My stomach tightens and I groan as she rolls it down the shaft. Once she's finished, she guides me to the promised land between her legs.

A slow smile spreads across my lips, making my approval of the direction she's pushed me in obvious. I rub the tip of my cock over her entrance, coating the condom with her cum. Then I glide back and forth watching as her mouth falls open, loving how much she enjoys the feeling.

"You're so fucking wet, Gabs." I groan. "So wet. And so sexy."

I stop at the entrance. No matter how ready I am. No matter how much I want to, I'm not going to push inside without her permission.

This is all about giving Gaby the power to control her own pleasure.

She raises her pelvis, taking me in ever so slightly, before lifting to take more of my cock and lowering until I'm out.

I grab her face, my breath hot and fast against her cheeks. Our eyes meet—giving her one last chance to stop before we go any further.

She touches my face with both hands and pulls me onto her. Then she ravishes my mouth. As we kiss feverishly, she reaches between us, takes my thick cock in her hand, and guides me inside. The action gives me the permission I need to push into her completely.

Quick. Hard.

On her terms.

Chapter Twenty-One

GABY

"Morning, sleepyhead."

When I open my eyes, I'm wrapped in the luxurious black comforter and surrounded by pillows. Landon stands next to the bed, fully dressed, sporting a gash encrusted with dried blood above his right eye and a purple bruise below it. It matches his left eye, the one that was hit by a puck when he blocked a shot at last night's game.

"What the hell happened to you?" I ask, clutching the comforter against my chest as I sit up.

"I've already seen your boobs, Gabs." Landon ignores my question. I know he's trying to get a rise out of me, but it won't work this time. I trust Landon with everything.

So I let go.

Landon's smile fades and his eyes pop open. Well, the right eye pops. His left eye is frozen in a perpetual squint. Immediately embarrassed by my boldness, I reach for the comforter, but before I can pull it up, Landon tackles me into his magnificent mattress.

"Who are you and what did you do with my sweet little introvert?" He drops his head to the valley between my exposed breasts and presses kisses along the sides of each one. I giggle as his hair tickles my neck and chin. "You're a little vixen."

Landon lifts his head and brings his face to mine, hovering close, almost close enough to kiss him.

I skim my fingertips across his eyebrow. "What happened?"

"Nothing. But for the record, it was worth it."

"Landon Charles."

"You never told me your brother didn't want you dating hockey players."

"Excuse me?" I try to sit up, but Landon won't budge, holding me in place.

"Joey jumped me when I stopped at your house to talk to your dad."

"What?" This time I press both hands against his chest and push him off me. We both sit up.

"I stopped by your house to talk to your dad this morning."

"Why? Why would you *ever* do that?"

"He asked me to."

"Oh."

A summons from Papa couldn't be good. Neither could Joey beating up my boyfriend, though he *did* warn me he'd do it.

Landon touches the fresh gash above his eye. "Totally worth it."

Twisting my hands in my lap, I ask, "Am I allowed to ask what Papa wanted to talk to you about?"

Landon picks up one of my hands and laces his fingers through it. "Mostly stuff you and I have already talked about."

I nod but keep my head down, my eyes on our joined hands. Leave it to Papa to talk to Landon about my personal business behind my back. He still doesn't trust me.

Typical Papa. Typical of my entire family.

Landon leans back and dips his free hand into his pocket. "He, um, he gave me this to give to you."

When I extend my hand, he drops a tiny yellow and blue pill into my palm.

Fuck.

"So he told you everything." I roll my wrist and watch the pill slide back and forth in my hand.

"I wish you would have."

My head snaps up. "You're angry with me?"

"No. No, I'm not." Landon releases my hand and slides his arm across my shoulder, bringing me close. "It's your business, Gabs. I just thought you trusted me enough to tell me."

I wiggle out from under his arm and grab the comforter, wrapping it around myself, as if a tangible object can conceal the level of embarrassment and shame inside.

"Telling someone I tried to kill myself isn't about trust." I jump off the bed, tugging the comforter with me. "It's about not wanting to reveal all the crazy to a guy you just started dating."

"I don't think you're crazy. I get it."

"You had a conversation with my father about my suicide attempt and everything is awesome. He doesn't know anything about it. I can only imagine how he told the story." I tug the heavy blanket a few more times, bringing it with me as I move toward the door. "I bet I came across as a weak little girl who tried to take the easy way out, right?"

Landon stands up. "No, he—"

"I don't care. I don't fucking care." The pill burns in my fist—a daily reminder of that one instance of cowardice. Instead of chuck it in my mouth, I throw it at Landon's face. He bobs, dodging it easily.

Landon glances behind him, to the spot where the pill landed on the hardwood floor. "Maybe you should swallow it instead of throwing it at me."

"Fuck. You." I spin around, dragging the monstrous comforter with me as I trudge down the hall and into the bathroom.

After dropping the comforter in the hallway and slamming the bathroom door with an appropriate amount of angry flair, I realize that all my clothes are in Landon's bedroom.

Thankfully, a discarded outfit lays in a heap on the floor in front of the shower. As I tug his oversized button-down shirt up one arm, Landon pounds on the door.

"I'm sorry, Gabs. I shouldn't have said that. Will you please come out and talk to me?"

"We don't need to talk. You and Papa already did that. You discussed all the most private parts of my life behind my back. I'm used to it from him, I just didn't think you'd ever join in." I slide to the floor and lean against the door.

"Your dad was worried about you. And when he told me you'd been skipping your medication—"

"I wasn't skipping, I forgot!" I bang my fist against the door behind me. "I usually take it in the morning when it's staring me in the face. But I've been waking up here and I just forgot."

Which is the absolute truth, despite my previous pill-taking issues. Still, Papa had no right to bring it up with Landon.

There's no sound from the other side of the door. To someone not used to confrontations with anyone except my brothers, a few seconds of silence feels like a lifetime.

Landon knocks again, much softer than before. "I don't think what your dad did was right. I don't think he should have handled it the way he did. Can we talk without this door between us?"

When I don't answer immediately, he continues, "I love you so much, Gabs. I've never been so happy. I've never been so proud of who *I* am since I met you. I don't want to make decisions for you or hinder your dreams or talk about things behind your back. I want to hold your hand and stand by your side, working through everything together. We're like fucking superheroes together."

I close my eyes and allow his words to swaddle me like a cozy blanket around a newborn. He knows me so well, he addresses my exact fears.

"Will you please unlock the door?"

"I never locked it."

Suddenly, the door rams my back as Landon attempts to enter.

"Oh my God!" he exclaims. "I'm so sorry!"

I scoot over to allow him inside. When I glance up, the tenderness and strength I've come to rely on radiates from his eyes.

If he ever wanted to run away, now is his chance. With me sitting on a cold bathroom floor, my arms wrapped around my torso to keep his humongous, dirty shirt closed around my tiny frame. Tears stream down my cheeks, depositing whatever eye makeup was still left from last night onto the front of the shirt.

Instead, Landon kneels in front of me with his bottom lip caught in his teeth. His eyes flicker as desire replaces tenderness.

"I've never wanted to fuck you so badly in my life." He reaches out, places his hands on my knees, and gently opens my legs.

My breath catches, but I never take my gaze from his. His movements wouldn't be scandalous in a fully-clothed situation. But in an intimate situation, with nothing but his shirt draped over my naked body, it definitely tips the sensual scale.

"I thought you wanted to talk."

"I did. I do." Landon shakes his head as if knocking out cobwebs. His lips quiver as he holds back a smile. "But you're sitting there, looking so fucking sexy in my roommate's shirt. I'm jealous, amused, and turned on all at the same time."

"What?" I yank the shirt and scan it. His roommate? "What roommate?"

A burst of laughter breaks Landon's fake serious expression. "I live with Varenkov. This is his place, actually. He's not here most of the time, obviously. But when he's in town he stays here."

Last season, the Monarchs called Aleksandr Varenkov up. Why is he here now?

"You mean to tell me a complete stranger's dirty shirt is touching my naked body? Gross." Shrugging and tugging, I peel the shirt off my shoulder.

"Let me do that." Landon inches closer, spreading my legs open farther to allow his hips in between. He reaches for the shirt but pauses before removing it. "Cool?"

"I want you to," I confirm confidently.

My heart, which has already sped up with his advancement between my legs, slams against my rib cage as he strips the shirt off, leaving nothing covering me. Instinct makes me cross my arms over my chest, but that leaves my lower body completely bare. The overhead bathroom light shines like a spotlight, highlighting every naked inch. "Can you please turn off the light?"

"Don't you want to see me? Am I repulsive?" Landon asks. He sits back on his calves and drags his T-shirt over his head.

"Funny." My shoulders shake with a silent laugh, though I don't take my eyes off the hard planes of his chest. "I'm embarrassed."

"You are so fucking beautiful." He grabs my hips and pulls me toward him until I lay flat on the floor. As he kneels between my legs, his hands grip the outsides of my bare thighs, his long fingers firm, but still. "I'll stop if you say no."

"I won't say no." My internal body temperature soars to new heights, bared completely to him. The cool tile feels fantastic against my overheated skin.

Landon leans over me, opens the bottom drawer of the bathroom vanity, and extracts a condom. Does everyone keep condoms in the bottom drawer of the vanity? Did I missed that lesson in health class?

"Can we *please* turn off the light?" I ask again.

"No deal. I need to see every inch of you." He stops ripping the condom packet open to trail a finger down the top of my right thigh.

I roll my eyes to the ceiling and turn my head to the side in embarrassment

"You're giving me a complex, Gaby." Landon leans over and drop a kiss below my belly button before straightening and gesturing toward his body. "You don't want to see all this in its fluorescent-lit glory?"

Instead of answering, I grab the waistband of his shorts and tug them down. Landon, obviously excited I'm taking charge, shucks them down to his thighs and leans onto me, flattening himself over my body. My feet lose their grip on the floor and a gust of air leaves my lips as his full weight falls.

Instead of entering me, like I expect, Landon grabs my waist with his strong hands and rolls onto his back, bringing me with him in one swift motion.

Suddenly, the tables have turned. I'm kneeling over him, our bodies completely ready for each other.

"You're in charge, Gabs." Landon holds my hips but keeps his grip loose enough to allow me to move.

"I don't—" I begin. There's no need to continue since Landon knows that everything sex-related we haven't done together is a new experience for me.

The blush in my cheeks spreads to my neck and chest, judging by the telltale tingle and warmth in those areas. I raise my hands to cover my face, but before I can hide, Landon grabs them and places them on his chest.

"Relax. You got this." He winks. Then he grabs my hips once again and lifts me so I'm hovering over his cock. "Just do whatever feels right to you."

Relaxing is easy when you've done something a million times, but when trying something foreign, it's next to impossible. Still, I press on —literally—sliding onto Landon slowly. His sharp intake of breath makes me pause and clench.

"Are you okay?" I whisper, panicked I might've hurt him somehow. Is he supposed to bend toward me? Should I lean forward so he's more comfortable?

Landon's eyes flash open. "You feel fucking amazing. Don't stop."

At his insistence, I start over, placing my hands on his chest and moving again. When I lean forward, Landon grabs my head and brings my ear to his lips.

"Lift all the way off and come back down again." His voice is scratchy, his breath heavy.

He can't see my nod because he's closed his eyes. Following his direction, I lift myself completely off before sliding onto him again. His eyes shoot open and his fingers dig into my skin with the contact.

This time, I know the squeeze means it feels good for him. I hide my smile behind the veil of hair that falls forward as I lean over Landon.

He lifts a hand to sweep the wavy brown locks out of my face. "I want to see that smile. I want to see how much you like fucking me."

"HOW WAS IT?" Landon punctuates his question by kissing my head while tracing figure eights on my skin with his fingertips.

"'Like riding a bike' would be a bad analogy because I've never done that before."

Landon chuckles but lets me continue.

"I just mean it was easy to figure out and, um, enjoy."

"I knew you'd like it." Landon smacks my bare bottom.

"Landon!" I lift my head off his chest.

"I knew you'd like that, too."

He knows parts of me better than I know myself. And he can teach me more than I ever dreamed.

"Every time I look at you I'm reminded of how lucky I am to have you in my life." He brings his hands to my head and massages my scalp. Then he gathers my hair and sweeps it to the side, before sliding his hands down my neck and back. He laces his fingers behind me and tightens his embrace. "Being with you makes me want to skip practice to kiss every inch of your bare skin."

When I smile, my lips brush the smooth skin of his chest. His heart beats under my ear.

"But if I lost my job, you'd never speak to me again. So I better get up and shower."

"Not funny."

"I know. You're ruthless." Landon bends down to place a quick kiss on my lips.

Suddenly, there's a violent knock on the bathroom door.

"You have your own bathroom, Landon!" a familiar female voice calls from the other side of the door. "You never should have agreed to switch bedrooms when you left for Charlotte, Sasha!"

"Who is that?" I whisper, racking my brain to figure out how I know the girl's voice.

"Varenkov's fiancée."

His answer doesn't explain how I know the voice, since I have no clue who Aleksandr Varenkov is engaged to.

"I'm giving you until the count of five, then Sasha's gonna take a piss on your bed."

Landon's lips twist in disgust. "She's usually pretty tame, but we should probably move this over to my bathroom floor before anyone takes a piss on my bed." Landon gets to his knees and twists around to grab his discarded T-shirt.

I fish Alekandr's shirt off the floor and hold it up. "Should I put this back on for my five-step walk of shame?"

Landon thrusts his shirt at me. "Don't even joke like that."

Another pound. Against my head.

"*Come on*, Landon!"

When he stands to pull his shorts on, I sit up and slip his T-shirt over my head, inhaling as it sails past my nose. The soft fabric smells like soap and sweat. I might sneak it home with me. Though, I'm sure he wouldn't deny me if I asked.

Landon helps me up while giving my appearance a thorough once-over before he opens the bathroom door. With my head lowered and my fingers gripping the hem of the T-shirt, I follow him out.

As we move, I spot the women's perfectly pedicured bare feet to the right of the doorway.

"Gaby? Gaby Bertucci, is that you?" the woman asks.

Recognition of the voice's owner hits me like a sucker punch. I lift my head quickly.

Auden Berezin. My brother's beautiful, blonde best friend since grade school. Drew has barely mentioned Auden since they graduated high school, so I assumed they'd lost touch. Until last year, when he suddenly wouldn't stop talking about her.

His random obsession makes sense now. He wouldn't give her the time of day back then, but now he wants her because Aleksandr has her.

"Auden. I—" What do you say to a family friend who catches you banging your boyfriend on a bathroom floor?

"*You're* Hermione?" Auden's eyes lower to my fingers tugging the hem of Landon's shirt. Then she lifts her wide eyes to mine as if realization sets in. "Of course, you are."

"What are you talking about?" I pat Landon's bicep and turn to question him. "What is she talking about?"

"Nothing." He tilts his head at Auden and sighs. "Socials. I call you Hermione on socials."

"Why?"

"I don't want to use your real name. My personal life is my business. So when I talk about you, I call you Hermione."

"Which makes sense because he's totally in love with Hermione!" Auden's sloppy ponytail swings as she gushes. But when her eyes catch

Landon's, she clamps her lips together and zips them closed with her thumb and index finger.

Landon shoots her an annoyed look. "Didn't you need to use the bathroom?"

A smile creeps onto Auden's lips as she crosses the threshold.

"Please don't tell Drew!" I blurt out as the wind gust from Auden shutting the door sends strands of hair into my face.

The door cracks open and Auden sticks her head out.

"Why?" both she and Landon ask simultaneously.

"I don't know. We're just really close and I'd rather tell him organically. Like bringing Landon to a family dinner or something. And Joey already beat him up, so—" I wave my hand toward Landon's black eyes, even though only one came from Joey.

"Oh my gosh! Joey did that? Both of them?" Auden opens the door wider and reaches out to touch Landon's eye.

Landon swipes her hand away with a growl before yelling, "Sasha! Get out here and take care of your woman!"

Auden backs into the bathroom, giving me a wink before closing the door behind her.

Chapter Twenty-Two

GABY

A FEW DAYS AFTER MY FREAK OUT AT LANDON'S PLACE, I'M RUNNING late for work. As I look over my shoulder, checking my blind spots before pulling out into the street, I notice what looks like an enormous bear waving his arms and running across the lawn.

Papa.

I slam the breaks and shove the gearshift into park before roll down the passenger side window. Though, I'm tempted to floor it and avoid the obvious outburst about to come at me.

"What the fuck is this, Gabriella?" he roars before he makes it to the window.

Papa's voice startles me. In all my years, I've rarely been on the receiving end of such a harsh tone from my father.

My head swivels like a lazy Susan, checking to see if any neighbors heard his outburst. He has some kind of newspaper in his hands, but since I haven't read it I have no clue why he keeps shaking it at me, more frantic with each step closer.

What could make Papa so angry? Had something gone wrong with the store? Despite our initial hiccups, Joey and I are trying to keep Papa's life the most stress-free it has been since, we imagine, his childhood.

A storm brews in his eyes as he hurries toward my car. His eyebrows and lips scrunch like a toddler's, the anger before the fit.

"I don't even know what you have there, Papa."

"I'm holding this week's *Metro Times*. And there's an ad for Three-One-Three Artisans in there."

Papa finally holds the paper still. The familiar mock-up ad Landon and I created jumps out at me, printed between advertisements for the Detroit Opera House's current show and the Detroit Institute of Arts' upcoming exhibit.

"Great placement," I murmur, excited to see our ad nestled between two legendary institutions.

Papa lowers the paper, giving me a full view of his rage. "That's all you have to say, Gabriella? 'Great placement?'"

"Well, I—" The realization of why Papa is so angry hits me like a snowball to the face. He thinks I placed the ad.

"I'm gonna need a little more explanation than that. And quick."

I shake my head. "I didn't run that."

"Come off it, Gaby."

"I didn't. I swear."

Sure, Landon and I created a mock-up of what an ad could look like using the photos I took at the hockey game, but I wanted to get Papa's approval before I placed any ads.

"You expect me to believe that?" He waits for me to nod before he speaks again. "You talked about a very similar advertisement months ago, and I specifically told you to forget about it. Now it's in a local newspaper. What am I supposed to think?"

The realization of how simple it is to tie facts back to people and still be wrong makes me suddenly sad for all of those falsely accused of real crimes with no way to prove otherwise.

"Did you ask Joey? Maybe *he* ran it."

"Did you give Joey a copy of this to run?"

The scrambled puzzle pieces fall into place as I shake my head "No." The only people who had access to that ad were me and Landon.

And I didn't do it.

I close my eyes, defeat pressing me into my seat like an elephant is in my lap. "I'll call the *Metro Times* today and make sure it doesn't run again."

"It shouldn't have run in the first place. I understand teenage rebellion. I went through it with your brothers. But this is different than a simple teenage angst. Why would you outwardly defy me regarding matters of *my* store? What's gotten into you?"

Landon.

Completely. Figuratively. Literally.

But the literal part isn't something you tell your father.

Ever.

"Sorry, Papa." My finger hovers over the power window button for the passenger side, overwhelmed by the urge to run away.

Away from my father. Away from the store. Away from Landon.

Papa leans into the car. With one blink, the anger melts away, replaced by a soft kindness. When he speaks again, his whisper holds a lilt of concern. "Have you been taking your medicine, Gaby?"

Just when I think I've gotten my life on the right track, and proven myself to be an asset to my family and my community, he brings it back to my weakness.

Everything comes back to my medicine. My depression. My craziness. My rape.

Perfection is restored by swallowing one pill per day.

"Yes." I move both hands to the steering wheel and squeeze, unable to make eye contact.

"I'm concerned."

"I'm fine, Papa. Can I go now?"

"Where are you going?"

"Work."

"Of course." Papa sighs and straightens up. His slight retreat allows me time to roll up the window and peel away from the curb.

I have to talk to Landon about placing the advertisement without my permission.

I'm already stressed out dealing with Joey, I don't need another complication to add to the 313 fire.

Chapter Twenty-Three

LANDON

WHEN I STEP INSIDE 313 ARTISANS, I IMMEDIATELY SPOT GABY AT the register smiling radiantly at her customer, keeping up the conversation as she as she wraps a glass mug in tissue paper. For some strange reason, watching her quick movements and easy banter with customers gets my blood pumping.

She has a distorted image of herself and I don't know how to get her to see the person everyone else sees. She thinks she comes across as quiet and introverted, yet every time I see her at work, she exudes confidence and power.

I've always seen it, which is why seeing Gaby at work has made my internal temperature spike since the moment I started noticing girls.

Now that we're officially together its next-level. And watching her smile sends my brain straight back to our sexcapades on my bathroom floor. Every time I touch her I want more, as if nothing can extinguish the embers of desire smoldering under my skin except for her kiss.

"Thanks, Shelia! Come back soon," she calls, waving to the woman wearing a bright purple fedora and a black frock splattered with paint.

Most people still see Detroit as a one-trick pony—an automotive, industrial town. Of course, that's the history, but there are so many other amazing things going on. I love seeing artists and creators in the community around Eastern Market.

"How's it going, sexy?" I ask, wrapping my arms around her from behind and kissing her neck softly.

"Hey," she says breathlessly as she spins around to face me.

"What the fuck, man? This is a family business."

Gaby jumps at Joey's booming voice. I ignore the anger by rolling my eyes and saying, "Nice language to use at a family business."

As he passes, he elbows me, pushing me into his sister. She braces herself by grabbing my biceps. I look down at her and grin, flexing under her grip. Her cheeks glow bright pink, but instead of letting me go, she gives them an appreciative squeeze.

"You have another customer, Gaby," Joey barks.

"We need to talk," she tells me as she releases her grip on my arms and moves toward the register.

I drop a quick kiss on her cheek before backing away. "I'll be hiding in the stuffed animal bin." I wink.

"I thought nothing was going on with you two, Gaby?" Joey asks, bagging the items as she taps prices into the register. "Didn't I warn you about him?"

"Don't even lecture me. You don't know him."

"I know all I need to know. And—"

"Excuse me." A customer holds up a blue T-shirt. "Do you have this in a large?"

"Go check," she snaps at her brother. "And mind your own business," she whisper-hisses as he trudges to the back.

I duck behind a shelf, laughing as she puts Joey in his place in the middle of the crowded store. There are more people in here than I've ever seen—which makes it even funnier.

The ad just ran and it's already working.

"I need to take a break. Five, ten minutes tops," Gaby tells Joey when he returns with a large T-shirt in hand.

Joey doesn't respond, which makes her huff. She looks up, searching for me. When our eyes meet, she nods to the door to the office in the back of the store. I wink and jog to meet her there.

"Did you place that ad in the *Metro Times*?" she asks as soon she closes the door behind us.

I throw my backpack on the floor and collapse into her dad's chair. Then I stretch my legs out, propping my heels on the desk one at a time, and cross my legs at the ankles. In five seconds, she'll be straddling me, so I might as well get ready for it.

"Turned out awesome, didn't it?"

Her top lip turns up in a scowl, eyebrows narrowing as she observes my position. "Why did you do that?"

"Wait." I lean forward, seeking clarification for the edge in her tone. "Are you mad at me?"

"Yes! You knew I wanted to get Papa's approval first."

"Your dad was never going to give you approval." I lower my legs, feet pounding the floor when they drop.

"He would have. Once I showed him the final product and brought it to him in—"

I interrupt her, "—in a logical manner. Yeah, I know. And that's bullshit." I rise quickly and walk around the desk to where she stands. "Your dad has never placed an ad in his life. And it wasn't going to happen now. The only way to go through with your plan was to do it. So I did it. And I'm not sorry."

"You don't know everything about us, Landon. You aren't the Bertucci whisperer."

"I know what you've told me. I did it to help you, Gabs. It proved you right."

"I don't need to be right. I need to be respected. And going behind Papa's back and placing an ad just kicked me down a few rungs on the ladder."

"I don't see it that way. It's already brought in customers. Ten people have walked into this store since I've been here. Four people purchased. That's a pretty good ratio, right? Better than zero customers and zero purchases."

"You're not getting it." She rubs her forehead in exasperation.

"No. *You're* not getting it. A simple thank-you would shut this entire argument down."

"Thank you?" Her eyes blaze. "Thank you for going behind my

back? Thank you for not giving me the heads up before my father reamed me for something I didn't do. Thank you for being the *man* who placed the ad so that if it does bring us business, it supports his misogynist mindset. Is that thank you enough?"

I open my mouth to tell her she's twisting my intentions. But before I say anything, I stop and let her words sink in.

She's right. I did go behind her back. I didn't think about the backlash she would get from her extremely old-fashioned—and stubborn—father. What I viewed as an act of kindness perpetuated her insecurities about not being taken seriously because she's a female.

Some people think patriarchy in families doesn't exist, but those are the people who only see things from their perspective and experience. If they haven't been a part of such a family—hell, a *culture*—they don't think it happens.

Detroit has so many rich cultural communities I've seen stuff I can't believe still happens many times. It might not be the norm anymore, but it still occurs.

I take her hands in mine. "I'm sorry, Gabs. I didn't think about any of that. I honestly didn't think about it at all. I placed the ad because I wanted to help. I thought I was doing something good for the store. And your family. And *you*."

Though I can tell she's still got loads of anger pumping through her veins, she squeezes my hands and gives me a half-smile.

"I'm sorry I was so rude. I just—" She exhales slowly, dropping my hands and rubbing her neck. "I'm so stressed out here. And I'm so used to being dismissed, I jumped to stupid conclusions."

"No. You were right. I didn't stop to think about how it would affect you, and I'm sorry." I tilt her chin with my fingers and lean down to kiss her. "Am I forgiven?"

She nods.

"Do you know how sexy you look when you're yelling at me? Clenched fists, scrunched nose." I run my finger down the bridge and tap the tip.

"A scrunched nose is sexy? Good to know."

Suddenly, someone starts pounding on the door. "What are you doing in there, Gaby?" Joey yells.

She spins out of my arms and kicks the door. "We're talking! Geez, dude!"

I laugh. "I'll get out of your hair. I actually stopped by to give you something."

I grab my backpack from the floor and dig around for a minute. Gaby leans over, trying to get a glimpse into my bag, but I throw up a shoulder so she can't see.

"Why is it quiet? What's he giving you? I will bust down this effing door." Joey pounds again.

Instead of listening to him whine or break the door down, I pull it open and step out. Though Joey and I are nose-to-nose, I lean forward slightly as if challenging him. Then I hold up the tattered paperback I'd brought for his sister. "It's a book."

"Break's over, Gaby," he says pointedly, scowling and stepping back.

She peers around me and addresses her brother, "Oh, you're so hard."

He flips the bird and turns around.

"Here." I hand her *Harry Potter and the Sorcerer's Stone.* "I have the whole series in here for you," I say, patting my bulging bag.

She flips the book from front to back then fans the pages, before running her finger over a few of the creases from when my brother and I dog-eared the pages. "Where did you get these?"

"They're mine. Well, first they were Jay's. Then he passed them down to me." I reach out and open the inside cover where a half-peeled sticker reads: THIS BOOK BELONGS TO JASON TAYLOR.

"You don't want to pass them to your brothers?"

"I'm pretty sure they wouldn't have the same appreciation you would for this particular set of books. Hope there's enough wear and tear for your liking."

Jason and I read the series so many times the books are almost falling apart. My parents bought our younger brothers a new set, but I held onto this one.

I knew she'd like the gift, but I wasn't prepared for the tear slipping down her cheek. I swallow hard, pulling her into my arms and hugging her to my chest. "Awww, Gabster."

When she pulls back, she wipes at her eyes. "I have never received such a thoughtful gift. I mean, I—" She laughs. "I love it. I love *you*. Thank you."

"I love you, Gabs." I kiss her. "Now, I'm leaving before your brother tries to kick my ass again."

"Wait!" She grabs my forearm.

"Yeah?"

I want her to drag me back into the office, but I'm pretty sure that's not how things will go with Joey all up in our business.

Using my shoulder for balance, she raises onto her toes, lifting herself to whisper directly into my ear. "So, um, this morning was really fun, but I wondered if—"

She steps back, dropping back to her flat feet as if embarrassed to continue. I immediately miss the warmth of her touch and the way her breath feels against my ear. She closes her eyes for a moment as if summoning confidence. When she opens them, she looks up at me through thick lashes and rasps, "I had this idea."

"Yes," I urge her to continue, shifting my weight from one leg to the other as if I need to make room in my baggy shorts for my swelling dick.

She lifts onto her toes again, brushing her lips against my ear as she speaks. "Maybe I could lay under you while you're doing push-ups sometime."

Confused, I purse my lips, squinting as I contemplate her request. "Why would you want to lay—"

After taking a second to picture what that would look like, I realize what she means and I swear my eyes bulge out of their sockets. I grab the sides of my head with both hands and arch backward. "Geez, Gabriella."

She shoots. She scores!

It took a while, but she finally managed to make me blush with a sexual comment.

In my peripheral vision, I notice Joey looking up from helping a customer. Gaby must notice too, because she puts her hands on my back and guides me toward the door, hoping to avoid another fight with Joey.

"Time to go. I'll see you later."

"You know that request is going straight to the locker room, right?" I tease.

"Landon!"

I slip out the door, laughing at the mortification on her face. As I walk to my car, I think about the cover of the book I gave Gaby—Harry Potter riding a broom with his arm extended trying to catch the Golden Snitch.

After all these years, I finally caught my Golden Snitch.

Chapter Twenty-Four

GABY

"WHAT DO YOU MEAN THERE'S NO ORDER THERE FOR US?" I chuckle. "They've had an order for us every Saturday for over eighty years."

My stomach tightens and I bolt upright in my bed as I listen to Sammy explain that he already talked to the delivery manager at the farm. Bertucci Produce did *not* have an order scheduled for today. There aren't any future orders for us in their system either.

"I don't understand. What happened?"

"I don't know. She said something about paperwork and changing their billing system. They stopped the shipment since we never responded," Sammy explains.

"With no heads-up? Couldn't they have called?"

"They did. They said they called Joe's direct line multiple times and left messages."

Damn.

Damn. Damn. Damn.

I knew I should have checked the voicemails at the store. I knew it!

Why did I trust Joey would take care of such an important part of the business? I should've gone behind him and checked every single thing he was doing, just like Papa asked. What started as an annoying inconvenience, is exactly what the store needed to stay on track with Papa gone.

And I fucked it up.

Think, Gaby, think.

"Okay." I swallow back tears. "I'm gonna call Jackie. She'll straighten it out."

I can handle this.

I *will* handle this.

A might-be genius idea pops into my head before I hang up. "Can you pick me up in your truck in about ten minutes? And bring any empty crates you have."

Time to get to the bottom of this. I've barely hung up with my cousin and my thumbs are already busy scrolling through my contacts to reach Jackie, the office manager at Mitchell Farms.

"Hey, Jackie, it's Gaby Bertucci."

"Hey, sweetie. What'cha need?"

The tone to her "Hey, sweetie" sounds anything but affectionate, but I'm used to it. After I accused her grandson of rape, she barely looks at me, let alone has a kind word. Still, I have to deal with her—with all of the Mitchells—for the business.

"We didn't get a delivery today. Just checking to make sure everything is okay. Is it running late?"

"Nope. Not running late. You never got us the billing change form we sent weeks ago. You never responded to any of our calls. I already told Sammy all this."

"Jackie, I'm so sorry we didn't get you the information you needed, but Papa had a heart attack and we've been picking up the pieces since."

"I know that, and I am so sorry to hear, sweetie," she says in the most condescending tone, thick with fake sugar. "But we both run businesses. We needed a form for our new billing system. Your father told us to fax them to your little art store so he could sign off. We did that, and you never returned it. We left multiple messages. There's only so much we can do."

"I understand that. It's my fault. I'm taking complete blame."

"Oh, are you now? Well, that's a change of tune."

Ever want to pounce through the phone and bitch slap a person?

A tiny—petty—part of my brain wants to drive to Mitchell Farms and ram one of their tractors into the pole barn they use as an office.

Instead, I ignore her jab—like I always do. "We've run on credit before. You know we're good for it. I can fax this information within the hour. I'll drive to the store now."

"This week's orders have already been delivered. But fax that information today, because we need to process it to have your order ready for next week."

"So there's no way to get an order today? What if I drove to the farm and picked it up?"

"Don't you *ever* set foot on this farm, Gaby Bertucci," she snaps. "We don't need any more trouble from you."

"This is completely out of line, Jackie."

"If you want to start the shipments back up, get that paperwork fa—"

Before she finishes the sentence, I press "End" and slam my phone into the mattress. The wood floor would've had a much more dramatic effect, but I don't want to pay for a replacement screen.

"What's up?" Joey asks, poking his head into my bedroom. He stands at my door shirtless holding a fistful of bedhead. I'm surprised he's already up. Usually, someone in the house has to wake him so he can fly into the store at the last minute.

"There's no produce delivery for the stand today."

"Why not?"

"We never completed some billing paperwork Mitchell Farms needed."

A flash of something passes over Joey's face, and he leans back. "I'm heading over to the store early today. I'll go back to the office and get that done first thing. And I'll, uh, check and make sure everything has been paid, too."

Without waiting for a response, Joey shuffles away from my door. A few minutes later, his footsteps pound the stairs.

The same scary part of me that wants to ram a tractor into the Mitchells' pole barn, wants to strangle my brother. Sure, he'll bust his ass to take care of faxes and invoices after the damage has been done.

When will the next shoe drop as other outstanding bills pile up on Papa's desk?

Anger pumps through my veins, propelling me out of bed and into the bathroom where I quickly wash my face and brush my teeth.

I've never had so many violent thoughts in all my life as I have in the last three minutes. Maybe I should take up yoga and live a life of peace and Zen.

At least Joey acknowledged he hasn't been keeping up with invoices since he'd been assigned as Papa's replacement. He should have shut his mouth and done the job, instead of resenting me for attempting to teach him the ins and outs of the store. If he needed help, he could have asked.

When Sammy's truck turns into our driveway, bright lights shine into the windows, reminding me to take a few breaths and get some composure.

I knew that Plan A (talking to Jackie), could have a sour ending, so I'd formulated Plan B just in case.

"Hey, Joey! I'm running out to see if I can help with the stand. I'll be at the store as soon as I can," I call into the kitchen, where Joey stands at the bar, hoovering a bowl of cereal.

"Okay. I've got it under control at the store, Gaby. I promise. Don't worry."

Don't worry.

Easy to say. Hard to do.

Chapter Twenty-Five

GABY

"Why are we going to your old place, Gaby?" Sammy asks.

"It's my backup plan," I answer.

Sammy stops his truck in front of 16301 Iroquois Street, where the first home I lived in once stood. The place I learned to walk, learned to ride a bike, learned to stick up for myself with two teasing brothers.

Nine years ago, someone burned it to the ground on the night before Halloween, which had long been known as Devil's Night in Detroit. Though there's been a citywide effort to lower vandalism and arson for years, even changing the name to "Angel's Night," crimes still occur—as we found out the hard way.

"Is this some sort of community garden?" Sammy asks as he jumps out of the truck.

"Nope. It's the Bertucci garden," I say proudly walking to the back of the truck. Standing on my tiptoes, I lean over and grab two empty crates from the bed. "Grab some crates. You're gonna help me harvest."

My heart soars, still proud of myself for starting this garden five years ago. Though, it started small, it's grown into a pretty big project. We usually donate our harvests to the Capuchin Soup Kitchen.

Never once did I think we'd need it in an emergency for the business.

Sammy's walking toward the fence as I retrieve crates. He turns around and cups his hands over his mouth as he calls to me. "Harvest what?"

Confused, I run to his side and examine the land. Something had raked over every row of produce. The gaping holes where vegetable plants had once grown are obvious from the curb.

"What the hell?" I exhale, dropping the crates and unhooking the latch on the chain-link fence.

The garden is big, the size of two plots of land—the spot where our house once stood and the plot behind it. Papa bought the vacant lot behind ours shortly after the fire. He'd had the land cleared and grated immediately because he'd originally planned to rebuild our house.

Seems silly, doesn't it? I mean, we live in Detroit. A place where people go missing every day. Senseless crimes happen every day. Houses burn down every day. And my dad wanted to rebuild, right there in that same spot.

Papa didn't want to walk away from the first piece of land he and Mama bought once they'd saved enough money for a down payment. Too many years. Too many memories. Too much pride.

We may have had to cut back or make changes through the years, but the Bertucci businesses continue to thrive in Detroit, despite our own tragedies. And Papa refused to give up on the city that's provided him and his family with a great life.

Papa scrapped the idea of rebuilding once he realized he could buy a beautiful old house with more square footage than our previous house and renovate for much cheaper than he would pay for new construction.

The decision relieved me, because I don't think I could have lived on Iroquois after the fire. The bitterness of loss would always be there, a ghost haunting us with the sadness of every wonderful memory burned in less than an hour. But at least we came out alive, right?

Since we owned the land, and we weren't going to rebuild on it, I asked Papa if we could plant a garden instead. At school we'd been studied urban farming, which communities throughout the city had been using as a productive way to fill the ever-growing number of vacant lots.

Various individuals and organizations started buying burned out houses and unoccupied plots of land and began planting gardens. Other than the obvious benefit of food production, the gardens created jobs for people as well as beauty in the vacant lots on the streets of Detroit.

Though my family has always had pride in our city, and in its people, I realized the Spirit of Detroit isn't just a bronze statue on Woodward Avenue. It's the people who continue to create ways to transform negative situations into something positive.

After a few years and countless discussions (actually, me begging relentlessly), Papa finally hired a few guys from the neighborhood to help him put down fresh soil. I picked out the fruit and vegetable seeds, and ten of my classmates helped us with the planting as a project for my high school's community service club.

Hope deflates with every cautious step, careful not to crush a patch of something plentiful, or at the very least, salvageable. A head of lettuce emerges every three of four plants, but the ones still there are infested with holes or hadn't grown to full size. The tomato vines, creeping up their wire trellises, loom above the garden devoid of most of their fruit.

I rub my eyes with my fingertips before raking them through my hair, pulling the strands toward the back of my head. "What am I gonna do?"

"If this was the backup plan, we're not gonna be able to open at the shed today." Sammy removes his faded, formerly navy blue Tigers hat and wipes his forehead with the back of his hand.

I was so wrapped up in the loss, I forgot he was even with me. Someone to witness my epic fail. Hell, someone to vocalize it.

For the first time in seventy-seven years, the Bertucci Produce stand at Eastern Market would be closed on a Saturday.

I turn my back to the ghostly garden and lace my fingers through the diamond-shaped gaps in the fence.

Part of me wants to blame it on Joey. He's the one who didn't correct our billing information with Mitchell Farms. He came in on his high horse, thinking he didn't need help from anyone and messed up the biggest thing he possibly could have.

But blame doesn't help.

Solutions help. And I couldn't even come through with a solution.

"We haven't been closed in over seventy years, Sammy." I kick the fence with my heel, still able to feel the vibration a second later. "Not since Great-Grandpa started the business."

"Yeah, well, no one in our family has ever had a heart attack before. There are some things you can't plan for, Gaby."

I know that, but it still breaks my heart. And makes me feel as incompetent as Papa already thinks I am.

One person going down shouldn't shut down a business. We should have systems in place by now.

I should have systems in place.

Dejected, I begin walking back to the truck. "Guess we should get going. I need to shower before I have to be at the store."

Just then, my phone rings.

I answer on the third ring. "Hey, Mama."

"Hello, my sweet." I can hear her smile through the phone.

She and Papa took a weekend trip to Traverse City, a welcome break for both of them after the stress of the past few months. I can always tell when Mama is stressed out because she's been up painting until all hours of the night. Worried about my dad. And she's still smiling every morning.

My mother, the epitome of survival.

"Do you know where Sammy is?" she asks me. "Uncle Sal said he hasn't shown up with the stand's delivery yet and he can't get ahold of him on his cell. It's not like him to be late."

I kick the tire of Sammy's old Ford pickup truck. "Yeah, about that. There won't be a delivery today, Mama."

"Excuse me?"

"The produce wasn't delivered."

"Come on, Gaby. This isn't the time to joke. That's been a standing delivery since before you were born. Since before *I* was born." She laughs.

"I'm not joking, Mama. Jackie sent some new billing paperwork to the store a few weeks ago. It—" I pause. I won't throw Joey under the bus. Not yet, anyway. "—I didn't get it filled out in time."

I drop my forehead against the door of Sammy's truck, wishing I could bang it until I have an idea for fixing this jacked-up situation.

"Why didn't you tell us earlier, Gaby? We could have prepared."

"Because I thought I had a solution. I thought I could use the veggies from the Iroquois Street garden."

"The garden?" Mama asks. "On Iroquois?"

"Yes—I—"

"Gaby, you didn't really think that would be a viable option, did you?" Her voice is soft, but ripe with disappointment.

"When Sammy and I got here, the garden had been picked over. Almost everything was gone. There's definitely wasn't enough to bring to sell."

For the first time, it dawns on me how absolutely ridiculous it was to think that stupid garden would be the solution.

Silence again. I hate silence.

"I'm sorry, Mama. I was—" The biggest idiot in existence. "I was just trying to help."

"I appreciate you trying to help, Gaby. I just wish you would have told me what was going on instead of trying to fix it yourself. We could have found a solution. Things like this have happened before. We could have handled it if we had known."

I have no words. No excuses.

I should have called Mama and Papa straightaway. My pride shoved my common sense inside a locker. I wanted so badly to be the hero. To prove to my family—my father—that I could do it. A girl, *their girl*, could run the family business.

Instead I messed it all up.

Sunk by my own ambition. Hadn't reading *Macbeth* a hundred times taught me anything?

"I was trying to handle it so you and Papa wouldn't be more stressed out than you already are."

"Well, that plan didn't work, did it, Gabriella? And because of your choices, we'll have to open late on our busiest day of the week. We easily could've brought in some produce from one of the stores hours ago." Mama sighs. "What in the world were you thinking?"

"I don't know."

When she speaks again, there's a hint of hesitation in her voice. "Are you trying to make Joey look bad because your father put him in charge of Three-one-three?"

"What? No!" I say, raising my voice when I have no right to be indignant. "I was trying to save his ass for not completing the paperwork."

"You just told me you were the one who forgot the paperwork. What's the truth, Gaby?"

I sigh, realizing the original lie I'd told to keep Joey out of trouble just blew up in my face. Like the decision to go to the garden before contacting anyone else.

The best laid plans . . .

"I don't know what's going on with you, but it's not okay. The stores have practically run themselves for years. Your father gets sick and they go to shit? It doesn't make sense. I know you weren't happy about Papa letting Joey run Three-one-three, but if you're intentionally sabotaging things so he gets in trouble, you should stop. Right now. This is not about your hurt feelings, Gaby. This is our livelihood. Our entire family relies on this business."

Shocked. Hurt. Angry. Those are the words that come to mind listening to my mother accuse me of sabotaging my brother.

"I tried to handle everything myself, so no one would have another thing to be stressed over," I whisper. "My intentions weren't spiteful, Mama."

"I really hope that's the truth, Gabriella. You need to make better decisions regarding the business, not go out on your own. We know you're young and still learning. That's one of the reasons Papa left Joey in charge. Why don't you go home for the day?"

"Come on, Mama!"

"You need a break. Go home."

It takes every ounce of self-control I have to not scream or throw my phone into the road.

I need to calm down. To think about the situation. To regain control.

I need comfort and safety.

I need Landon.

Chapter Twenty-Six

GABY

AFTER SAMMY DROPS ME OFF AT HOME, I GRAB A FEW CRATES OUT OF his truck.

He lowers his window and leans out. "What are you doing with those?"

"I'm going to go back to the garden to see if I can salvage anything for the soup kitchen."

"Good thinking. Sorry about the garden, Gaby." He'd said it a few times on the short ride to my house, and though each time it had made me well up with tears, this time I let them fall.

I nod and turn away, instead of letting Sammy see me cry. I don't want his sympathy. I know my poor decisions caused this situation. Mama's accusations tick through my head again.

I hadn't deliberately sabotaged Joey, but I *did* put my stupid hero complex above the good of the business; above the good of my entire family.

Hadn't I read this fable countless times? When you actively seek your moment in the sun, it blows up in your face.

After throwing the crates in my trunk, I climb in the front seat.

And cry.

Calling Landon is out of the question, with all my hiccups and snorts, so I pull out my phone and send him a quick text.

Me: Need to see you. Can I come over in an hour?

I wipe my eyes with my fingertips and wait for a return text. For the first time in my life, I wish I listened to my grandma's advice to always keep tissues in the car.

Landon: Of course. You ok?
Me: No. I mean, yes, I'm ok. It's a long story.
Landon: I'm here for you. I love you.
Me: Love you too. See you soon.

I toss the phone onto the passenger seat and drive back to the garden with a lighter heart, knowing I'll be with Landon soon.

Once I arrive at Iroquois, I extract a small spiral notebook and pen from my glove compartment. Then, I wander down each aisle and take stock of what's there, throwing a random fruit or veggie into my crate.

After Papa cleared both plots of land, he'd invested in an irrigation system for the garden, a maze of hoses along the dirt. Near the lettuce, I notice one of the hoses lay severed in half.

Maybe I shouldn't have jumped to the conclusion that a person, or people, had been stealing from the garden. It looks like an animal chewed it. I drop my notebook and pen and crouch next to the hose, flicking the frayed rubber with my index finger as I survey the damage. Definitely an animal.

I dust my hands off on my jeans before grabbing my notebook and pen and standing up. I jot myself a note to have someone come out and replace the hose.

Technically the garden has two street fronts, but only the Iroquois Street side has a swinging entrance in the gate. Not that it matters. It's an old-school, waist-high chain-link fence surrounding the area, so the lack of entrance gates wouldn't hinder intruders. Anyone, including children, would be able to climb or hop over the fence.

The last crop I want to check is all the way in the back, near the opposite street. I selected that location for the raised bed of strawberries because I know how crazy strawberries can grow. After a preschool project about planting, I begged Mama to help me plant them in our backyard when I was five years old, because they were my favorite fruit.

About a year later, after being mesmerized by a book about fairies during story time at school, I created a fairy garden amid my treasured strawberries.

She started me off with two fairies attached to long, thin sticks. Magic zapped through my fingers when I pushed those sticks into the ground among the juicy, red strawberries. A secret world that only Mama and I knew about came alive. For my seventh birthday she'd bought me a beautiful, pink, sparkly fairy cottage and a miniature birdbath with a crystal ball sparkling inside.

A few days after the fire, Mama and Papa brought me and my brothers to see the ruins of our childhood home. They said we needed closure, but at the time it was pure torture. I didn't want to see my home reduced to a blackened wooden frame. Everything was gone. Everything.

I stood there staring, horrified that the place that had once represented everything had burned to nothing. I wanted to get back in the car and go, until I remembered my garden. Had the fire reached the backyard? My strawberry garden? My fairies?

I released Mama's hand and ran to the backyard, ignoring Papa's cry for me to be careful as I kicked up dust and ashes on my path to the back. I never ran close to the house, just through the debris scattered across the lawn. When I reached the backyard, I found the garden covered in a thin layer of gray ash but still there.

Still alive. Still thriving.

And hidden among the strawberries, under a gross, grimy film, were my fairies—and their house. And their itsy-bitsy birdbath with its beautiful, shiny crystal ball.

I snatched them all up and carried them back to the car. Instead of planting them in the yard at our new house, I tucked them away in the bottom drawer of my nightstand, among all my socks. Where they stayed until high school.

Once the garden had been planted, and each type of fruit and vegetable had its place, I dug the forgotten fairies out of my sock drawer and hid them among the new crop of strawberries. Under those vines, the fairies were home.

I know exactly where they are, but take the long way around to check out the entire strawberry patch before taking a careful step into the middle and pushing the foliage away. My fairies smile at me from under the green blanket of leaves and vines. The iridescent paint on their wings shimmer in the sunlight.

Is it stupid that I continued to check the welfare of plastic garden figurines? Maybe. But as the only toys salvaged from the fire that seized every physical memento from my childhood, I didn't care.

Even at nineteen, the fairies bring me a sense of peace.

"Mission Accomplished," I say as I stand up.

The unmistakable sound of clanging on the chain-link fence made me turn. Out of the corner of my eye, I watch a large figure in a bright red T-shirt jump over the fence, from my garden onto the sidewalk.

I hesitate before calling out, which is the smart thing to do before spewing venomous words at someone in Detroit. I don't live in fear, but I know how to keep myself safe and what battles to pick.

Instead, I creep to the fence slowly and peer over. The intruder hadn't gone far. He's kneeling with his back to me in front of two little boys. Both boys' fists overflow with perfect, plump strawberries.

The intruder says something I can't hear to the boys and turns his head slightly toward the garden.

My stomach churns and I grab the top of the fence. I swallow a clump of air, trying not to throw up.

I croak one word to the profile I recognize.

"Landon?"

My sight seems distorted, as if I'm looking through the wispy edges of a cloud.

Was this entire day a figment of my imagination? A nightmare?

I rub my eyes, but quickly realized and I can't wipe it away because this is real life.

Upon hearing his name, Landon glances at me, then back to the boys before cranking his neck toward me again, as if in disbelief. "Gabs? What are you doing in there?"

"What do you mean what I am doing in here? This is my garden. I just saw you jump the fence. What were *you* doing in here?"

"That's the rich lady who's farm it is. She don't ever share." One of the boys says to him.

"This is your garden?" Landon asks, his eyes scanning the garden, rather than meeting mine again.

"Yes. I told you about it, remember?"

He couldn't have forgotten.

The Harry Potter books he'd given me after I told him the fire took out my prized first editions of the series had been lost in the fire sit proudly on my dresser. A thoughtful, treasured gift from him after I'd revealed my own family's biggest Detroit tragedy.

Landon finally looks me in the eye. "I didn't—" he begins.

"Didn't what, Landon?" I interject.

I squeeze my eyes shut and pause. I have to stave off the tears and keep a strong voice right now, even though I want to sink down and army-crawl under the empty vines where the stolen strawberries once hung. I open my eyes but clench my fists at my side. "Didn't know? Didn't steal?"

The taller of the two boys leans into Landon and says, "Old girl is maaad."

Landon, still on his knees, glances at the boy and puts a finger over his lips. Then he stands up and moves toward me. "It's not like that, Gaby."

I take a step back. Toward my garden, toward my car, toward my old world. The world where Landon was just a crush, not a real person with the power to help—or hurt.

Out of nervous habit, I press each of my knuckles with the pad of my thumb. I hear the pops and crunches on the first go-round, but keep methodically squeezing to calm myself. Or maybe I'm directing the pain somewhere other than my heart.

"Why would you steal from us? From *me*?" I yell.

Confrontation is becoming easier for me, which makes me sad. I don't like this side of myself. But I can't back down, either, because it was Landon who helped me find my strength—and my voice.

"I didn't know this was your garden," he explains.

I laugh, a hollow, sad chuckle. "Okay, why would you steal from *anyone's* garden? This isn't a rich community."

"I was trying to teach them not to steal."

"By stealing?"

"I wasn't—"

"You have the fucking strawberries in your hand! I saw you jump over the fence!"

"Oh my god, just listen for a minute." Landon's voice rises from relaxed and patient to an annoyed growl.

"How are you going to justify this, Landon? Because you're such a good person from such a good family?"

"No, I—"

"Or the old, I play hockey so I'm above the law? Is that the excuse? Because you're a big fish in a small sea right now, Landon. I doubt anyone outside of Metro Detroit would even recognize you."

"Gaby, please calm down. You're not making sense right now. You're acting crazy."

Trigger enabled.

"Crazy?" I ask. "Yeah, I'm crazy to be upset about someone stealing from the garden I started on the grounds where my house burned down to help people who don't have access to reasonably priced fresh produce. It's crazy that I've given every harvest to the local soup kitchen for the last four years. That's totally crazy."

"That's not what I meant and you know it. Stop for a second and listen to me."

"Listen to you." I chuckle. "I'm so damn sick of listening to everyone else. And doing what everyone tells me is best for me. How I should feel. How I should act. What I should do. I'm so over that bull-shit." I point a finger at him. "*You're* the one who told me to stand up for myself, right, Landon? But you just want to be the next guy who gets to have his way and tell me what to do. You feel invisible in your family, so you went after me, quiet little Gaby, who won't stand up to anyone. Guess your plan backfired."

"That's fucking bullshit. I think you know me by now to know—"

"You're right, Landon," I interrupt, on a roll with my insults and throwing all common sense and compassion out the window. "I do know you by now. The man who never had to work for anything in his life steals from someone's garden when he could easily buy the food."

Landon staggers back as if I landed a hook to his cheek or a jab to his gut.

"You're right, Gaby, I've never had to work for anything my whole life—including women. This relationship just became too much work for me."

The last few months flash before my eyes as Landon turns around and walks away.

I stand, shaking with rage, in front of the garden I created to be a symbol of resilience and perseverance after tragedy.

Instead of directing my anger at Papa, Joey, or Jared Mitchell—I threw it all at Landon.

Like the house that formerly occupied the land of the garden behind me, my relationship with Landon took months to build, and less than five minutes to go up in flames.

Chapter Twenty-Seven

GABY

MY BEST FRIEND CATAPULTED HERSELF INTO SAINTHOOD FOR driving from Chicago to hang out with me this weekend. I didn't even have to ask. I told her Landon and I broke up, and she jumped in her car.

True friendship is worth a million relationships.

"He's a guy, Gaby. You have him on this invisible pedestal, but he's just a guy," Michelle reminds me.

"He gave me confidence, ya know? He brought out a different version of me. With Landon by my side, the quiet, book-nerd store clerk seemed cool. Even *I* believed it."

"First off," she interrupts before letting me continue my pity parade. "You are cool. You've always been cool. Your problem is that you've bought into the ridiculous notion that people who fit a certain mold in society are 'cool.' You're nineteen years old and more well-read than half the country. You can run your family business with your eyes closed."

"That is so sexy," I mock her rolling my eyes. "I'm gonna orgasm."

She ignores the vulgar comment."It is. Smart people run the world."

"Rich people run the world," I correct her.

"Smart people find rich investors to bring their ideas to fruition." She huffs.

I lean back and lift my gaze to the ceiling. "Sorry. I understand your point. I'm being a particular sort of bitch today."

"You compare yourself to people who are nothing like you. Do you want to be a woman who hangs around bars hoping to bang a hockey player?"

"No."

"No. You threw mints at the mean girls. That's something you and I would talk about doing after the fact. Not something you'd ever do in real life," Michelle agrees.

"Exactly! In what universe would I ever confront anyone, let alone girls who had been talking about me behind my back?"

"Landon-Land."

"Yep." When I fall back on my bed, I feel a stuffed animal lodged between my shoulder blades and the mattress. I reach under to pull out the fuzzy friend, then chuck it across the room.

Michelle reaches up with both arms and catches it in midair. "Don't take it out on Paws."

As she turns it over in her hands, I realize it's a replica of the fuzzy stuffed tiger I'd thrown at Landon the day of Papa's heart attack.

"It's not just Landon. You do it with all guys." Michelle stops flipping the tiger.

I turn my head toward her, too exhausted to sit up. "Do what?"

"Put them on a pedestal. It's not just you," she adds quickly. "A lot of people do it, whether it's with celebrities or singers. We have these ideal images of people, and when we see them as human beings, it deflates what we built them up as. Maybe you should focus on seeing people for who they are."

I nod. She has a point. I do think of some people as larger than life. Like when I thought Landon could never like me because he's a professional hockey player and I'm plain old, never-went-to-college, never-left-her-parents'-house Gaby.

"Oh my God," I whisper. "The misogyny is so ingrained, I don't even realize I'm perpetuating it."

"What?"

"I'm all 'I am woman. Hear me roar,'" I begin. "In reality, I'm perpetuating the misogyny I grew up with." I bang my hand on my desk. "I'm amplifying the patriarchy I'm trying to dismantle."

"Now that you know, you do better."

"Tell me something about Landon that makes him a regular old human being like us," Michelle encourages the conversation.

"I don't want a Landon-bashing ceremony, Michelle."

"See! That's what I'm saying. It's not bashing. The things that make him human aren't bad. Those qualities make him the man you love."

Part of me wants to tell Michelle about Landon's selfish feelings about his brothers, but that would be bashing because Landon is entitled to feel jealousy just like anyone with siblings. You can't deny someone their feelings simply because you disagree or don't understand. And that's what Michelle's trying to say.

Why do I automatically think flaws are the qualities that make us human?

"I get it," I say after a few minutes of contemplation. "He puts his pants on one leg at a time."

Michelle gathers her long, brown hair and tosses it behind her back. "So what happened exactly?" She settles deeper into the zebra-print beanbag on my floor.

"I went to the garden to see what I could pick to bring to Capuchin's and Landon was there. Taking the food and handing it out to kids."

"Taking the food from your garden?" Her eyebrows veer together.

"Yes." I sit up on my bed.

"Did you see him take the food?"

"Uh, yeah. Strawberries. I literally caught him red-handed."

"Did he know it was your garden?"

"No. He knew we had a garden, but I never told him our old address or anything. He couldn't have known that particular garden belonged to us." I drop my head into my hands in my lap. "He didn't know."

"Still, he was taking food from *someone's* garden. Whether he was feeding kids or not. "

"I'm a horrible person." I fall back onto the mattress. "He was feeding hungry kids from a garden we don't use."

"But he didn't know that, Gaby. I understand why you got upset. You created that garden to give food to the needy."

I laugh. She's right. "My hero complex kicked in."

"Hero complex." She scoffs. "Don't twist your best quality into a negative.

"That garden could have been some elderly couple's only way to get fresh produce. He could take those kids to a grocery store and buy them food for a month."

"But it *wasn't* an elderly couple's." I slam my fist onto the bed. Angry at myself, not at my best friend. "It's a well-off family's garden and those kids know we only harvest a couple times a year. They probably saw all that food sitting there and wondered why it was off-limits. I thought I was helping the hungry by giving it to the soup kitchen. I could've been giving it to them."

"Gaby. You were helping the hungry. You were doing a wonderful thing with that garden. I understand why you freaked out."

This is my moment to come clean and confess without having to sit behind a screen listening to a dude in a robe on the other side tell me to say ten Hail Marys and three Our Fathers to absolve me of my sins.

"I wasn't upset because he gave away my donation to the soup kitchen. I mean, I was, but that wasn't the entire reason I freaked out."

"Okay." She wrinkles her nose. "Why did you freak out?"

I take a deep breath, just like I would if I were kneeling in that creepy little room in the back of the Catholic church where my family has been parishioners since before I was a glint in my parents' eyes.

The room with the painting on the wall with those weird eyes that follow you no matter where you stand. A mocking reminder to mere mortals that we can't get away from judgment.

"There was a huge mess up at work, and we didn't get our produce delivery for the shed at Eastern Market. I thought I could use the fruit and veggies from the garden to save the day. But it had been raked over and there was nothing left.

"When I returned to see what was salvageable, I saw Landon

jump over the fence and give the kids the food. I blew up at him because I was pissed I didn't get to be the hero. Turns out I'm the villain."

She snorts. "Yeah right. That garden doesn't yield a fourth of what the stand needs for a Saturday."

I stare at her, unamused.

"You didn't know, Gaby," Michelle's voice is quiet but steady. "You reacted as anyone would have in your situation."

"Really? Anyone would have blown up seeing someone give hungry kids food?"

"That's not what I meant. You were upset for a different reason. You took it out on Landon and those kids. Was it smooth? No. But it's not unforgivable."

I sit up and face her, folding my legs in front of me. "You don't think I'm a horrible, selfish person?"

"Gaby Bertucci, you are the least horrible person I know. Your whole reason for creating that garden was to give the food to a soup kitchen. I remember—I helped plant it." She smiles and leans forward in the beanbag. "And I know for a fact that you've called and ordered pizzas at the end of your shift and left them on the bus bench outside your store for hungry people to have something to eat. And I know you were the one who started your family's tradition of volunteering at the soup kitchen every Thanksgiving."

"Everyone does charity work. It's not a big deal." I swallow the lump in my throat and shrug.

"Fine. You overreacted because you were trying to prove yourself to your impossible father. Does that damn you for all eternity?"

"No, but it lost me the best person to come into my life—" I pause. Michelle and I aren't normally sappy with each other, but she just sapped the crap out of me, so I feel comfortable returning the favor. "—since you."

"Quick! Hit me with some stupid song lyric before I start crying," Michelle says.

"'Cause baby I'm gifted. You see what I mean? USDA-certified lean. I'm the man,'" I sing.

"It's a bit telling of what's going on in your subconscious when that's the first song that came to your head, Gaby!" Michelle bursts into laughter.

While I hope The Killers wrote *The Man* to be as cringy as possible to poke fun at arrogant males, I'm sure some guys use it as their theme song.

"What now?" I ask when our giggles subside.

"Now, you get him back."

Just as I open my mouth to ask how I hear footsteps stomping down the hallway toward my room.

Papa barrels in, a man on a mission as he waves a newspaper in the air.

"Shit." I hiss. I know what it is even before he stops fanning it around.

"It's in there again, Gabriella! Two weeks in the *Metro Times*. I thought you said you would cancel this ad." He thrust the paper in my face. "Can't I count on you for anything anymore?"

His comment is so unnecessary, that I almost feel smug about the ad.

I lift my eyes from the paper to Papa. "I called, Papa. The print run had already been finalized for the week. I couldn't change it. It won't be in there next week."

"How am I supposed to believe that, Gaby? You already told me you canceled it." Papa shakes the paper at me as if his angry words hadn't emphasized his points enough.

"Call the *Metro Times* yourself, if you don't trust me."

"I have no clue what's been going through your head recently. I had a heart attack and you lost your mind."

Lost my mind?

I lost my boyfriend. I lost my family's confidence in my ability to make good decisions about the store. But I hadn't lost my mind. Well, not over this.

"Sales were up four hundred and fifty percent after that ad ran last week. Four hundred and fifty percent!" I jump to my feet. I only come up to Papa's chin, but it makes me feel better.

"Excuse me?"

"You haven't been in the store to see it, or read the reports, but I have. The store was as packed as any Saturday at the shed. And people didn't just window shop, they bought. That ad increased our traffic significantly.

"Landon may have run that ad without our permission or knowledge, but I, for one, am glad he did. I worked my ass off to make that ad. I took photography lessons in my free time and shot all the photos. I bought a computer program with my own money and learned it so I could create an ad that would highlight our family's presence in the community, and convey the hip, cool vibe of our new store and its products. I think it turned out fantastic."

"Are you kidding me?" Papa asks.

"No. Someone should be proud of the work I've done to generate business for the store. If it has to be me, well—" I reach over my shoulder and pat myself on the back.

The slow crinkle of him squeezing the paper his angry grip draws my eyes to his hands. His other fist hangs clenched at his side and his eyes widen, as large as ping-pong balls, as I pat my own back.

Papa has never hit me. Not once, as far as I can remember.

But right now, Papa's eyes swirl with anger he's never directed at me before, and for a split-second, I think he might slap the shit out of me.

"Keep smirking, Gaby the Great. You think you're so smart. Let's see if the business generated from these ads"—He shakes the paper at me again—"is a fluke."

He spins around and stomps back down the hallway. I hadn't realized I'd been smirking. Must've been my I-don't-have-Landon-so-I-don't-give-a-rat's-ass-about-anything face.

"How will we know if we stop the ads?" I whisper, turning back to Michelle.

Silence descends on my room like a rain cloud in Seattle.

"Maturity isn't my strong point, is it?"

"He called you 'Gaby the Great.' That's gotta count for something, right?"

"Yeah, I don't think he meant it as a compliment." I burst out laughing. Nervous laughter of a woman with nothing to lose.

I finally stood up to Papa over the ad.

I lower myself onto my bed and search for my phone. I need to call—

No one.

Because I messed everything up with Landon. I bite my bottom lip to keep from crying, but it doesn't help, and my top teeth catch on the chapped flesh when my lips quiver.

"Gaby!" Michelle jumps off the beanbag and lowers herself on the bed. "Your dad will get over it. He's probably shocked you stood up to him."

I shake my head, as tears run down my cheeks. "It's not that. It's . . . I want to call Landon."

"I'm sorry." She puts a hand on my shoulder.

"My first thought was to call him. He would be so proud that I didn't back down."

"Well, you stood your ground, that's for sure."

I look at my best friend through tear-filled eyes and smile. "Did you just Tom Petty me?"

Michelle shrugs. "You gave me no choice with that setup."

"You're the best." I laugh as I wipe my tears.

"You needed to smile. Things will get better, I promise."

Chapter Twenty-Eight

GABY

When I arrive at work the next morning, there's a line of people down Russell Street and wrapped around the block. The queue is so long, it blocks the entrance to the parking deck I usually park in.

I try to keep abreast of any large events happening around Eastern Market so I'll be prepared for traffic delays. Nothing was on my radar for today, but there must be some sort of event.

As I walk past the crowd, I notice how many of the people are wearing Aviators and Monarchs jerseys.

It isn't until I reach the front door, that I realize where the massive line begins.

Why in the world does 313 Artisans have a line around the block?

Puzzled, I select the key for the front door from my keychain and insert it into the lock.

"Are you Gabriella Bertucci?" a girl leaning against the front door asks. The rectangular name tag on the lapel of her polo shirt reads: ERIKA—Detroit Aviators.

"I am," I say, pausing before turning the key.

"Awesome. I've been waiting for you to open the store so I can set up."

"Set up for what?" I ask.

"For the signing," Erika answers, glancing at the people behind us.

Without speaking, I unlock the front door and usher her inside. She pulls a rolling suitcase behind her.

"Forgive me, but I have no clue what is going on," I admit once we're in the store. I close my eyes and rub my forehead, feeling like an idiot for showing my ignorance in front of potential customers.

"Pavel Gribov and Luke Daniels are signing here today from ten to twelve. You didn't know?" Erika asks.

I flip the lock on the door so no one else will be able to enter. "No. What? I—"

Erika doesn't wait for me to answer. She kicks into full gear, shoving two of our display tables together and lifting a pile of shirts off one of them.

"Can you find another place for these?" She shoves the stack of T-shirts into my chest.

Once she's cleared the merchandise off the tables, she unzips her suitcase, removes a black tablecloth, and drapes it over the tables. When she flips the fabric down, the Detroit Aviators logo sits front and center. Then she retrieves two boxes out of the suitcase and fishes a tiny, silver box cutter out of her pocket.

I'm dazed and feel like an idiot just standing there. "Erika, I'm so sorry I didn't know this was happening. I would have been prepared. What can I do?"

"There's a box of Sharpies in my suitcase. Can you grab a few and put them out?"

I nod, grabbing the markers and scattering them on the table. Erika sets two stacks of papers on the table—eight-by-ten photographs of Gribov and Daniels.

She pulls a buzzing cell phone out of her pocket. "Yep. Yep. Let me see." She holds the phone against her ear with her shoulder. "Is there a back door the guys can come through?"

"Yeah."

As I explain how to get to the back entrance, she relays the directions to the person on the other end of the call.

"Thanks." Erika presses a button on her phone and stuffs it back in her pants pocket. "They'll be here in a few minutes."

"What's going on?" Joey asks.

Wow.

He showed up early today.

"Two Detroit Aviators players are signing here from ten to twelve," I tell him as if I'm the one with all the answers.

"Gaby, you didn't—" Joey has an 'Oh-shit' look on his face. Papa must not be far behind him.

"I didn't."

"Like the ads in *Metro Times*?" He asks, the tone of his voice dripping with accusation.

"I didn't do that either. Joey, I swear."

"Then how?"

"Landon Taylor set it up," Erika says matter-of-factly, cutting through the family bullshit. "The Aviators Director of Creative Services was supposed to call you yesterday, Gaby. Sorry about that. We had some communication problems." She points to the back. "Is the door this way?"

When I nod, she strolls past us and through the EMPLOYEES ONLY door that leads to the office.

"I'm on your side, Gaby, but Papa was straight-up pissed about the advertising thing."

"I know, I know." I glance at the front door. "But what can we do? Look at the line."

Joey brushes past me, unlocks the front door, and pops his head out. "I can't even see the end!"

"What's that saying?" I ask. "It's easier to ask for forgiveness than permission."

He turns the key. "If even a tenth of those people buy something, you won't need forgiveness."

"Well, that's a start, but we need them to come back. And tell all their friends, too." I bite my lip.

"Good job, Gabster," Joey tells me. "You knew exactly what this place needed."

"Landon did it."

"Landon may have set it up, but I know this was one of your ideas. It was really smart." Joey gives me a quick hug. "Sorry I've been a huge pain in the ass. It's hard being a Bertucci who hates retail."

Everyone is selfish to an extent. Everyone looks out for their own happiness. It's easy to get caught up in our own problems.

I always felt shafted, because Papa wanted one of his boys to take over Bertucci Produce just like he and his brother had. I never stopped to see the situation from my brother's eyes. As much as I wanted to prove myself to my father, so did they. In their own way, by doing what they loved to do, not being forced into the family business.

"Chairs?" Erika yells, her head the only thing visible through the back door. "Do you guys have two chairs?"

"I'll get them," Joey tells me, touching my shoulder as he walks by.

I follow him, slipping into the office to grab a box of business cards and flyers. I place small piles 1 around the store, even on the Aviators signing table. If someone doesn't purchase anything today, they might grab a card and remember 313 Artisans as the shop for unique, locally crafted gifts.

For the sake of the store, I hope today goes well.

"Do we get chairs?" Pavel Gribov asks. He straightens the black Aviators logo baseball cap on his head.

"Stop being a whiney little bitch and put on a fake fucking smile before I call someone else to sign with me," Luke snaps.

I bite my lip to keep from laughing, glad Luke directed his annoyance at someone other than his former photography student. "The chairs are coming. I'll check on them."

As I move toward the office door, Joey comes out with metal folding chairs hooked under each arm. He leans them against the table and opens the first one, setting it down in front of Gribov.

"Thanks." Gribov huffs. Then he plops into the chair and leans back. Part of me wishes he'd fall backward. Not get hurt or anything, just bust his ego a little bit.

"Good thing you used me in the ads, Gaby. Taylor could never draw a crowd like this," Luke teases as he unfolds his chair and sets it down.

Joey nods thanks and moves toward the door, ready to flip the lock and let the crowd in when he's given the word.

"You have Taylor to thank for your crowd of devoted fans, Lukey." I pat his shoulder. "He's the one who switched out the photo."

"He's smarter than I give him credit for."

"'Lukey?'" Gribov elbows Luke. "You sign like this today." He reaches across his teammate and grabs one of Luke's headshots. Then he pretends to sweep a marker over the photo. "Lukey Daniels. Number 19."

Luke chuckles. "That shit would be a collector's item. It would go for thousands on eBay."

"Do you guys want a water or pop or something?" Joey asks from his post at the door.

"I'm good," Luke says.

"Vodka?" Gribov asks, which earns him a slap upside the head from Luke.

"I have a flask in back if you want me to get it." I nod to the office door.

Gribov's eyes widen and the first smile of the day, not directed at Luke, creeps onto his face.

"I'm kidding."

He mutters something in what I assume is Russian, because it certainly isn't English.

"Ready, guys?" Erika asks. The guys both nod. "All right, Mr. Bertucci. You can unlock the door."

I take a deep breath and watch Joey. He stands still craning his neck to peer out the window.

"Joey!" I yell.

He looks back in. "Yeah?"

"She said you can unlock the door."

"Oh, sorry, I heard her say 'Mr. Bertucci.'"

"Yeah, that's you."

Joey laughs, deep and loud. "Hell, no! That's Papa. That's *Nonno*!"

"Just open the door." I giggle. Leave it to Joey to be confused by his own last name.

He cranks the key in the lock, before stooping to flip a metal latch on the bottom of the second door. Then he pushes the doors open and disappears behind the surprisingly orderly crowd flooding through the entrance.

"Single file!" Erika calls out. "Line starts over here." She directs people to her by waving her arm.

A rush of adrenaline flashes through me. If half of the crowd stays to shop and a quarter of them buy something, I'll be a happy girl. If more people purchase, I'll be ecstatic.

After organizing the line and getting started, Erika walks outside to talk to the crowd still waiting on the street.

At first, I stand next to Luke and Gribov, helping direct people, answering questions, and assisting the guys. Within thirty minutes, there's a huge line at Joey's register. I excuse myself from the capable hockey players and jump on the second one.

On a normal Saturday, hundreds of people pack into every nook of Eastern Market. 313 Artisans feels like a major part of it for the first time since we opened.

"HOLY SHIT!" Joey leans against the door. "That was the craziest day in the history of existence. How do stores that are busy all the time keep up?"

"Hopefully we'll find out." I smile.

Excitement shakes my fingers as I tap the keys to print out the report I want to view. There's no question whether that was the busiest day in 313 Artisans' history or not. We've never had that many people in here.

I need to see the numbers.

Numbers are real. Tangible.

Papa can't brush off numbers.

"Holy shit," I mimic my brother's curse as I scan the paper jumbled with revenue this store's printer has never seen.

The report matches the numbers from a Saturday at the shed, our longest-running, most frequented produce stand. We'd rung the most we ever have on both registers. Granted, beating any previous day's sales wasn't difficult, but the sheer amount is still an accomplishment.

Papa will be surprised—and hopefully proud.

On a day that came as a total surprise to both of us, Joey and I set aside all the hard feelings, came together, and rocked the event Landon set up.

As the Beatles famously sang, "We get by with a little help from our friends."

And family.

Chapter Twenty-Nine

GABY

Can you meet me at 16301 Iroquois at noon? Please. Please please please.

THE TEXT I SENT LANDON THIS MORNING DIDN'T HAVE MUCH detail, but since he hasn't responded to any of my voicemails or texts over the last two weeks, I didn't put too much effort into it.

Sending him a time and place seemed like the best plan. If he agrees to meet me in person, I can explain everything.

I pull four S-shaped hooks out of my back pocket and begin fastening the new sign to the chain-link fence in front of the garden. My fingers quiver as the minutes tick closer to noon.

After I finish hanging the first sign, I open the gate and walk to the back where I hang a replica of the sign facing Burns Street.

Now, anyone who passes the garden on either street will understand the intention.

The picnic blanket I keep in my car lays in a clump on the grass. I pick it up and flap it a few times, releasing the folds and crinkles from it being tucked away in my trunk. Then I drape it over the sign to block the words until Landon arrives.

If Landon arrives.

When I look at my watch, the hands read quarter past twelve. Exactly one minute since the last time I checked.

I wouldn't blame Landon for not showing. I probably wouldn't come back to the spot where someone accused me of stealing, either. Maybe he thinks I'm setting him up. Po-po waiting for him on the next block to catch him in the act and throw him in the slammer.

When Landon pulls up, I'm walking heel to toe along the curb, balancing with my arms extended like I did when I was a little girl. Trying to keep my balance even though there's no high-stake reason to do so.

Only this time there is. If I fall off, it will be the end of everything I gained with Landon.

"Sorry I'm late. I couldn't find the address," he says, stuffing his hands in his pocket.

"No worries." I believe him. If you input 16301 Iroquois into a navigation system, it doesn't register since there's no house on this plot anymore.

"Interesting you bring me back to the scene of my crime." The low voice I love acts like shock paddles, causing a rush of blood to my heart.

"The scene of *my* crime," I correct him, jumping off the curb onto the patch of sparse brown grass that separates the sidewalk from the street. "I'm sorry I overreacted. I'm sorry I freaked out. I should have let you explain."

When I envisioned how this moment would go, I squared my shoulders and looked straight into Landon's eyes. I summon every ounce of whatever charm he thought I had to lure him in originally.

I'm bold. I'm strong.

In my head.

But standing in front of him, faced with real confrontation, reminds me of the strengths I don't possess. I can't look at him at all, let alone into his eyes. So, I apologize to the hot pink laces weaved through my black running shoes.

"I know you think I'm a horrible person because I was upset that you were giving kids food. But I'm not, I swear. I—"

"Look at me, Gabriella."

My head shoots up immediately, responding to his command. I've missed his smile and his eyes that anchor me. I've missed the strength his presence brings out in me. And how his presence helps my newfound fearlessness transcend my timidness.

Landon steps toward me and reaches out to touch my face. "I'm not angry with you. I don't think you're a horrible person. I could never think that."

"But I—geez, Landon. I freaked out. I freaked out because you gave hungry kids food." I pause and shake my head because it's not the truth. "No. I freaked out because I was an idiot. Trying to be a hero and not thinking of anyone else."

"No, you didn't. You freaked out because you'd reached your capacity for stress. I'm not blind, Gaby. I know how much pressure you've been under. Shot down by your father, trying to work with a frustrating brother, and you saw me giving food away from a garden you started from ashes—literal ashes."

I try to lower my head, but Landon reaches for my chin and cups it firmly, tilting my face to his.

"I knew those boys had been stealing food from this garden. I didn't know it was your garden, but I knew they were stealing from someone's garden."

"It wasn't right to make you feel bad about it. You are an amazing person, Gabs. No matter how angry I was when you didn't listen to my explanation, you didn't deserve another punch in the gut. Especially from me."

"I'm the one who delivered the blow." I drop my gaze to the cracked sidewalk.

Landon lets go of my chin. "In a way, yes, but I acted like an idiot. I let you walk away. I didn't fight."

"There wasn't much to fight for." I look at him. "A crazy girl who got mad because you let hungry kids have food. You were right. And I want to remedy the situation."

"'Remedy the situation?' Are we all business right now?" he asks.

"What else should we be?"

"Do you really need to ask me that?"

"Yes," I nod. "Because I don't know which way is up right now. You threw me for a loop, Landon. You changed my life. You changed how I portray myself to the world."

"I could say the same thing about you."

"Bullshit."

Landon places his hands on my shoulders. "Why do you think you don't affect people, Gabs? How can you not see that you *are* the good in the world? Do you think I've been angry because you called me out for taking food from your garden? I'm not. You were right.

"I've been giving you time to cool down. To make sure you really want to be with someone like me. I treated you like your family has your whole life, going behind your back and making decisions for you without your permission. I placed those ads and set up that signing without asking you. I acted like the misogynist male you've been trying to break free of your whole life."

"It worked. It all worked. We've never been so busy. Consistently."

"That's not the point," he argues.

"I don't care about the point." I reach up and take his hands from my shoulders, holding them firmly and bringing them in front of us. "You were right. You did act a little like every other man in my life, but you did it because you had faith in me and my ideas. Not because you were trying to keep me in my place. You knew I was too timid to place those ads without my father's consent. And you knew we needed advertising just as much as I knew it. I have to stop the victim mentality and start being part of the solution."

"You are the solution. Your ideas are the injection of enthusiasm that your family's stores need. I'm sorry I got so pissed off at your comment about not having to work for anything."

I bring his hands to my lips and kiss them. "I shouldn't have said that. It was anger in the moment talking."

"But, again, you were right."

I shake my head, but Landon continues.

"You were right. Compared to my little brothers, I've been handed everything. The best training. The best coaches. Parents who supported me and paid for me every step of the way. And there I am sniveling over two little boys who were born with nothing. Parents who chose drugs instead of them. People who used them for welfare money and discarded them when that wasn't enough." Landon closes his eyes and shakes his head.

"But I shouldn't have used your feelings against you. It wasn't my place to judge."

"I'm glad I told you. And I'm glad you used it against me. I couldn't get out of my funk until you called me out."

"I think it's human nature to rationalize things in our heads to get inner justification for feelings and decisions. We all do it," I admit, releasing his hands.

And I'm one of the worst. The proof is in the garden behind me.

"I've seen such a huge change in you, Gaby. From the quiet girl who threw stuffed tigers at me to get my attention to the girl who stood up to me and kicked me to the curb."

"I'm pretty sure *you* kicked *me* to the curb, but whatever." I smile and shrug my shoulders.

"No. I got pissed off and stormed away like a little boy. You put me in my place."

"Thank you for placing the ads. And setting up the signing. It kept the store running. I know it did. Papa would never admit it, but Three-One_Three was going down fast."

"They were all your ideas. I just ran with them," Landon says.

"Why did you use the pictures of Luke? I thought the plan was to use you in the ads. Hometown boy? Local hero? Long-time shopper?"

"Because none of this is about me." He puts his hands on my biceps, holding me firmly. "This is about the next generation of your family's business. *Your* business."

"But it could have been your first endorsement contract," I tease.

"Yeah, then all the guys would razz me about sleeping with my boss." He lowers his face and presses his lips on mine. "I love bringing color to your cheeks. So easily embarrassed."

"Don't make me bust out a German polka on you." I don't even care about the embarrassing way I always blush around him. I'm just happy he's back by my side to put it there.

"It wasn't a polka!" Landon says in faux exasperation.

I wrap my arms around him tightly, unable to find a better way to express the pure joy filling my heart. "I don't even know how to thank you. Hugging is all I have."

"Can't. Breathe. Gaby." He coughs out each word until I release my grip. Then he drops his head. "And I happen to know hugging is not your best move. You can thank me with your closeted vixen ways later."

I ignore his comment. "Can I show you something?"

"Does it have to do with your closeted vixen ways?"

"No. Get your mind out of the gutter. We're still making up here." I step back to make it clear we still have business to discuss.

"We could make up at my place." Landon moves closer to me and dips his face into the curve where my neck meets my shoulders.

"Seriously? Can I have one more minute of apology time?"

"Yes." Landon straightens.

"Like I said before, you were right. I had no reason to yell at you about feeding hungry children. My pride and disappointment in how I handled things got in the way of seeing the bigger picture."

"Gaby," Landon begins.

"Shhh." I lace my fingers through his and lead him to the sign I covered with a blanket. "You were right. You're a man, but you were right." I wink. "So I did this."

I yank the cover off the sign and watch Landon's expression change from confused to delighted as he reads it.

COMMUNITY GARDEN

IF YOU NEED IT, TAKE IT.

IF YOUR NEIGHBOR NEEDS IT, TELL THEM.

IF YOU HAVE THE MEANS, REPLANT.

TOGETHER WE CAN MAKE A DIFFERENCE

HELPING EACH OTHER

BE KIND, LOVE HARD.

"This is amazing, Gabs." Landon faces me. "You didn't have to do that."

"I know I didn't. But it made so much sense. Why would I harvest this garden and give it to the soup kitchen, which has its own farm, when I could share it with the people in the community?" I push flyaway strands of hair away from my face. "This was my street. These were my neighbors. The families around here can benefit from this garden. And I know the ones that can help with it will. I can't believe I was so selfish before."

"Giving your harvest to a soup kitchen is not selfish." Landon grabs my shoulders.

"I know. I just meant that good can be done with the food right here. I don't need to bring it anywhere else."

"It's absolutely awesome. The way your mind works is absolutely awesome. Do you ever think about yourself?" Landon asks.

"You know I do. That's how we got into this mess."

"Let's stop right now. No more. You wanted to help your family in a bad situation. That's not being selfish."

"I love you." I close the gap between us and bury my face in his chest.

"I have never been so lucky to be loved by someone." Landon wraps his arms around me and brings me into his warm, hard body. The meaty arms, muscular torso, and masculine smell I missed so much in the last few weeks. "Can we make up for real now?"

"And by that you mean going to your place, right?"

Landon's lips spread revealing his perfect set of teeth, Cheshire cat–like.

"You're such a smart guy." I back out of his embrace and bend to retrieve my picnic blanket from the ground.

Landon smacks my butt which almost knocks me flat on my face. Thankfully, I throw my arms out to brace myself just in time.

He laughs, grabbing my waist as he realizes what happened. Before helping me into an me into an upright position, he holds my hips still and grinds his pelvis into my ass.

"Geez, Landon!" I tuck the blanket under my arm, brushing the dirt and gravel off my hands, trying to ignore the arousal blooming between my legs.

He eyes the blanket as I shake it free of loose debris on the way to our cars. "You wanna spread that blanket in the garden and make up in there?"

"In front of the fairies?" I fake a gasp.

"Fairies?"

I dismiss his question with a wave of my hand. "A story for another time."

"Business mogul. Book nerd. Closeted vixen. Fairy believer. You never stop surprising me, Gabs."

EPILOGUE

Gaby

GETTING UP FOR WORK THE MORNING AFTER A BLISSFULLY AMAZING night with Landon was hard. All I wanted to do was stay wrapped in his warm embrace, but duty calls.

I have a newfound excitement for my role at our stores.

"Do you know why I let Joey run this store?" Papa's question comes out of nowhere like a random rainshower on an otherwise flawless sunny day.

"Long-standing Bertucci male-chauvinist tradition?" I deadpan.

There's no reason to be sarcastic, but I'm so fed up with patriarchy and keeping my feelings inside.

"What?" Papa's narrow eyes and forehead wrinkles.

How is he surprised by my comment?

"Bertucci Produce has always been run by men and it always will be." A defeated sigh escapes as I finally give voice to the truth I realized long ago. "And since Drew is into hockey, Joey's the one. The golden boy. The heir to the Bertucci legacy. I've known how it would play out since the day I was born."

"Gaby, come in here." Papa waves me into the office.

Uh-oh. A closed-door meeting. Maybe I had the right idea to keep my mouth shut all these years.

Nah. I would have blown up at some point. Better to get it all out on the table now when I'm finally at peace with myself.

I scan the store to make sure it's safe to leave for a few minutes. Joey's at the register, smiling and laughing with the customer he's checking out. Sammy's flipping through a T-shirt rack, helping another person find a certain size.

The store is fine. Better than fine.

Joey's line is three customers deep, and various people wander through the aisles, browsing the artwork or smelling handmade candles.

The store has done a complete one-eighty over the last few months. Pride pushes my shoulders straight and holds my head high as I enter the office and settle into the blue paisley chair across the desk from Papa.

A few months ago, I would've put my head down and fiddled with my hands in my lap, waiting for Papa to rail me.

But not today.

Today, I raise my chin and look my father straight in the eye. I'm stronger, and ready for whatever he throws at me. It's time to own my feelings and opinions rather than deny them.

"Gaby," Papa begins. He reaches over the desk, extending his hand.

What's going on? Is he sick again?

My heart beats faster. Fear and confusion propel me forward to take his hand.

"When I retire, you will take over every single Bertucci entity I manage. *You*, Gaby. Not Joey. Not Drew. You."

I pull back in surprise, but Papa holds my hand and squeezes it.

"You've been by my side since you were four years old. You know every inch of the stores. You can probably run them better than I can. Definitely better than your Uncle Sal," he quips with a wink.

"What?" I ask, too fearful of the "but" that must be coming next to get excited.

There has to be a *but*, right?

"I can't believe I've been so blind all these years. I've taken you for granted and I apologize. I assumed you knew."

"How could I know, Papa? You shot me down when I was prepared to manage the store. You let Joey run it. Joey—a person who'd never set foot inside the place."

"Do you want to know why I let Joey run this store?"

"Yes." My answer is loud and adamant.

"Bertucci Produce—the shed, the two stores—that pays our bills. That keeps us afloat. Hell, it keeps our entire extended family afloat. But this store is new. We're testing it out, trying to get your mother's artistic pipe dream off the ground." He chuckles. "I would never let your brother run one of the produce stores. We'd all be on the street within a week."

This time I laugh. His scenario is only a slight exaggeration. Bertucci Produce is a whole different beast. Joey could've been a bagger, at best.

Papa continues, "I'd like Joey to get his life on track. I thought giving him responsibility here would get his mind in the right place. Think about the future and what he wants to do." Papa releases me and rubs his face with both of his hands. Then he rests his elbows on the desk, clasps his fingers, and sets his chin on them. "But it doesn't seem like I've accomplished anything except getting you extremely upset with me."

"It's okay, Papa. I've been upset for a while. I'm just vocalizing it now," I admit honestly.

He releases his hands and pounds the desk. "I always thought your anger was normal teenage-girl angst. Glad to know it's because you think I'm a chauvinist pig. I can work with that."

"Papa!" I grab his hand. "I wish you would have told me. We could've saved a lot of unnecessary teenage angst."

"Honestly, Gaby, I didn't realize I was being chauvinistic. Other than the Joey thing, what do I do that makes you think I'm president of the He-Man Women Haters club?"

Though I have no clue where he came up with that club name, I don't hesitate to respond.

"You never listen to my ideas. But if Sammy or Uncle Sal or some other *man* suggests it, then you listen. You do it all the time. I think you're only happy about the Aviators player signing we had because

Landon set it up. A man had to be involved or it wouldn't have gone off as well as it did."

Papa's eyes widen in shock, and he leans back in his chair. "You think it's because you're a woman."

"It sure seems that way from my perspective."

He nods. "I understand that now. And I apologize for not giving you a chance." He leans back, rubbing his cheek and laughing as if remembering something funny. "You've been feeding me fabulous, grandiose ideas since you were eight. Sometimes when I look at you I still see that girl, not the smart, driven nineteen-year-old who's ready to have more control."

I smile and straighten my posture, delighted by his comment. "Come on, Papa," I cajole him. "It's a little bit because I'm a woman. I mean, you don't listen to Mama either."

"I don't? Then why are we sitting in the office of a local artisan store we financed with our own money to help your mother fulfill her dreams of selling her artwork?"

"Well, I just meant—" I begin.

But he's right. 313 was Mama's vision—her dream, her baby, though she doesn't work here. Her contribution is the art—her paintings, sketches, and sculptures. She's also the liaison between the artists we showcase.

"I didn't realize I came off as such a caveman, Gaby, especially to my one and only daughter. I've trusted you with decisions for years. You're smart and capable, and *you* created the plan to get customers into this store, no matter who ended up carrying out that plan." Papa stands up and walks around the desk, stopping in front of me and extending his arms. "Can you forgive me?"

A tear slips down my cheek as I register all the wonderful things Papa just said. I jump up and crush him with a hug. "I love you, Papa."

He wraps his arms around me and doesn't let up until I'm the one pulling away. My favorite kind of hug.

"Can I ask you one more question?" he asks, still holding me.

"Sure."

"Did you choose not to go to college because of what happened with the Mitchell boy?"

Oh no.

I can handle dancing around the rape with Mom, but when Papa brings it up, I want to hide like a jack-in-the-box and break off the crank so no one could make me pop out.

"No. I—school isn't my thing. You saw my report cards." I try to shrug out of Papa's arms, but he won't let me go.

"You're an intelligent girl, Gabriella. Your report cards changed after the rape."

And there *it* is. The word that must not be used.

Papa continues, "Are you scared to go to college because of what happened?"

"I don't know."

Lie.

Truth: I do know. I never admitted it, even to myself. I refused to set foot on a college campus since the rape. Every time I visit Michelle at Loyola, I make up some lame excuse about wanting a hotel room close to a concert venue or Michigan Avenue shopping to avoid staying at her dorm.

I still haven't figured out what I'll do when Drew graduates and I'm expected to be at the ceremony. On the same campus *it* happened.

"Landon brought it up. I can't believe I never thought about it." Papa shakes his head. "I don't want to push anything at you, Gaby. But I don't want you to miss out on life because of fear. There are other options. Online classes. You can live at home."

"I'll think about it, Papa." I inspect a piece of dog hair on his sweater, which is still inches from my face since he's not letting go of me. "I suck at online classes. And I'm—I'm not ready to think about that right now."

"Okay." Papa strokes my hair. "But when, or *if*, you are, please let us know. We can help, Gaby. We'll do whatever is best for you."

"Speaking of Landon," I begin. Papa put his thoughts out there, now it's my turn. "Did you and Mama start this store because you didn't want me to have to work with the Mitchells anymore?"

Papa's body stiffens, tightening his embrace. "He's a perceptive boy, isn't he?"

"Outsiders usually are."

"To an extent, yes. You know we can't leave the family business. Not right now, at least. Your mother and I thought if we could make this store profitable, we could give ourselves some distance from the produce side. We needed to find a place where you could work without the fear of seeing that asshole every day. And if this store is successful, maybe we can open other branches. Maybe in a mall, or I don't know." Papa shakes his head.

"It kills me that we can't walk away from the Mitchells and their bullshit. It pisses me off that *Nonno* would rather keep his business ties strong than his family safe. As your father, I want to do everything I can to protect you. Even if it means giving my brother control of the produce business."

My grip on Papa tightens as tears stream down my cheeks.

How many times had I cursed my father for going along with *Nonno's* business bullshit? How many times had I bitched and complained—including today—about his plan to bump me out of the picture because I'm a woman? Just knowing he's willing to give up the business for me proves he's amazing.

"Is it time to talk about the great and powerful wizard, Landon Taylor?" Papa asks, backing up slightly to hold me at arm's length.

"Shhhh!" I glance at the door to make sure it's still closed.

"You two have gotten quite close, Gaby."

"He's the most wonderful person," I say. I can't keep the smile off my face. "He's had a positive influence on me."

"I see that. And I'm glad." Papa releases me from his arms. "I like him, Gaby. And he comes from a good family. But you might want to tread lightly. He's a hockey player. Hockey players travel. They get traded. They have a lot of fans."

"I know." I reach back and fluff the hair from my neck, where Papa's massive arms crushed it. "I'm not ready for forever yet. I'm too young. But I like who I am with him. And I'm excited to roll with whatever life has for both of us."

"And you love him."

"I do." I drop my eyes to the floor, convinced Papa could see memories of sex with Landon in the blush of my cheeks.

"Your mother and I are here if you need us, Gaby. Love is beautiful. But it's not always easy. Relationships take a lot of work."

"Tell me about it. You had to open an art store to keep your woman happy."

Humor seems like the best way to deflect conversations about love —or worse, sex—that Papa may be hedging toward. I can't handle another birds-and-bees talk. The first one, with Mama fumbling through a demonstration with a condom and a flashlight, embarrassed me enough.

Papa opens the door to the office and we both step out into the store.

"Chill, she's right there." Sammy points at me. I look up to see that he's speaking to Landon.

My boyfriend bounces on his toes like he's waiting for the gunshot to start a marathon. He rushes toward me.

"I'm going to the NHL, Gabs!" Before I can react, he sweeps me into his arms and spins me.

"That's amazing!" I wrap my arms around his neck and hug him. Then I raise my head and kiss his cheek. "I knew it would happen. The Monarchs were just slow."

Landon sets me down but doesn't let me go. His hands settle on my hips and he presses his lips on mine. I kiss him back with gusto, despite my father being inches away from us.

"It's not the Monarchs. I got traded."

"What?" I pull back but stay close because I don't want him to take his hands off me. I glance at Papa as he inches by us to greet a customer. "Traded to where?"

In the grand scheme of things, *where* doesn't matter. Landon would go to whatever team wanted him and would play him. All of his hard work is finally paying off.

"The Wings. And they aren't even sending me to Grand Rapids first. I'm gonna be playing in the NHL right here in Detroit."

The extreme surprise—and joy—I feel multiplies with every head that swivels toward us as Landon makes his announcement.

A chorus of cheers erupts, popping the imaginary Gaby and Landon bubble surrounding us. Perfect timing, as if the crowd realized

I wouldn't be able to form words or thoughts or even sounds after Landon's announcement.

Everyone's happiness rallies around our local hero, who'll be playing hockey in his hometown. What's better than being able to follow his career and root for him without wavering from fierce home-team loyalty?

I'm thrilled he'll be fulfilling his dream right here. In the city we were both born and raised. In the city we're slowly trying to help put back together, one small step at a time.

"That's so ridiculously fantastic," I whisper in his ear. "You know I would've been ecstatic for you if you'd been called up Charlotte, too, right?"

"I know. It's one of the reasons I love you, Gabs. You get it." Landon looks around the bustling store. "I'm glad I'm staying. It looks like Three-One-Three is gonna need my help."

"And that's why I love you, Landon. You get it."

Thanks for reading POWER PLAY!
I hope you love Gaby and Landon!
If you thought they brought the heat and heart, it's nothing compared to the passion between Pavel and Kristen in UNSPORTSMANLIKE CONDUCT, the next Detroit Aviators Hockey romance.

Read UNSPORTSMANLIKE CONDUCT now!

"Henry has created such wonderful, flawed, and relatable characters in a storyline that tugs at the heart, and it became much more than just another sports story."
- ★★★★★ Reader Review

Turn the page to read an excerpt of Unsportsmanlike Conduct...

UNSPORTSMANLIKE CONDUCT EXCERPT

KRISTEN

"Latin dancing?" Sia whines as we stand in the doorway of one of the ship's many nightclubs. "Do we have to go here?"

"Yes," I whisper, closing my eyes and letting the music penetrate my ears. After spending my entire childhood in dance classes, I still get lost every time I hear an infectious beat.

"Did you really think Kristen was gonna let us walk by this place without going in?" Lena asks. She knows my love affair with dancing.

The room explodes with flashing lights, pulsing strobes, and glowing neon backdrops. Across the way, multiple people dance on a huge stage. A few at the front of the stage seem to be giving instructions. My limbs itch to get up there and help, but this is my vacation, so I fight the urge to teach and set my sights on the floor instead.

"They have a lesson going on up there." I point to the stage. "Why don't you try it?"

Sia purses her lips and shakes her head. "I'd rather watch you."

With a smile, I grab her hand and weave through the crowd to the dance floor, where I let the pulse of the music take over. Who can hear a Latin beat and not want to shake something? The compelling pull makes it impossible to stand still.

Though I knew it wouldn't be anything like the sultry Latin Fridays back home at Diablos in Royal Oak, I thought a Latin club on a cruise had promise. Within thirty minutes, I realize the dance floor holds far more people with Sia's skills than mine. Instead of expecting to find a partner who can keep up with me, I slip into instructor mode and teach Sia and Lena a simple salsa.

Tons of bodies bump, bounce, and gyrate around us. It's hard to loosen up and let the music take hold while trying to sidestep each predatory pelvis. I'd much rather groove with a guy who stays in his zone than someone who tries to grind every girl in the vicinity.

As I put weight on my back foot, rocking away from one particular creepy dude, someone catches my hand and tugs me forward into his hard chest.

What kind of guy dared to grab me when I haven't been giving off those vibes?

Bracing myself, I press my palms against a soft black button-down shirt. Pasha stands in front of me with an adorably arrogant smirk on his face. Instead of speaking, he holds his arms up in a formal dance position. Intrigued, I take his hands and he immediately leads me in a succession of smooth salsa steps.

It isn't intricate choreography only two dancers who have practiced together would know, just a series of basic Latin dance steps. He leads and I follow. But nobody else on the dance floor knows that. To them it probably looks like a scripted routine straight out of a musical.

And damn! Pasha can move.

Instead of keeping the typical position, he releases my right hand and steps closer to me. He places his hand on my waist while keeping his eyes locked with mine. His slight change in position makes the moves harder for me to complete since I'm accustomed to being led by a partner with a rigid form who leaves space between us. That's how I learned during my eight years of ballroom classes and competitions.

Pasha's steps are flawless as we float across the floor. For the first time in years, I have to pay attention and count steps. Our intense eye contact and proximity make every seductive move a million times sexier.

A trickle of sweat rolls down my back as I heat up from the exercise and being so close to him. Every time he steps forward, our bodies are inches from mashing together. I've seen couples perform sexy salsa dancing in competitions and practices, but I've never participated. Probably because I've never been with a partner who had the effortless confidence Pasha has.

If I take my gaze from Pasha's, I'll lose my count, so I can't tell what the rest of the crowd is doing, but when hoots and claps thunder around us, I know we've gained an audience. The song morphs into another, and I finally close my eyes, breaking the intensity of his gaze. Pasha tugs me into his arms and hugs me.

"You surprise me." Despite our close proximity, Pasha has to yell over the music.

His comment makes me laugh because he's the one who surprised me.

"I never would have pegged you as a dancer." My breath is still heavy from the activity.

"Why?"

"You're bulky," I say, trying to think of the right word.

"What?" He pulls back, as if I've insulted him.

"Sorry. I just meant you're bulkier than the partners I'm used to," I explain. "I've always danced with tall, slim dudes. None of them were as muscular as you."

Pasha's lips slide into an easy smile. Instead of responding in words, he places his hand on my waist and guides me into another step. This time it's a merengue to match the sultry music, which is much easier to follow in the tight proximity he likes to hold me in. In fact, it's the perfect dance for the way he likes to hold me.

He takes another step closer, placing his leg between mine. He releases my grip and slides his hand against the back of my neck, pulling me close as we rock and step in time with the music. I swallow back the desire pulsing through me.

Read UNSPORTSMANLIKE CONDUCT Now!

BE KIND. LOVE HARD.

At the beginning of my career, I vowed to give a portion of royalties from each of my books to charity. I choose charities that are close to my heart and that are involved in my books in some way. Visit the Be Kind Love Hard page on my website to learn more about each charity.

A HEARTFELT THANK YOU TO EACH ONE OF YOU
SOPHIA X

A portion of the royalties from the sale of POWER PLAY will be donated to RAINN and Earthworks Urban Farm.

For information on helping victims of sexual assault: RAINN.org.
For information on an Urban Farm that helps feed the hungry:
Earthworks Urban Farm

#BeKindLoveHard

REVIEWS ROCK

THANK YOU so much for taking the time to read POWER PLAY. I truly appreciate every single one of you. If you enjoyed reading POWER PLAY as much as I enjoyed writing it, it would mean the world to me if you would consider leaving a review on Amazon.

(If you really loved the book, copy and paste the same review to Bookbub & Goodreads!)

SOPHIA X

PLAYLIST

Complete Playlist on YouTube: SophiaHenryOfficial

Lazaretto - Jack White

Willing to Wait - Sebadoh

Get Hurt - The Gasoline Anthem

Screen - Twenty One Pilots

Shut Up And Dance - Walk The Moon

I Need My Girl - The National

Always Take You Back - Night Terrors of 1927

El Perdón - Nicky Jam and Enrique Iglesias

Reggaetón Lento (Bailemos) - CNCO

Raise Your Glass - P!nk

Don't Let Me Down, Gently - The Wonder Stuff

Prefect Memory (I'll Remember You) - Remy Zero

Titanium - David Guette (feat. Sia)

How Was It For You? - James

(If You're Wondering If I Want You To) I Want You To - Weezer

Demons - The National

Graceless - The National

Fight Song - Rachel Platten

Skyscraper - Demi Lovato
Énchame La Culpa - Luis Fonsi & Demi Lovato
Pressure - The 1975
Falling For You - The 1975
All My Heroes - Bleachers
I Wanna Be Yours - Arctic Monkeys
Levitating - Dua Lipa (feat. DaBaby)
Thinking Out Loud - Ed Sheeran
Someone To You - BANNERS

ALSO BY SOPHIA HENRY

<u>*DUO SAINTS AND SINNERS*</u>

SAINTS

SINNERS

<u>*ROMANS AUTONOMES LIÉS AUX SAGAS*</u>

EVEN STRENGTH

Saints & Sinners/Aviators Hockey Crossover Novel

<u>*SAGA AVIATORS HOCKEY*</u>

JINGLE BALL BENDER

BLUE LINES

<u>GERMAN</u>

<u>*MATERIAL GIRLS SERIES*</u>

OPEN YOUR HEART

LIVE TO TELL

CRAZY FOR YOU

<u>RUSSIAN</u>

<u>*SAINTS AND SINNERS SERIES*</u>

SAINTS

SINNERS

DON'T MISS OUT!

Sophia Henry's mailing list is the place to be if you like steamy romance novels that tug at your heart strings. Stay notified of new releases, sales, exclusive content. sophiahenry.com

MERCH STORE

Choose kindness and love with everything you've got. It's not just a motto. It's a way of life. Grab some motivational or bookish merch today! shopkrasivo.com

ABOUT THE AUTHOR

USA Today Bestselling Author Sophia Henry fell in love with reading, writing, and hockey all before she became a teenager. After graduating with a Creative Writing degree from Central Michigan University, she moved to warm and sunny North Carolina to enjoy the remainder of her winters.

She spends her days writing steamy, heartfelt contemporary romance novels hoping they resonate with and encourage others. When Sophia's not writing, she's hanging out with her two high-energy sons, an equally high-energy Plott Hound, and two cats who want nothing to do with any of them. She can also be found watching her beloved Detroit Red Wings and rocking out at as many concerts as she can possibly attend.

Sophia Henry's mailing list is the place to be if you like steamy romance novels that tug at your heart strings. Sign up at sophiahenry.com